STALKING GROUND

ALSO BY MARGARET MIZUSHIMA:

Killing Trail

STALKING GROUND

A Timber Creek K-9 Mystery

Margaret Mizushima

CROOKED
LANE

NEW YORK

Published in the United States by Crooked Lane Books, an imprint of The Quick Brown Fox & Company LLC.

Crooked Lane Books and its logo are trademarks of The Quick Brown Fox & Company LLC.

Library of Congress Catalog-in-Publication data available upon request.

ISBN (hardcover): 978-1-62953-833-4
ISBN (paperback): 978-1-62953-834-1
ISBN (ePub): 978-1-62953-835-8
ISBN (Kindle): 978-1-62953-836-5
ISBN (ePDF): 978-1-62953-837-2

Cover design by Melanie Sun
Book design by Jennifer Canzone

Printed in the United States.

www.crookedlanebooks.com

Crooked Lane Books
34 West 27th St., 10th Floor
New York, NY 10001

First edition: September 2016

10 9 8 7 6 5 4 3 2 1

To my husband, Charlie,
with gratitude for his never-ending support

Chapter 1

A bead of sweat rolled down Deputy Mattie Cobb's face beneath the plastic guard on her helmet. She tilted her head to keep the sweat from going into her eyes and caught a glimpse of the sky. Not a cloud in sight. It was unseasonably warm for October in Denver—much warmer than in Timber Creek, where forest and meadow soaked up the sun's rays. Here, the rays hit pavement and bent back upon themselves.

She'd been assigned the lead on a mission at an industrial park south of Denver. A jewelry store had been robbed at Cherry Creek Mall, and patrol officers had followed the suspects to this location. Reports indicated at least two armed suspects, possibly three, had escaped and then abandoned their Dodge Intrepid in this parking lot. Mattie and her K-9 partner, Robo, were expected to track and apprehend the fugitives.

Three unfamiliar officers—called by code names Red, Blue, and Green—fanned out behind her as backup. The officers carried AR-15 rifles and Mattie a Glock 17 handgun.

Mattie signaled for them to gather around. "The park is laid out in a rectangle. There are four rows of three buildings each. Starting on the left, we'll call that row one, then two, three, and four. We'll number the buildings, starting with one, two, and three in the first row." Mattie counted off the buildings one through twelve, pointing out each row. "We'll go where Robo takes us. Any questions?"

She waited a beat. When there were no questions, she keyed on the transmitter she wore on her shoulder and spoke to the sergeant in charge. "K-9 One reporting. In place and ready."

"Copy, K-9 One. It's a go."

She rolled her shoulders inside her Kevlar vest to loosen the knots that had formed. Sweat rolled down her spine.

Stay focused. Don't get distracted. And listen to your dog.

Robo, a ninety-pound male German shepherd, stood at her side. He wore a Kevlar dog vest and his blue nylon tracking harness. "Are you ready to work?" she asked, using excitement in her voice to increase his prey drive. Robo jumped on his hind feet, careful not to paw at her.

She unsnapped the leash from his collar and fixed it to her utility belt. Today, she would let him search off lead. She'd grown to trust her partner's obedience, and she knew she should allow him to follow his own instincts. Robo's instincts were sometimes all that stood between Mattie and a life-or-death situation—not just today, but every day they were on duty.

She raised her hand to signal the start of the mission. "Okay, Robo. Let's go to work."

He trotted beside her as she went to the passenger side of the Dodge. After opening the front door, she gestured toward the seat. "Scent this."

He whiffed briefly, his delicate lips fluttering, and then headed away from the car, nose to the ground. Mattie signaled the others to follow as she jogged behind Robo, matching his pace. He led her down the asphalt alley between rows one and two. Mattie scanned the tops of the warehouses and spotted a vent that might hide a sniper. She crouched, pointing at it.

Officer Green studied it through his riflescope while the other officers followed, staying in a tight group.

Robo led them to the end of the building, his ears moving forward and back as he monitored the sounds in front and checked on Mattie behind. He seemed to be remembering his training to keep only a short distance between them and not to run off too fast, so she could act as backup for him. His Kevlar vest looked heavy and hot, and his paws left damp prints. She hated that, but it couldn't be helped. He needed the protective equipment as much as she did.

At the end of building one, Robo paused and sniffed in two different directions. Mattie noted the position. If she was reading Robo's signals correctly, the fugitives had probably split up at this point. Robo headed down one of the scent trails, tracking the scent he picked up on the passenger seat.

"They split up here," she said to the other officers. "Red and Blue, you go that way. Green, come with me."

She hurried after Robo. He headed into a narrow passageway between two buildings. It was filled with air-conditioning systems, ductwork, and vents. "Robo, wait," she said, and he stopped.

She scanned the area, the back of her neck tingling. She checked Robo and noticed the fur at his neck lay flat, no hackles raised. The fugitive had come this way, but he wasn't close now.

"Go on," she told him. "Search."

Her dog slipped into the area with Mattie close behind. She looked back over her shoulder to check on Green. He was scanning all directions: forward, upward, and back. Doing his job. No need to instruct him.

Robo dodged behind a heat vent. His tail splayed on the ground behind the vent, and Mattie knew that he'd sat, indicating he'd found something. She moved forward to where she could see him. He was sitting beside a bundle, and when she came around, he touched it with his nose.

He'd found a leather purse wedged into a crack between the ductwork, not quite out of sight but not readily apparent. If an officer gave the spot a cursory glance, he might miss it.

"Good boy." Mattie picked up the purse. Opening it, she found it filled with jewelry. She showed it to Green. He nodded, taking it from her and slipping the strap over his shoulder to carry.

Mattie had thought the passenger might be the one to carry the stash. Pleased that she'd asked Robo to sniff the right seat, she waved a hand back toward the scent trail.

"Robo, search."

Robo backtracked out of the narrow space and headed on beyond the next building. He'd successfully followed the fugitive into the passageway to find the stash and then picked up the trail to follow him back out. This was a significant improvement in his skill level for tracking. Her dog never failed to amaze her.

At the end of the building, Robo paused and circled the area for a thorough sniffing. Mattie read his movements to mean that one or more scent trails had merged with the one they'd been following. She conjured an image of two fugitives splitting off behind while the one went to hide the stash and then joining together at this point.

"Wait, Robo," she said. She keyed on her transmitter. "Officer Blue, do you read me?"

"Affirmative, K-9 One."

"Do you have a visual on our suspects?"

"Negative."

"Come to the southwest end of building six to rejoin for backup."

"Copy that, K-9 One. Over."

Mattie waited until she spotted the other two officers rounding the end of the first row of buildings. She turned back to Robo. "Okay, Robo. Search."

With his nose to the ground, he headed toward the end of the third row of warehouses, across a wide, open space dotted with several parked vehicles. As Mattie ran after him, she scanned the area, finding too many places where a fugitive could set up an ambush. She started to pull back, but Robo was hot on the trail. He darted ahead, hackles raised. Mattie reacted at once. "Robo, here. Come!"

Robo whirled and headed toward her. A shot fired. The bullet hit the pavement, missing him by mere feet.

Mattie shouted at Robo to heel, and she ran in a zigzag pattern to take cover behind a white industrial van. Green stayed with her while Red and Blue hunkered down behind a delivery truck on the other side of the parking lot. She assessed the situation. No one had been injured, and Robo stood safely beside her.

She opened radio contact to everyone. "Do we have a location on the shooter?"

Officer Red responded. "Behind the third vehicle down, gray van."

She peered around the end of the van that covered her. A bullet smacked the pavement a foot away from her. She ducked back behind the van, making sure Robo stayed behind her.

"Red and Blue, provide a diversion. Pin down the shooter with firepower. Green and I will move forward in front of the vehicles."

Mattie crept forward. "Robo, heel." They neared the front of the van, Robo so close it was as if they moved as one. Green stayed directly behind them.

When she rounded the front of the van, she could see a space between the building and the fronts of the next three vehicles that would provide cover.

"Fire now," she ordered.

Shots rang out from across the parking lot. Mattie raised a hand and gave Green the signal to follow. Crouching, she jogged down the narrow passage with Robo at heel, stopping at the last vehicle, a white utility truck with racks on the side.

"Are there keys inside?" she asked Green, her voice quiet and firm, hiding the fact that her stomach clenched with nerves.

He moved down the passenger side, staying hidden from the shooter. "Affirmative."

"Can you drive this truck real slow and shield me so I can get to the shooter?"

His face lit up with a smile. "That's an affirmative, K-9 One."

She turned on her transmitter. "Green and I plan to flush this guy out. Provide cover. Then move forward when you can."

Green opened the passenger door and disappeared inside the truck. Moments later, the truck's engine roared to life. Mattie checked Robo. He was still latched on to her left heel, following her every move.

"Good boy, Robo. Heel." She kept the utility truck between her and the shooter as Green backed it slowly out of the space. The other officers continued to fire, trying to pin the guy down and neutralize him. Green drove the truck down the parking lot with Mattie and Robo creeping alongside.

Within seconds, the shooting stopped from behind the gray van. A black form materialized in the van's shadow. The fugitive ran toward the building and slipped through an open door before Mattie could draw a bead on him.

She spoke to all the officers. "The suspect moved into building nine."

Red and Blue left their position and ran to join her.

"Move the truck in front of the door," she told Green, "and take cover behind it. Watch this exit. And watch for the other fugitives. Remember, we have at least two suspects out here, maybe three."

She scanned the parking lot. "Red and Blue, split up and go to the other side. There's probably another exit. Make sure we don't lose them that way."

Robo danced from side to side on his front feet as the two officers broke away and ran in different directions. But he stayed at Mattie's heel without her having to prompt him. Green had taken cover behind the utility truck. She sprinted toward the open door, Robo close beside her, but stopped short of the opening. Taking cover at the door's edge, she peered into the building. The dim light inside revealed nothing. She blinked and refocused.

"Scent this," she spoke to Robo quietly, pointing at the invisible scent trail the fugitive had left when he charged through the doorway. "Search."

Nose to the ground, Robo entered with Mattie immediately behind him. Static erupted on her headset.

"Halt!" Officer Red shouted. And then she heard the sounds of his breath as he started to run.

"Robo, wait." She paused and listened, her eyes scanning the warehouse she'd just entered. The place was filled with rows of containers stacked from floor to ceiling, and a skid-steer loader was parked close by. Narrow alleyways branched off between the rows. She hurried to take cover behind the skid-steer.

Officer Red's voice came into her headset, loud and breathless. "K-9 One. We've apprehended and neutralized two suspects. Do you copy?"

"Affirmative."

"Both suspects are unarmed. Neither one is the shooter. I repeat, we do *not* have the shooter."

"Copy that," Mattie said. "How many exits?"

"Two. Your entry and one at the north end."

"Green and Blue, guard both exits. Red, come inside to back us up. Can you make that happen?"

"Affirmative. Hold for one minute. Over."

With her heart pumping more energy than she knew what to do with, Mattie waited until she saw Officer Red appear in the doorway. He signaled that he'd spotted her.

Mattie lifted the face guard on her helmet and shouted toward the back of the warehouse. "You are surrounded by police! We have blocked all exits. You cannot escape. Surrender at once."

Silence.

Pulling her face guard back into place, she directed Robo toward the scent trail. "Robo, search." As they moved forward, she signaled Officer Red to follow.

Robo led Mattie into a narrow passage between the rows of boxes, while Red covered her back. A wave of claustrophobia enveloped her as the boxes towered above, threatening to fall and crush. She focused on Robo's back, watching the hair bristle and rise on the back of his neck. She scanned up and down the passageway, looking for signs of an ambush.

They reached an intersection, and Robo turned right. Mattie made the turn almost at the same time he did, her weapon held ready to shoot. Gliding down the narrow passage with his nose to the ground, Robo picked up speed. Mattie stayed close.

They came into an open space. Mattie spied the fugitive, moving away from her at an ungainly pace, his shape bulky in the dim light.

"Robo, take him!"

With lethal silence, Robo darted after the man. He leapt, striking the runner's right arm. The gun hit the floor and skidded, scrapping against the concrete. Robo's growls filled the space as he used his weight to pull the man to his knees.

Mattie approached cautiously, signaling Officer Red to pick up the gun.

"Out!" the fugitive cried. "Robo, out!"

Robo turned more vicious, growling and giving the man's arm a fierce shake. Mattie smiled. Robo's tail was waving.

This is what he lives for.

A full suit of bite gear with extra padding around the arms and hands protected the fugitive from her dog's terrible jaws. She let Robo have his fun for a few more seconds before she decided to call a halt. "Robo, out!" Mattie used a loud, firm voice to instruct him.

Robo broke away at once and backed up a step, tail still waving.

"Guard!"

Her dog crouched into guard position, mouth open, teeth exposed, jowls dripping.

"Have you had enough, Sergeant Madsen?" Mattie asked the fugitive.

The large man in the bite suit stayed on his knees and raised his hands in surrender. Mattie saw his smile beaming from behind the protective gear he wore on his face.

"You can call him off now, Deputy. I give up."

"Robo, down."

Robo dropped into a down position, but his posture said that he was ready to go again any time.

Madsen, Robo's trainer, pulled off his helmet. Sweat glistened on his shiny, bald head and dripped down to roll across the tattoo of a policeman's badge above his right ear. He grinned up at Mattie. "Well, he's surely your dog now, Deputy. No doubt about it."

Mattie smiled back. "He's every bit the dog you made him, Sergeant. No one could ask for a better partner."

"Congratulations. Now go play with your dog, and we'll debrief here in a few minutes, after I get the hell out of this goddamn bite suit."

Mattie told Robo to come with her as she pulled off her helmet and walked out into the sunshine. She felt the sweat drip down her scalp, and she ran her fingers through her hair, inviting the breeze to cool her head. Robo gamboled alongside, nosing her utility belt.

"Just wait a minute," she told him. "Let me take off your vest first."

She undressed Robo, gave him some water, and then took out his tennis ball, his reward for a successful exercise. Mattie tossed it out into the parkway. His nails skittered and caught as he turned to run after it.

Officer Red saluted her and gave her a quick smile before turning to uncuff his two prisoners. They all started to peel off their protective gear. The Simunition they'd used for the exercise was a form of nonpenetrating ammo, but it could still pack a punch on an unprotected body. These trainings were critical for Robo to teach him new abilities and to keep his entire skill set sharp. Not to mention how they enhanced the bond that was growing between Mattie and him as partners.

Mattie played with Robo, looking forward to an evening of drinks and camaraderie with her fellow trainees. She threw the ball and her dog bounded after it, bringing it back with a jaunty step and a proud look on his face. He gave it up readily and backed off, waiting for the next throw with eagerness apparent in his toothy grin. He would retrieve the ball as many times as she could throw it.

Her cell phone vibrated in her pocket. Pausing, she took it out, noticing the call came from the sheriff's office in Timber Creek. "This is Deputy Cobb."

Chief Deputy Brody's gravelly voice rumbled through the receiver. "We've got a situation here, Cobb. We need you to come back tonight."

"What is it?"

He paused for a split second. "Adrienne has gone missing."

Adrienne Howard, Brody's girlfriend. "She's missing?"

"Yes. She disappeared yesterday afternoon. I haven't seen or heard from her since."

Mattie tried to think of what to say next. Brody wouldn't want to hear it, but Adrienne could have left town on her own. Maybe even to get away from Brody; she doubted that any relationship with the chief deputy could be easy.

"She's been missing only twenty-four hours?"

"Sheriff McCoy authorized filing a missing person's report, even though it's a day early. There's no doubt about her status. When can you get back to Timber Creek?"

Mattie didn't share his certainty, but there was nothing she could do about it. "I have one more debriefing and then I'll leave. I should be back in about five hours."

"ETA at seven o'clock this evening, then?"

"Yes."

"Come right to the station. The sheriff or I will be here."

"Affirmative. See you then."

"And Cobb . . . thanks. We need your help on this one."

"Sure, Brody."

She disconnected the call, reflecting on the strain she'd heard in Brody's voice. He really was infatuated with the woman. She hoped he wasn't in for a big letdown. Right now, she'd bet that Adrienne Howard had run away from him. Even though Brody wasn't on her best-friends list, she'd hate to see him brokenhearted.

Chapter 2

Cole Walker, DVM, tied the last knot, picked the scissors out of the stainless steel tray his daughter Angela was holding for him, and snipped the suture. He leaned back on his heels and inspected the neat row of stitches he'd placed on the horse's leg.

"Thanks, Angel," he said, using the nickname he'd given his fifteen-year-old daughter when she was a toddler. "Now could you get that blue wrap from the counter?"

She turned away to retrieve it.

"This wound is superficial," Cole told the owner, Garrett Hartman. "It should heal well, though it's likely to leave a scar."

The craggy rancher pushed his Stetson back on his head. "That's okay. This fella works cows, not the show circuit."

The quarter horse gelding stood steady and quiet in the stocks, a metal stanchion designed to hold horses while they were being worked on. His dark bay coat glistened in the overhead light that Angela had switched on as the sunlight waned. After dinner, she'd come out to the clinic to help Cole with this emergency while his youngest, eight-year-old Sophie, stayed at home with their new housekeeper, Molly Gibbs. Since his attempts at day help had all been tremendous failures, Cole was trying something new: a live-in housekeeper. He was desperate for this new arrangement to work out.

Angela handed him the wrap, her fingers pale and thin against the blue elastic bandage. She reminded him of his ex-wife, willowy and blonde, while his youngest took after him, sturdy and brunette.

"Leave this bandage on for two days and then take it off to check the wound. If it looks clean, you can apply an ointment that I'll give you and rewrap it. If you're concerned about how it looks, give me a call, but I don't think you'll have any problems with it." Cole rolled the bandage over a gauze pad he'd placed on top of the sutures. "How's Leslie doing these days?"

Cole noticed that Angela watched Garrett, awaiting his answer. He and his wife Leslie were the parents of one of her best friends, Grace, a girl who'd been murdered a few months ago.

Garrett cleared his throat. "She's doing as well as can be expected, I guess. We're awful lonely. You could come out and see us sometime, Angie, if you want."

The girl nodded. "I'd like that. Maybe tomorrow after school?"

"Sure, I'll tell Leslie."

"Can Mrs. Gibbs take me and Sophie out together, Dad?"

"Okay," Cole said. "Would it be all right for Sophie to visit too, Garrett?"

Lines crinkled the weathered skin around the corners of Garrett's light blue eyes. It did Cole's heart good to see his friend smile, something lacking the last few times they'd visited.

"Sure," Garrett said. "Leslie will be glad to see both you girls."

Angela ran a hand down the gelding's back and then used her fingers to rub in a circular motion along each side of his spine. Cole recognized the technique Adrienne Howard had taught her for relaxing the muscles that connected to the vertebrae. The gelding's eyelids drooped as he visibly melted under her touch.

Although many owners across the country were using therapeutic massage to help rehabilitate performance horses with strained muscles and injuries, Cole had to wonder if it would ever catch on with the ranchers around Timber Creek. Adrienne seemed dedicated to learning and practicing these specialized techniques, and she'd been willing to work at no charge, so several of Cole's clients had offered their horses to help enhance her training. Only time would tell if she could turn her volunteer work into a form of income.

"Dad, what did you find out about Adrienne?" Angela asked as she continued to massage the gelding. "Did you call her work?"

"Yeah. The lady I talked to said they don't know where she is."

"What's this about?" Garrett asked.

"Adrienne Howard. She works and lives out at Valley Vista hot springs. She's a massage therapist the kids and I met about a month ago. She's been coming to the clinic to practice massage on horses."

"She was supposed to come this afternoon, but she didn't show," Angela said.

"Maybe she forgot," Garrett said. "I seem to do a lot of that lately."

Cole shook his head. "I doubt it. She had several appointments, and it's not like her to miss them."

"There's no reason for concern, is there?" Garrett said.

But Cole could read the concern in his friend's eyes anyway. And why wouldn't he worry? After what happened to Grace, they all did. "I don't know what to think. Anya, the therapist I talked to, told me Adrienne worked yesterday morning at the hot springs, business as usual. She was scheduled to have the afternoon off, but she didn't come home last night. I don't know . . . maybe she just decided to take off. People do that sometimes."

"I'd sure be worried," Garrett said with a frown.

"Apparently her coworkers notified the sheriff's office that she's missing."

"Have you called Mattie to ask her what's going on?" Angela asked.

"No, Mattie's in Denver today at a training exercise. She'll be back tomorrow. I'll check in with her then."

"We need to do something before tomorrow, Dad." Angela's tone sounded reproachful, nothing new to Cole. He'd had a hard time pleasing his eldest lately.

"I'm sure the sheriff's office is taking care of things," Cole said, hoping that would put her mind at ease.

But Garrett wasn't ready to rest easy either. "What if she's the victim of foul play, like our Grace? We need to see how we can help find this lady. I'll call the sheriff's office and see if he wants to mobilize the sheriff's posse to search for her."

Cole had joined the sheriff's posse himself after Grace's death last summer. The group of mounted volunteers helped with crowd control at county events and rodeos, as well as search and rescue in the local wilderness area.

Angela was giving Cole a look that he found irritating. "It's a big country we've got here," he said, trying to explain. "I don't know where we'd start to look. Maybe Adrienne decided to leave town on her own. We don't know yet if she's truly missing."

"Well, we've got to do something to find out. We can't just sit around and wait," Angela said.

"We might not have a choice." Cole finished wrapping the gelding's leg and stood. "I tell you what. I'll call Sheriff McCoy and see if they know anything yet. Why don't you go ahead and load this guy, Garrett. Maybe by then we'll have some answers."

Cole released the end of the stocks and swung the side bar wide, so Garrett could back the gelding out. Its shod hooves scraped the concrete floor as it moved out of the equine treatment room. Angela followed Garrett and the horse outside, leaving Cole alone as he pulled out his cell phone and scrolled to the sheriff's office phone number. The trouble with drug traffic through town last summer had made him cautious, and he'd placed both Deputy Mattie Cobb and the sheriff's office on his contact list.

A woman answered the phone. "Timber Creek County Sheriff."

Cole identified himself. "I'm a friend of Adrienne Howard's, and I'm worried about her. I'm wondering if I could talk to Sheriff McCoy."

After only a brief time on hold, Cole recognized the sheriff's voice immediately. Its deep, rich timbre was unmistakable. "Hello, Cole. I understand you're calling about Adrienne Howard."

Cole explained the relationship he had with Adrienne and how she'd missed her appointment earlier in the day. "The kids and I are worried about her, so I thought I'd call and see if anything had changed."

The sheriff hesitated, as if choosing his words carefully. "We're taking her absence seriously, Cole. I'm concerned enough that I've authorized a missing person's report."

"I don't know Adrienne very well, but it seemed out of character for her not to show up today. Is there anything I can do?"

"What time were you expecting her?"

"At three o'clock. She schedules horse clients at my clinic."

"That's good to know. We need to interview people who worked with Adrienne. Can you make a list of clients that she's seen in the past few weeks? We'll need names and phone numbers."

"We have some confidentiality issues that would prohibit me from doing that, but I'll do my best. Angie and I can make a list tonight and get permission for you to call. I don't anticipate any problems with that. We'll have it for you as soon as possible."

Garrett and Angela came back into the treatment room, Garrett's eyes searching out Cole's. The grief that lingered in his friend's face caused an icy tingle to run up Cole's spine, giving him a bad feeling.

"I have Garrett Hartman here at the clinic with me, Sheriff. If you get a lead that calls for a search party, let us know and we'll activate the posse." Cole hesitated but decided to go ahead and ask. "When do you expect Deputy Cobb to return?"

"She's on her way right now. We expect her around seven."

It seemed odd, but knowing Mattie would return soon made him feel a little better.

Cole said good-bye and disconnected the call. He shared the details he'd gleaned from the sheriff with Garrett and Angela. Anxiety pinched his daughter's face. She'd formed a bond with Adrienne while they worked together here at the clinic. Angie had been through a lot lately. First his divorce, then Grace's death, and now this. The strain was beginning to show.

"Come here, Angie," Cole said, sheltering her under his arm and bringing her close for a one-arm hug. "The sheriff wants us to make a list of Adrienne's clients. That gives us something we can do to help."

"You and your sister are still welcome to come out after school tomorrow," Garrett told her.

Angela nodded. "Tell Leslie hello for me."

Garrett's face lightened somewhat. "I surely will. She'll be happy to hear from you. I'd better get on the road now."

Cole and Angela followed him outside and watched him drive away, down the lane that led past the house and then out to the highway. Cole put his arm around Angela's shoulders while they stood, and she seemed to take comfort from the gesture.

"Let's clean up and get started on that list. I need to call everyone before we turn it over to the sheriff, and I'd like to get it to him tonight."

"Okay."

As Cole followed her into the clinic, he thanked his lucky stars that his own daughters were here with him, safe at home. If he lost one of them, the way the Hartmans had lost their Grace, it would kill him. The girls' mother had checked out of their lives last spring and seemed to have turned her back on them. He still couldn't understand what Liv was thinking. He may never. Didn't she know what she was doing to her kids?

While he cleaned up the treatment room, he thought of Adrienne. She was dedicated to her profession and was a bundle of energy. Did she have a mother that worried about her? A father? He knew very little about the woman except that she was kind, caring, and had a gift for easing tight muscles in people and horses.

He hoped that everything would be all right and that someone would hear from her soon.

Chapter 3

Shortly before seven, Mattie drove past the lane that led to Cole's clinic. The new Ford Explorer the county had purchased for the K-9 unit had eaten up the miles between Denver and Timber Creek, so she'd made excellent time. She glanced down the lane but could see nothing, shrubs and trees blocking her view of both the house and the vet clinic. The property felt familiar. Since meeting Cole Walker and his daughters last August, they'd become friends.

She started to call Cole to tell him she was back in town but decided that would be silly. Although they shared dinner once in a while and spent occasional evenings sitting on his front porch with his kids—watching Robo and the Walkers' dog, Belle, play and talking about everything from dogs to stars and constellations—it wasn't like they were a couple or anything. Nothing like that. They were friends; that was all.

Mattie wished she'd been able to at least catch a glimpse of him.

Within minutes, she pulled up in front of the Timber Creek County Sheriff's Department, parked her SUV, and unloaded Robo from the back. He'd slept most of the way, and now he trotted beside her at heel, waving his tail, fresh and sassy. She, on the other hand, felt like it had been a very long, hot day. She wished she had time to go home and shower, but it couldn't be helped. She'd promised Brody seven o'clock, and now she would deliver.

She was surprised to see Rainbow sitting at the dispatcher's desk. Her shift should have ended hours ago. Relief crossed the dispatcher's face when Mattie and Robo came through the front door.

"Oh, Mattie," Rainbow said, quick tears welling, her voice almost breathless. She brushed a strand of blonde hair back away from her face. "Thank goodness you're here. I know you were supposed to have the weekend off, but we need you. Adrienne disappeared, and I think something bad has happened to her. You know how you get that feeling in your gut sometimes, that feeling of dread? Well, I've had it all day. You know what I mean, don't you?" Rainbow paused for a breath, searching Mattie's face with reddened eyes.

Rainbow had made friends with the hot springs crowd early last summer, and evidently she'd become close friends with Adrienne Howard.

"I know what you mean," Mattie said. "But why do you feel that way? Maybe she's just decided to leave town for the weekend, to take a break."

Rainbow shook her head. "No, Adrienne would never do that. She would never go away without telling someone—she knows we'd worry. Besides, she loves her life. She was unhappy before she came here, but she loves what she's doing." Rainbow glanced at Brody's office, and Mattie followed her gaze. His door was closed. Rainbow continued in a near whisper. "She loves Deputy Brody, too. She would never leave him. He's about to go crazy with worry, you know."

"What do you think happened to her?"

"We don't know." Rainbow's voice caught. "I think she went on a hike yesterday afternoon and something happened. Maybe she fell or twisted her ankle."

Brody's door opened and he came through it. "Cobb. How long have you been here?"

Mattie couldn't believe how bad Brody looked. Shadow darkened his unshaven jaw, and his icy blue eyes appeared bloodshot and tired. She guessed he'd not slept since Adrienne failed to show up last evening. "I just got in."

Brody started toward the briefing room. "Come with me. Rainbow, notify the sheriff that I'm starting to brief Deputy Cobb."

"I will," Rainbow said, reaching for the phone. "Do you want him to come back to the station?"

"That's his decision. He told me to let him know when Cobb arrived."

"Got it."

"He went home for dinner," Brody said to Mattie as she followed him into the briefing room, Robo at heel. Her dog seemed to love that heeling position, the lesson they'd reinforced during the training exercise today, and he chose to stick by her side without being told.

The dry-erase board had been wheeled to the front of the room, an eight-by-ten blow-up of what looked like Adrienne's driver's license photo posted at the top. Mattie recognized her: pretty face, blonde shoulder-length hair, gray eyes, and a happy smile. She also recognized Brody's handwriting on the board. He'd summarized the investigation to date. Evidently, he didn't share her suspicion that Adrienne left town of her own free will, and it was obvious that Rainbow didn't either. And both of them knew the woman much better than she did.

"Sit," Brody said, gesturing to a chair.

Robo sat at Mattie's heel.

She glanced down at him and suppressed a smile. He was panting slightly, his deep brown eyes meeting hers as if anticipating her next wish. He was being such an obedient guy today.

"I'll stand. I've been sitting for hours. What do you have so far?" she asked.

Brody pointed to the top of the board where yesterday's date was written. "Missing since Wednesday afternoon. Worked at Valley Vista hot springs yesterday morning, took the afternoon off. Presumably went for a hike. Took her car. Left her purse, money, credit cards at home."

That last detail influenced Mattie's opinion: no one ran away without money and credit cards, unless they'd established a secret bank account somewhere and wanted to disappear without a trace. Could Adrienne have done that kind of planning? And if so, why?

"Deputy Johnson and I have driven over half the county last night and today, checking places I know she likes to hike. Covered Ute Canyon, Butterfly Pass, Old Flowers Trail, and the others listed here." Brody waved a hand down a long list of hiking trails near Timber Creek. "Her car isn't parked at any of the trail heads."

"Have you issued a BOLO on the car?" Mattie asked.

"Yes. This afternoon."

The door behind her opened. Mattie turned to see Sheriff McCoy enter the room. A large African American man, Abraham McCoy exuded quiet confidence. His serene expression countered Brody's anxious one, and she appreciated the calming presence the sheriff carried with him.

"Welcome home, Deputy Cobb," he said. "Thank you for coming back early."

"Not a problem. I hope I can help."

"We anticipate needing Robo to search as soon as we locate Miss Howard's car." McCoy took a seat at a table. "Go ahead, Chief Deputy," he said to Brody.

Mattie turned her attention back to the board. Brody indicated the next point: *Mother—Velda Howard.*

"Velda Howard is Adrienne's mother, but they're estranged. I contacted her this morning to see if she knows anything. She lives in Hightower." Hightower was only about thirty miles from Timber Creek. "She hasn't talked to Adrienne for six years. Had no idea that she moved here. She says Adrienne left home for California six years ago with her high school sweetheart, Kevin Conrad. She hasn't heard from her since."

"Why are they estranged?" Mattie asked.

"Mother didn't approve of her choice of boyfriends."

Mattie nodded and looked at the next point: *Kevin Conrad.*

"I found the old boyfriend today. He's still living in California. Spoke with him on the phone. He and Adrienne split up five years ago. Said he didn't know where she moved, didn't talk with her after she left."

Brody had literally covered a lot of territory; no wonder he looked so exhausted.

"Was the split amicable?" She was wondering if foul play from an ex could be involved.

"Yes, according to him. He's married now and has a kid."

"And were you able to confirm that he's actually in California, both today and yesterday? He hasn't been here in Timber Creek?"

"Yes. He gave me the name of his employer. I confirmed the phone number from a public source. He was at work both days. It's legit."

Brody's hand moved to the next point: *Residence/Employment—Valley Vista Hot Springs.* "Dean Hornsby—what a piece of work that guy is—won't give permission to search the yurt where she lives or the one where she does massage. And Judge Taylor won't issue a search warrant until Adrienne's been missing forty-eight hours."

Hornsby, the owner of the hot springs resort, had been a suspect in the Grace Hartman case. Detective Stella LoSasso, who'd helped with the case, had dubbed the ineffective and soft-looking man "the tampon king of Arizona." He'd sold an inherited personal-products business prior to moving to Timber Creek and investing the proceeds into Valley Vista hot springs, hoping to turn it into a popular, yet rustic, health spa. No, the man wouldn't be willing to assume the risk and responsibility for permitting an unwarranted search. But maybe Anya, the other massage therapist, could provide information.

"Have you talked with Anya Yamamoto yet?" Mattie asked.

"Yes. She confirmed Miss Howard was missing this morning," McCoy said. "She believes that Adrienne went hiking yesterday afternoon, which is also Deputy Brody's opinion."

Rainbow's too, Mattie thought.

Brody pointed to the next item: *Massage Therapy Clients—Cole Walker.* This point surprised Mattie. She didn't know Cole was involved at the hot springs.

"Adrienne has been working with Walker at his clinic, doing massage on horses," Brody said. "She was scheduled to be there at three o'clock this afternoon, and he called in after she didn't show. We don't know for sure yet, but this means she might've gone on a stable or farm call yesterday afternoon instead of a hike. Adrienne keeps her own horse client schedule, and no one else seems to be privy to it. Walker is putting together a list of clients for us to contact. We'll follow up to see if she had an appointment with any of them or if she mentioned where she might be yesterday afternoon to anyone."

"When will we have that list?" Mattie asked.

"Any time now. He planned to call each one to skirt around confidentiality issues."

Mattie nodded. "Maybe we can get someone at the hot springs to do the same. We should interview all of Adrienne's clients. Who knows what they discuss during a session? Maybe one of them will have a lead."

"I'll call Anya Yamamoto and suggest it," McCoy said.

Brody added *Massage Therapy Clients—Hot Springs* to the board.

Mattie thought of something else. "What about her cell phone, Brody?"

"I'm not sure where it is. She always keeps it with her."

"I'll see if Ms. Yamamoto can find it at the hot springs," McCoy said. "Any other ideas for next steps?"

"I have a few more trailheads to check for her car," Brody said.

"Have you alerted the forest rangers on that BOLO? Sandy Benson and her crew were the ones who found Grace Hartman's car for us," Mattie said.

"Yes, I spoke with Ranger Benson," McCoy said. "They're on it."

Mattie looked at Brody, taking in his haggard appearance. "With all due respect, it's important for you to get some sleep tonight, Brody. Tell Benson where you want the rangers to search and then go home. Once we find that car, we're going to need you on the ground. Not everyone can take on those hiking trails, you know. You and Johnson are the only ones who can keep up with Robo and me."

Brody straightened and stared at her hard. She stared right back at him.

"Deputy Cobb's right," McCoy said. "We need to employ all the help we've got, and the rangers can take over searching the trailheads into the wilderness area. Now, is there anything else we should discuss?"

The thought crossed Mattie's mind that there was still a possibility that the woman had decided to rabbit on her own, but she kept it to herself. It appeared she was the only one in the room who had doubts. Sheriff McCoy took the utilization of resources seriously, and his commitment appeared to be 100 percent. She remained silent.

"Deputy Cobb, call Dr. Walker and see if he has some people you can interview," McCoy said. "Let's get started on that list."

"I'll call Benson," Brody said.

"You need to go home, Deputy Brody," McCoy said. "We'll notify you if we get a serious lead."

Brody didn't respond. Instead, he turned to write *Cell Phone* on the dry-erase board.

"Tomorrow I'm going to establish a tip line and run it through the front desk. The weekly paper will run the ad in the morning," McCoy said.

Mattie nodded and prepared to leave, looking down at her partner. During the discussion, Robo had lain near her feet and followed their conversation with pricked ears.

"You ready to roll, Robo?" she asked.

He scrambled to his feet and followed her out to the lobby where Rainbow still sat at the dispatcher's desk, her reddened eyes dark with fatigue.

"Why are you working the night shift?" Mattie asked her.

"Sam Corns couldn't come in tonight."

"You can turn it over to the answering service, can't you?"

Rainbow shook her head. "I can't take that chance. Someone might call in about Adrienne. Unless it's an emergency, we wouldn't get the message until morning."

Mattie paused and took a long look at her friend. Usually perky and dressed in flowing garments, today she wore a T-shirt and khakis, her blonde hair scraped back in a ponytail with wispy strands falling down. Rainbow had brought Mattie soups and casseroles while she was recuperating from an injury she'd sustained when making a dangerous arrest last August. If there was any woman in this town she could call a friend, Rainbow would be the one.

Until recently, Mattie had believed friendships were like baggage, and she'd preferred to travel light through life. Lately, though, she'd allowed a few people to breach the walls she'd put up around herself. She cared about Rainbow and hated to see her so distressed.

"Notify the answering service to call me if anything comes in," Mattie said. "Then go home and get some sleep. We need you on the day shift. Sheriff McCoy says a tip line will be advertised in tomorrow's paper."

A tear slipped down Rainbow's cheek. She blotted it with a tissue she held ready and looked away. "I just can't keep myself from imagining her out there in the forest somewhere, hurt and suffering. I'm so afraid for her."

Mattie reached out and put her hand on Rainbow's arm. "Worrying like that isn't going to help. Being here to answer the phone tomorrow will."

Rainbow dabbed her eyes, looking down at her lap. "You're right. I'll make sure the answering service knows to call you on your cell phone."

"Perfect." Mattie withdrew her hand.

"I promise I'll stay on this until we find her, Rainbow. Robo and I will do everything we can to bring Adrienne home."

Rainbow gave her a thin smile. "I can't tell you how much better I feel, just knowing you're back home. If anyone can find her out there, you two can."

The K-9 unit's reputation for tracking had been elevated last summer. Mattie hoped that under these new circumstances, Rainbow's confidence in them wouldn't be misplaced.

After saying good-night, she went to the staff office to call Cole. She swiped to her contacts list and tapped on his number.

"Hello, Mattie," he answered. "I heard you were coming back tonight."

He sounded happy to hear from her, and something gave her heart a squeeze. "And I heard you're helping us get leads on people who might know something about Adrienne Howard."

"Angie and I are working on that right now. Almost done."

"Good. I want to get some names and numbers from you so I can get started."

"All right. Here goes." Cole dictated the first part of his list while Mattie recorded the information.

"I didn't know that Adrienne was working with you," she said when they finished.

"She's working with some of my clients' horses. Volunteering for now, but I think she plans to expand her career in that direction eventually."

"Do you think she was seeing a client yesterday afternoon?" Mattie asked.

"So far every client I've called has told me 'no' to that question. I don't track her schedule, though, so I don't know."

"Her friends think she might have gone hiking." Mattie wondered how well Cole knew Adrienne. "Do you know anything about where she might have gone?"

"No, I'm sorry I don't. I know very little about her beyond her massage skills for horses. I don't know anything about her personal life."

Mattie felt a vague sense of relief but stayed focused on her own business. "Deputy Brody has searched several trailheads for her car. We also have the rangers looking."

"Good."

She paused, deciding to venture into territory that he'd already shared. "How are things going with Mrs. Gibbs?"

"Well, the jury's still out. So far the verdict seems split."

She smiled, thinking he might be speaking in code, since he was working at the clinic with Angela. "Let me guess. Sophie for, Angie against."

"You've got that right." His voice reflected the smile that Mattie could picture, soft with a little sideways quirk. She heard a lighter voice murmur in the background. "Angie says to tell you she knows we're talking about Mrs. Gibbs."

Angela was a hard one to slip past. Mattie's smile widened. "Oh."

"She wants to talk to you."

"Sure. Pass me over to her."

Angela's voice came into the receiver. "Mattie?"

"Hey."

"Hey." The teen's voice sounded tight and stressed when she continued. "I'm worried about Adrienne."

"We're on it, Angie. We're doing what we can to find her."

"Do you think someone shot her and buried her in the mountains like Grace?"

Mattie's breath caught. The poor girl. No teenager's mind should have to conjure that image as her number-one fear. "We have no evidence whatsoever that would point to that, Angie."

"I've just been thinking, you know."

"I know what you mean. Sometimes we can't help but think of the worst. Especially when such a bad thing happened so recently. But nothing indicates that Adrienne could be a victim of foul play." She tried to soothe the girl. "We hope she's out in the high country, took a wrong turn or something, and she'll either show up soon or we'll find her. Once we find her car, we'll know where to look. And the rangers are helping us with that."

"Okay, that sounds good. Can we help you search if you find her car?"

"Maybe, but the last thing we want is for people to get lost. We have a list of volunteers we can turn to who are familiar with the wilderness area around here if we need them."

"I want to help."

"I'll write you in at the top of my list to call if the right job turns up."

"Thanks, Mattie." Again there was a voice in the background, this time much deeper. "Dad wants to talk to you again."

"Okay." Mattie and Angela exchanged good-byes.

"So you'll let us know if there's anything more we can do?" Cole asked.

"Yes. I'll stay in touch."

"Thanks." He paused, and she wondered what else he wanted to say. "Be careful, Mattie."

"Always. Good luck on the other thing—Mrs. Gibbs."

She could hear his smile in his words. "Thanks, I'll need it."

As she said good-bye, she realized how even the sound of Cole's voice seemed to relax her.

Setting her personal life aside, she refocused and picked up her phone. It was eight o'clock, and she had a lot of calls to make before it grew too late. She hoped someone would know something that could turn up a lead.

Chapter 4

Friday

Mattie startled awake, rose onto one elbow, and blinked at the clock. Shutting off the alarm, she shivered in the cold bedroom and then felt a puff of warm breath against her shoulder. Robo stood beside the bed, chin resting on the mattress, staring at her. In response to her eye contact, he huffed and circled in excitement, nails clicking against the hardwood floor.

She put her head back on the pillow and closed her eyes, pulling the quilt that her foster mother had made for her up over her chin. The room went silent. She knew that Robo had returned to his post beside the bed and would be using his eyes to will her to stay awake with all the intensity he could muster. And if there was one thing her dog could muster, it was intensity.

She peeked at him again. His mouth broadened into a grin. "Okay, I'll get up."

While Robo did his happy dance, Mattie rolled from the bed and hurried to the window to close it. She'd slept with her bedroom window open for as long as she could remember, winter and summer alike. The autumn chill lingered in the room while she quickly dressed in gray sweatpants and a T-shirt that had "Timber Creek Sheriff Dept." stenciled across the front in solid, black letters. She donned socks and running shoes, grabbed a hoodie, and headed toward the front door of her house. Robo darted ahead, tail waving.

Out on the porch, she could feel a breeze that intensified the chilly air, blowing from the northwest—the direction from which Timber Creek received most of its cold fronts. She sniffed. Snow? Checking the sky, she thought of Adrienne Howard. If Adrienne was lost somewhere in the wilderness, an incoming storm didn't bode well.

After stretching, Mattie struck a path for T-hill, her typical run. Vigorous morning exercise made Robo a much better partner at the office, and it was a crucial part of their routine. With him keeping pace beside her at heel, she headed up the steep, rocky pathway. Near the top of the hill sat a letter *T* built with rocks, kept whitewashed by each year's high school freshman class. She jogged straight upward, running toward it.

On the way down, her cell phone rang. Mattie pulled it from her pocket and checked the display. Her foster mother.

"Good morning, Mama."

"Good morning, *mijita*."

Being called "my little daughter" always warmed Mattie's spirit. "You're up early."

"Ha! You always say that."

She smiled. "You'd think I'd be used to you getting up before the sun by now."

"*Si*. Come over for breakfast."

"I don't have much time."

"It's ready for you."

"I'll be there in about twenty minutes."

Putting her cell phone back into her pocket, Mattie sprinted for home, Robo matching her stride. After feeding him, she hurried to shower and dressed in record time. Then she loaded Robo into the SUV and drove the few blocks to Mama's house, the foster home where she'd spent her last few years in the system.

She told Robo to wait in the car and headed across the yard, passing Mama's collection of plaster of paris yard ornaments: small chipmunks, squirrels, and rabbits frozen in mid-scurry. Skirting around the side of the white stucco house, she entered through the kitchen door, stepping into a different world filled with lovely aromas. Mama T never sent anyone away hungry, and she cooked up love in every bite. Mattie's mouth watered.

"What have you fixed for me today?" she said as she entered the kitchen.

Mama T put down her long-handled spoon and turned from the wood-burning stove for a hug. Mattie placed her cheek against the woman's silvery streaked black hair, which was pulled into a bun at the nape of her neck. She held onto the small comfort for a moment until Mama let her go. Stepping back, they grinned at each other, Mama T's smile showing a gap or two where teeth were missing.

"This morning we have huevos rancheros with green chili and tortilla."

"Mmm . . ." One of Mama's old standbys. Grabbing up a hot pad, Mattie went to the stove to lift the black porcelain coffee pot with the white speckles. "Can I pour you a cup of coffee?" she asked.

"*Si, gracias.* Then sit." Mama placed two plates heaped with food on the table.

As was their habit, Mama uttered a brief prayer of gratitude and then they ate in silence. Mama always insisted that her guests savor each bite and not waste time with chitchat. After they finished, she spoke. "Your brother called."

Mattie had been waiting for him to call for months. He'd called Mama T last August, asking her to see if Mattie wanted to reconnect, and then nothing. Of course he had to call now, just when she needed to focus on work and finding Adrienne. "What did he have to say?"

"That he is glad you will talk to him. He took your cell phone number and your home number both. He said he will call you soon."

"Okay. How did he sound?"

A frown line formed between Mama's brows. Apparently she considered the question important enough to give it her full concentration. "He sounded tired. And maybe at first, afraid you would not want him to call you. Then he sounded relieved. Happy. But still tired."

Her foster mother could gather a great deal from even a short phone call. During high school, Mattie learned she could hide nothing from her Mama T.

"He said to tell you thank you, and he looks forward to talking to you."

Mattie couldn't help giving her head a slight shake. Her brother Willie was a mystery to her. She'd hoped, for all the years since they'd been separated after Willie was sent away, that he would find her someday. And now that he had, he'd delayed their reunion for months. It didn't make sense. She preferred tackling this kind of situation head on, not waiting around for the moment to fester.

"Did he leave you a phone number?"

"No. It's strange. I asked for it, but he said no, he would call you."

"Well, I guess I'll just wait to hear from him then. Thank you, Mama, for being the middleman on this. It seems kind of crazy the way he's handling it."

The lady smiled. "Middlewoman," she said, her eyes twinkling. Then she sobered. "It does seem strange. Like he's hiding something. I hope it will be all right."

Mattie touched her warm hand and then stood to carry her dishes to the sink. "Don't worry. This is good. You said so yourself."

"I did, *mijita*. And so it is. Now you go to your work. You have much more important things to do than washing my dishes."

Mattie hugged Mama T and let herself out the door. On the way to the car, she suppressed a shiver. She zipped her jacket, pretending it was the cold air that caused it. But she couldn't hold back the bad feeling she had swelling in her chest. Was it about Willie? What if he didn't call? She'd been unable to retrieve Willie's number because Mama T still used an old-fashioned rotary phone on her kitchen wall. Detective LoSasso had suggested they subpoena her foster mother's phone records to find the number, but Mattie hesitated to abuse a system meant to trace criminals and not long-lost relatives.

Or was the bad feeling caused by something else, something that lay hidden out there that she had yet to discover?

Whatever it was, she didn't like this feeling of dread one bit.

★

Cole could smell bacon cooking when he came down the stairs for breakfast. He was mentally thanking his sister for finding Mrs. Gibbs, until he heard that dear woman's voice wafting up the stairway alongside the scent of bacon. Her Irish brogue colored her speech, and her angry tone heated up the kitchen.

"Ye'll not be going to school in that outfit, young miss. Not while I'm in charge, anyway."

Cole resisted the urge to turn around and head back to his bedroom. He sighed and trudged into the kitchen to face the battle. He sought out Angela—for he knew it must be his eldest drawing fire—and recognized immediately what had instigated the housekeeper's censorship.

In addition to a stony face, Angela wore an extremely low-cut tank top that Cole hadn't seen since summer. "What's wrong with it?" she asked.

"It's shameless, it is. I'll not have you parading around school with your bosom exposed."

The last thing Cole wanted to talk about at breakfast was his teenage daughter's bosom. Angela had vacillated between being his right-hand girl and acting out since school started. He understood the difficulties a teenager faced, but he felt compelled to stand behind the housekeeper and present a united front. Especially since he agreed on this one. "Mrs. Gibbs is right, Angie. You need to go upstairs and change."

"I've worn this shirt to school before, Dad. You didn't complain about it then."

After receiving his divorce papers, Cole had been in a depressive funk when school started last summer. Back then, he probably hadn't noticed. "I don't remember that, but I'll take your word for it. Letting you wear this shirt was my mistake. Let's not repeat it. Go change, Angie, before you miss the bus."

"Dad."

How can she load such disgust and disappointment into one syllable? "Do what I say. Hurry up."

Throwing him a look that would kill a lesser man, Angie left the table. Cole turned his attention to his youngest, Sophie. She looked rather self-satisfied after witnessing her older sister's defeat and was dressed in a freshly ironed pink blouse, her brown curls tied up on top of her head with a gauzy pink scarf. Mrs. Gibbs's work, no doubt. Belle, their Bernese mountain dog, sat beside Sophie, eagerly watching for anything that might drop. Cole smiled. Belle knew who was the messy one in the family.

"Good morning, sunshine," Cole said to Sophie as he made his way to the coffee pot.

"Hi, Daddy," she said, taking a bite of scrambled egg. "Mrs. Gibbs made breakfast."

"Mmm . . . I could smell it on my way down the stairs. Thank you, Mrs. Gibbs."

Standing at the stove with spatula in hand, the woman gave him an approving nod, probably more for backing her up with Angela than for his expression of gratitude. She wore her gray hair in tight curls around her round and ruddy face. She'd only been with them for a few days, but so far she appeared to prefer more formal dress—black trousers with creases and neutral colored blouses that had a look of starch about them—rather than the denims and T-shirts that Cole and his youngsters were used to.

"How do you like your eggs, Dr. Walker?" she said, brandishing one above the skillet.

"Please, call me Cole," he told her for the umpteenth time. She gave him a slight shrug.

"Scrambled is great. Two please." He took his seat beside Sophie, relishing her smile, a childish greeting around the toast she was taking a bite out of at the same time. "Do you have your backpack ready?"

"Yes, I do. Today we're going to start a science lesson about stars. Mattie showed us the dippers and the North Star, so I'll have a head start."

"Sounds good, little bit." He looked at Mrs. Gibbs, wanting to draw her into the conversation. "Are you all still planning to go out to the Hartman place after school?"

"Yes," Sophie said, while Mrs. Gibbs said, "We will."

"Do you need directions?" Cole asked.

"Angela can show me the way, can she not?"

"I'm sure she can." Cole hoped Angie was in a better mood when the time came.

Mrs. Gibbs set his plate—piled high with steaming eggs, four strips of bacon, and toast—in front of him. He could get used to this. Since he'd taken over kitchen duty, they'd had nothing but boxed cereals to choose from in the morning.

"Mrs. Gibbs, I appreciate this more than you'll ever know."

The crow's feet deepened around her green eyes when she smiled. "Oh, I have a notion how much you like your bacon. Most men do."

Cole dug in, eating quickly so that he could get to the office.

"What would you like for dinner?" Mrs. Gibbs asked as she sat down at the table with her own plate.

Dinner. On the table after work. One that he didn't have to cook himself. Would wonders never cease? "I'll leave that entirely up to you. I'm easy to please."

"Hamburgers," Sophie chimed in.

"We'll see," Mrs. Gibbs told her. "Now run upstairs and brush your teeth. It's almost time to go out for the bus."

Sophie got up from the table, smacked a kiss on top of Belle's head, and headed up the stairs. Belle took off after her, limping only slightly from the gunshot wound she'd sustained last summer. After Sophie left, Mrs. Gibbs spoke quietly. "Young Angela isn't very pleased with me."

"She'll get over it. She's a good kid, but I think she's gotten used to calling her own shots around here the past few months."

"I'll try to respect that. But I feel I must express my own opinion when I see something that the girls are doing that I don't agree with."

"Of course. And I'll back you up when I can." Cole might be desperate to have help around the house, but he wouldn't turn over the raising of his kids to an outsider. "One thing I learned lately is that I've got to be involved with my kids, and we made a pact to communicate with each other. So I'll have to express my opinions, too. Often you and I will agree. Sometimes we might not. Then we'll have to work things out."

Mrs. Gibbs gave him a skeptical look. "We shall see."

It sounded ominous. "I'm sure we can work together. We just need to keep each other in the loop." He pushed back his chair, ending the conversation. "Thank you for breakfast. That's a mighty fine way to start the morning."

"And what do you want for your lunch?"

"I'm used to a sandwich, but I can make that myself. I never know when I'll be able to take a lunch break."

"I'll leave something made for you in the refrigerator."

Clearly Mrs. Gibbs knew her way into a man's heart. "Thanks. As long as I have fruit, chips, and sandwich fixin's, I'm a happy camper."

The kids came down the stairs together, Angie picking at Sophie's hair in a teasing way but dressed in a more acceptable shirt. Cole decided not to comment on it, gave both girls a hug, and saw them out the door. They headed up the lane toward the highway to catch the school bus.

He felt autumn's chill in the air and instantly thought of Adrienne Howard. He scanned the sky. Wispy gray clouds spread over half of it from the west, and they looked like they were filled with wind. As if proving him right, a light breeze lifted some dry leaves and scattered them across the lane. If a storm was brewing, the warm Indian summer might be coming to an end.

Leaving Mrs. Gibbs to her own means, he said good-bye, pulled his pickup truck out of the garage, and headed down the lane to his clinic.

Chapter 5

Cole's assistant, Tess Murphy, arrived at the clinic shortly after him. He'd never paid much attention to the way his assistant dressed before, but the discussion at home must have triggered a new awareness. He noticed that today she wore a wild-patterned T-shirt under her white jacket, and her red hair stood up in stiff spikes.

"Hi, hi." Tess gave him her usual twinkly greeting. "How goes it with Mrs. Gibbs this morning?"

"We're getting along fine." A private man, Cole had never liked to air his personal life, so he switched the subject. "What do we have on the schedule?"

The phone rang, and Tess answered. He looked at the schedule while Tess opened the computer screen for the intake of new clients. After tapping in information, Tess held out the phone, covering the speaker. "This is Carmen Santiago. New client—Dark Horse Stable. Wants to schedule an ambulatory visit for a sick stud horse. It's way up in the mountains, so I thought you might want to prioritize."

He nodded, tucked the phone against his ear, and headed for the treatment room to prepare for his first client of the day, a routine cat exam with inoculations. "This is Dr. Walker."

"Carmen Santiago. I need an appointment as soon as you can work us in."

"Tess told me you're having trouble with your stallion. What's going on?"

Her voice was low-pitched and melodious, and she had a slight Spanish accent. "He acts like he's in pain. Stiff through the hind legs—doesn't want to walk."

"Are the muscles in his back and hind legs hard, like they're in spasm?"

"Yes."

"Did you exercise him right before the symptoms started?"

"Yes. We'd just finished his first morning workout."

"All right," Cole said. "He could be tying up. It's a condition that sport horses can get after working out real hard. Are you familiar with it?"

"Yes, I've seen it before. But this seems different. There are also muscle tremors."

"Those can occur sometimes. Do you have any pain reliever?" Cole mentioned a common analgesic that most horse trainers kept on hand.

"I do."

"Start him on that." Cole explained the dosage. "I'll be up as soon as I can. Where is your place?"

"We're located about twenty miles out. Go ten miles toward Hightower and turn north on Soldier Canyon Road." She then described a series of twists and turns that led up into the high country.

"I didn't realize you were so far out. It will take me about an hour to get to you. Make him as comfortable as you can." He heard the front door to the clinic open and knew his first patient had arrived. "I'll have Tess do some rescheduling. I can leave here in about twenty minutes."

He made arrangements with Tess to reschedule his morning and took care of the cat. Then he checked supplies in the mobile vet unit that sat in the back of his pickup truck, climbed in, and headed west on the highway going through Timber Creek toward Hightower.

The first few miles were smooth sailing through lush meadows that swept away on either side of the road. Feeling a pang of guilt, he drove past his childhood home, a cattle ranch where his parents still lived. It had been months since he'd visited. His mother was a difficult lady, and he felt she was partially to blame for his divorce. He'd found out too late that his mother had criticized Olivia constantly, and his ex-wife blamed him for not stopping it.

Good Lord, how could I stop something I didn't even know was happening?

After he turned off onto Soldier Canyon, the road forced him to pay attention to his driving. Covered in gravel and ruts, it climbed a steep grade through pinion, limber pine, and ever thickening trees. Finally, after ten miles, he topped the last hill. From this vantage point, he could see a clearing in the valley and the red metal rooftops of several buildings, one a large barnlike structure. He kept the truck in low gear as he made his way toward the place, down through the heavy evergreen forest and pockets of aspen with golden leaves that shivered in the breeze. It seemed like an isolated location for a training stable, but many folks loved the mountains enough to put up with the distance.

He found the entry to the stable easily enough. It was the only one along this stretch and was marked well with a log archway. A wooden sign swung from the top, embossed with the name Dark Horse Stable. He drove under the arch and followed a narrow lane a half-mile through the forest until a clearing opened up.

The lane split to the left where Cole could see a huge log home perched on a rise. Its vaulted roof rose above a wall of glass, exposing a forest view for its occupants as well as a view of the stable off to his right. He followed the right fork and drove toward the barn, made of solid red metal panels. After driving around it, he could see a flat space had been cleared on the other side where a well-groomed racetrack had been built. A bay thoroughbred streaked around the track, its black mane and tail streaming, running full out with a small rider perched on top. Cole shut down his engine and paused for a moment to enjoy the sight of the beautiful and powerful animal.

A man of Hispanic descent approached the truck, and Cole got out to meet him. As the man came closer, Cole could make out his saddened expression, and he was reminded of a bloodhound: long face, sad droopy eyes. He extended his hand. "I'm Dr. Walker."

The man offered a limp handshake with a well-calloused hand but didn't state his name. *"Patron,"* he said, waving his other hand toward the racetrack.

Cole didn't understand much Spanish, but he knew the man was telling him that the boss was out there on the horse. "Okay," he said, making his way toward the track. He could see now that the rider was a woman, presumably Carmen Santiago.

The rider pulled up and slipped from the saddle, landing lightly on her feet. The man hurried to take the horse's reins.

"I'm Carmen," she said, extending her hand.

"Dr. Walker." Her handshake was so firm that for a moment he thought he'd entered an arm-wrestling contest.

Carmen, also of Hispanic descent, was gorgeous. She wore her long, shiny hair pulled back and secured at the base of her neck in a black braid. Her flawless skin was a deep tan, the same color as Mattie's. She looked at him with earnest brown eyes so dark they were almost black. "Thank you for coming so quickly. I'll take you to see Diablo."

He followed her toward the barn. Near the entryway, a huge Doberman went ballistic at the end of his chain. Seeing the great jaws and flashing white teeth as the dog snarled and thrashed to get loose, Cole hoped mightily that the chain would hold.

"I see you have a guard dog," he said.

Carmen shouted at the dog in Spanish, but he ignored her and continued to struggle to get free. "Yes, we imported him from Germany. He's supposed to be a fully trained protection dog, but he's not as obedient as he should be. We allow him to patrol the grounds at night. These horses are very valuable."

Nothing like having a poorly trained dog roaming the property at night. He hoped the dog didn't bite an innocent person by accident. They'd continued to walk as they spoke and soon moved from the sunlight outside into the subdued light of the barn. The central alleyway had stalls and rooms branching off on either side and smelled of hay and horse manure. Wheelbarrows, pitchforks, rakes, and small stacks of hay sat at intervals down the alley. It was neat and well organized, a place for everything and everything in its place.

"He's in this first stall," Carmen said. "We gave him the medicine you suggested, but he doesn't seem to be feeling any better."

Cole peered over the stall door. The black stallion moved stiffly around the stall, clearly in pain but too agitated to stand still. Sweat ran in rivulets down his neck and torso, dripping from his chest and belly. Muscle fasciculation, fine muscle tremors, ran through his entire body. The sight shocked even Cole, who was somewhat used to seeing animals in pain.

He followed Carmen into the stall. She murmured sounds of comfort, and the stallion let her clip a lead rope onto his halter. "I didn't know if I should tie him or let him move around. I called to ask, but your secretary said you were on your way. He seemed too nervous to tie, so I left him alone."

"That's fine. That's what I typically recommend. He's sweating more than I would expect. How long has he been like this?"

"Since a little before eight o'clock this morning."

Cole still suspected this was an acute episode of exertional rhabdomyolysis, commonly known as "tying up," but it was worse than any case he'd seen before. He ran a hand down the horse's back, over his rump, and down the hind leg near the stifle—hard as stone beneath the skin, no body fat. This thoroughbred was in peak racing condition, so a lack of body fat didn't come as a big surprise. Unfortunately the hardness in the large muscles of the back, rump, and hind leg didn't either. It indicated spasm and confirmed his suspicions.

Cole used his stethoscope to listen to the stallion's heartbeat—eighty-eight per minute, indicating severe pain.

"Will he let me get a temp while you hold him?" he asked.

"Yes. He's usually hard to work with, but today he seems too sick to care."

Diablo—not the type of name you give a gentle horse. Nevertheless, the stallion stood in place, muscles quivering, while Cole temped him. Not elevated. Usually there was a slightly elevated temp with rhabdomyolysis.

A loud crash from down the alleyway echoed through the building. From the same direction, a horse snorted and kicked the wall in his stall. Diablo jumped and pulled back on the rope, dragging Carmen with him. Cole sidestepped to move out of the way and then reached to help Carmen, but she was already bringing the huge stallion under control.

Carmen frowned, obviously displeased. "One minute. I'll be right back," she said, handing Cole the lead rope.

Although Cole stayed with Diablo, he could hear Carmen's voice from farther down the alley, reaming someone out in Spanish. He didn't understand what she was saying, but her tone made it clear that someone was getting a reprimand, and he was glad he wasn't on the receiving end of that tongue-lashing.

While she was gone, Cole pulled open Diablo's lips and pressed the gum above his teeth to check capillary refill time—several seconds, prolonged. Again, not quite what he'd expected. Typically the gums were reddened and capillary refill was quick. But with this much sweating, Diablo was probably becoming dehydrated or toxic.

Carmen quietly slipped back inside the box stall.

"I'm going to need to set up an IV and give him some fluids," Cole told her. He looked around the stall, choosing the best place to set things up. "We'll tie him here by his hay after I get it established, and I can hang the bag up above. I'll go get my supplies out of the truck and be right back."

Cole found the supplies he needed, carried them back to the stall in a stainless steel bucket, and let himself back in. "There'll be a needle stick to put in the IV," he told Carmen. "Just let him circle around us if he won't stand still. I'll stay with him."

Carmen murmured to the horse in Spanish while Cole approached. He blocked the jugular vein in Diablo's neck with one hand while he inserted the needle. Leaving the flexible catheter in place, he withdrew the sharp needle and secured the external part with tape. The stallion tolerated the procedure well, not moving after the first flinch. "I need to draw some blood before I set up the fluids."

"What are you testing for?"

"I want to measure some enzymes and minerals in his blood. This amount of sweating might throw something off."

Cole drew the blood sample from the IV and then administered sedation. He squeezed a dose of anti-inflammatory medication through a tube placed into Diablo's mouth. The stallion thrust his tongue against it and bobbed his head but swallowed the paste anyway. Cole hooked up a bag of fluid and held it high. "This will take a few minutes," he said. "Go ahead and tie him now, and I'll hang this up above."

After hooking the bag on top of the feed bunk, Cole stepped back to observe the horse. "Let's give him a few minutes."

Still uncomfortable, Diablo shifted his weight as he stood with his back slightly hunched, the typical stance expected from rhabdomyolysis.

"Does this horse get grain or sweet feed?" Cole asked.

"Yes."

"I need you to put a hold on that, but keep some grass hay in front of him. We'll try to make him feel better so that he'll keep eating. You'll have to keep him as quiet as possible."

"Shall we keep him tied up?"

"No, let him move around on his own. But hold off on any other form of exercise. I'll let you know what the lab results are tomorrow."

With a frown of concern creasing her brow, she studied Diablo. "This horse means a lot to me. I can do whatever treatment you recommend. Just tell me what you want me to do."

"I'll leave medications and show you how to give them and what to watch for. Keep an eye on him and call me with an update around four this afternoon. Call sooner if he gets worse or if you have a question." Cole picked up his stethoscope. "I'll want you to count his heartbeats per minute."

"I have my own stethoscope. I'm used to what a normal heartbeat sounds like."

Cole thought Carmen appeared experienced enough to leave the stallion in her care; he was too sick to transport to the clinic anyway. Diablo's heart still raced, but there was nothing more Cole could do for him now. He outlined a treatment plan with Carmen while the IV fluid finished dripping. Then he disconnected the tubing, recapped the end, and prepared to leave. Carmen accompanied him as he left the barn. The Doberman rushed to the end of the chain, coming to a hard stop and barking a fierce warning.

Cold wind blasted, and Cole pulled his jacket close. Gray storm clouds filled the sky. At the truck, he put away his supplies and moved to get into the driver's side where he took a moment to jot down a list of instructions for Diablo. He gave it to her along with a business card. "I should come back tomorrow or Sunday to check on him, unless he's had a sudden turnaround for the better."

Taking off her glove, she offered another handshake, and this time it felt warm and soft and her hand felt small in his. "That will be fine," she said. "Thank you for coming so far to take care of Diablo."

Cole said good-bye and climbed into the cab of his truck. Out on the racetrack, two men wrestled with a beautiful chestnut horse, its red coat glistening with sweat. It tossed its mane, reared, and struck out at the man who approached with a saddle. The guy dodged the flailing hooves, barely getting out of the way in time.

High-strung thoroughbreds. Must be hard to manage.

Cole did a three-point turn and drove down the lane to leave the property, pulling out his cell phone, intending to call Tess to tell her he was heading back to the clinic. No signal. He placed the phone back in his pocket. He'd call her once he got down from the high country; maybe he could reach her when he hit the highway.

Chapter 6

Wind buffeted the SUV as Mattie steered around the last curve leading into Timber Creek. After having exhausted all the potential leads on the list that Cole had given them and some additional names that Anya Yamamoto had shared, she'd decided to ditch searching by phone and drive along some of the county roads between the hot springs and Cole's clinic. Perhaps they'd get a lucky break and she and Robo would find Adrienne's abandoned car—if one could consider that kind of thing lucky.

Mattie's cell phone rang as she neared the town. She glanced at the caller ID. It was Cole. She used her new vehicle's hands-free feature to connect. "This is Mattie."

"Hi, I'm just checking in to see how things are coming along with the search for Adrienne," Cole said.

"Nothing solid yet."

"So none of the people I listed could tell you anything useful?" He sounded disappointed.

"No, but thanks for helping with that. It was worth a try."

"I'm on my way down from a stable up in the mountains. It's looking pretty ugly up here. I'm afraid a storm is coming in."

Mattie looked at the sky layered with gray clouds. "Yeah, it's starting to look bad down here, too."

A silence deepened between them, and Mattie knew they were both thinking of Adrienne and what this storm meant if she was up in the mountains somewhere, unprotected and exposed to the elements. Neither of them seemed to want to say it.

"Hey, do you want to come for dinner tomorrow night and test out Mrs. Gibbs's cooking?" Cole asked. "It's proving to be a winner so far. Besides, I'd like to see what you think of her."

Why would he care about that? She was familiar with dinner invitations to the Walker home, but she couldn't imagine that he'd seriously be curious about her opinion of the housekeeper. "I'll have to see where we are with the case. I don't want to say I can come and then not be able to make it."

"Can I tell her it's a 'maybe'? One more person for dinner shouldn't be a big deal, and you can come if you're able."

"All right."

She could hear the smile in his voice. "Good. I hope to see you then."

Feeling herself relax, Mattie smiled, too. After disconnecting the call, she reached to turn on the radio. She tuned to a station out of Denver to listen to a weather forecast. She didn't have to wait long to learn what she needed to know.

"An arctic front is moving into Colorado, bringing strong winds and the first snow of the season to Colorado's high country. Temperatures will drop to the low thirties here in Denver, and we'll need to batten down the hatches. Expect winds around forty miles per hour with gusts up to sixty. Our snow forecast is for six to eight inches in the mountains above ten thousand feet for tonight. But don't be disappointed, folks, we can expect snow by tomorrow night even down here in the Mile-High City. Stay tuned for more details."

Having heard enough, Mattie switched off the radio. At about eight thousand feet, Timber Creek would most likely receive its first snow of the season by tomorrow night. The wilderness area around them would probably get hit tonight. Even without snow, she figured the temperature would plummet in the high country today from the seasonal sixties to frigid twenties with a wind-chill factor that would sink toward zero. She shivered and turned up the heat. She hoped Adrienne was someplace where she could do the same.

Back at the station, she unloaded Robo and went inside. Rainbow took off her headset and stood up from her desk.

"Mattie! I was just about to call you. Sheriff McCoy wants to see you right away. We've got a hit on Adrienne's car."

Her heart did a double step. "Where?"

Rainbow's face paled as she said the words. "Way up Dead Man Gulch. A logger reported it to Sandy Benson. He noticed it yesterday and got concerned when it was still there today. Especially with the storm coming, you know. So he called it in, and now you've got to get up there and let Robo find her."

Mattie squeezed Rainbow's hand as tears welled in her friend's eyes. "Where's the sheriff?"

"In his office."

Mattie crossed over and tapped on the door. "Come in," he said.

He was halfway across the room when she opened the door. Excitement had replaced his typically unflappable expression. "We found Adrienne's car."

"Rainbow told me."

"We've caught a break. The car isn't parked at a trailhead. It's at a pull-off on a logging trail up Dead Man Gulch. This is a rugged area, not a typical place for people to hike. In fact, it's not near any groomed trails."

"I wonder what she was doing there."

"I'm not sure, but we need you and Robo to head up there. Here are the directions to get to the site and the GPS setting." He handed her a handwritten list. "Is it clear enough?"

She read the note. "Yes, sir. How about Brody? Is he coming with me?"

"He and Deputy Johnson are already on their way."

A pet peeve niggled at her. She hoped they wouldn't disturb any scent trails. She'd call him on the way and tell him to stay inside his own vehicle until she could get there. "How far ahead of me are they?"

"Hard to say. They were already near that area when Benson called."

It might be too late; they were probably out of cell phone range. "I'll be on my way, then."

"And Mattie . . ."

Mattie turned back toward him, surprised that he'd used her given name. He was always so formal.

"Don't take any chances out there," he said. "We've got severe storm warnings forecasted for the high country, and temperatures will fall tonight. Make sure you get down off that mountain in time. Take your winter gear."

"It's already in the car," she said, thinking of Adrienne. "We may need riders on horseback for a rescue mission."

"Cole Walker has volunteered to help organize that. I'll give him a heads-up, let him know there's that possibility."

"With this storm coming, I think we'd better send a couple riders up to the area now to wait at the scene. Then if we find her and need help with evacuation, we won't waste any time."

McCoy paused, thinking it over. "I hate to activate volunteers unnecessarily, but I agree with you on this one. I'll make the call."

"Thank you." Mattie left his office, Robo at her side.

Holding out a paper bag, Rainbow intercepted Mattie as she started past the dispatcher's desk. "Here's a sandwich and some fruit for you to eat for lunch on your way up, and there's a bottle of water in there, too." Mattie could see the distress in her face. "Take care of yourself out there. I don't want you to get lost, too."

She took the bag. "Thanks. I keep supplies in the car, so don't worry. We'll do our best to bring her back, Rainbow."

Mattie hurried to the Explorer, reloaded Robo, and settled into her own seat. She plugged the GPS coordinates into her system and then pulled out of the parking lot. She tried to call Brody's cell phone but was disappointed when it went to voice mail.

Gravel spattered against the bottom of her SUV as she drove fast on the county road. A cloud bank loomed over the jagged northwestern horizon, gray and ominous. For the most part, she headed into the wind. Although she didn't feel hungry, she reached into the paper bag on the seat beside her to grab the sandwich. If Robo found a scent trail that led into the wilderness, her body would need fuel to keep up with him.

The first thirty minutes of the journey weren't too hard. But the road grew narrow and pitted as she climbed toward the gulch, leaving behind pinion and juniper to go up into a forest of towering ponderosa and lodgepole pine. It reminded her of the day Robo found Grace Hartman, and she hoped today wouldn't end in the same kind of tragedy.

She'd thought Robo's discovery of a body was nothing short of miraculous; he'd never been trained in cadaver work. But a phone call to his trainer Jim Madsen had cleared up the mystery. He'd said, "Hell, Deputy, that must be the smartest dog on the planet you've got there. We tested him once on cadaver work before we decided to train him for narcotics detection. The way I figure it, the damn dog must've remembered what to do."

It didn't surprise Mattie; she already knew her dog was a genius.

The GPS guided her onto a little-used road deformed by signs of washout. Steep walls of timber defined the sides of Dead Man Gulch as the road followed a narrow stream upward. Groves of aspen provided color ranging from yellow to gold to orange, their leaves quivering in the wind that plucked them from limbs and sent them skittering along the roadbed. Her outdoor temperature gauge said forty-four degrees, then forty-two. The nighttime plummet had begun.

Robo stood behind her in his compartment, watching out the windshield.

"We're going to work," she told him. He pricked his ears, licking his lips in anticipation.

She found the next turn and swung onto a small logging road. It wouldn't be far now, and she felt anxiety mingle with the sandwich she'd consumed. The narrow road grew steep and even more rugged. Remembering that Adrienne drove a compact sedan, Mattie wondered why she would drive all the way in here. It could be done—Brody's cruiser was also up ahead—but why would she want to expose her car to the possibility of damage? She could've parked down below and hiked up this way if she was interested in exercise and scenery.

Mattie glanced at the clock. Twelve thirty. They were still on Daylight Savings Time, so the sun would set around six thirty. Twilight might last for another hour if they were lucky. Brody's silver and blue cruiser appeared between the trees. She'd reached the right spot.

As she pulled up behind Brody's cruiser, she could see Adrienne's charcoal-colored Escape. And it looked like Brody and Johnson had already been all over it. The front doors and hatch back were open. Johnson stepped back from where he'd been searching inside the back compartment and straightened his long, lean form to full height to wave at her. In his bulky winter jacket and cap with earflaps, the rookie looked like a kid. A kid who happened to be six foot two.

Mattie gave him a frown instead of a wave. She might not be able to reprimand Chief Deputy Brody for sullying her scent trails, but she could let the rook know he'd done wrong. Since the pullout could hold only the two vehicles that were in it, she parked on the road, set her emergency brake, and exited the SUV, taking her heavy coat with her. Arctic air hit her broadside, chilling her body immediately. She pulled on her coat while she walked to join her fellow deputies.

"I hope you haven't disturbed a scent trail," she said to Johnson by way of greeting.

Brody exited the back seat of the car. His head was uncovered, his coat unzipped, and his face haunted and hollow. "We've got to get a move on this, Cobb. We're running out of time."

"Not a time to skip protocol, Chief," she said. "Did you find anything useful in there?"

"Nothing. It's clean. No blood stains in front or back."

His reply spoke volumes about what he feared most. "How about her cell phone?"

"No. There's nothing in here except the car's documents and manuals in the glove box and her music and a few personal items in the console. Her jacket's in the back seat."

"Great. Leave that right where it is and don't touch it. I'll use it for a scent article." She turned to go back to her Explorer.

Robo was watching for her out the side window of his compartment, and he bounced on his front feet when she approached. Mattie grinned at him, his excitement contagious. She opened up the door and he bailed out, prancing beside her, eyes locked onto hers.

"Do you want to go to work?" She began the patter she used to rev him up, and he almost levitated in his happiness. After giving him some water to moisten his mucus membranes and increase his scenting ability, she put on his blue nylon tracking harness and matching work collar. He stood at attention, allowing her to adjust his equipment. When Robo finished getting dressed for work, he settled into his responsibilities immediately. It happened that way every time. He watched her while she put on her own equipment, a utility belt filled with her supplies.

Robo walked beside her as they approached, while Brody and Johnson stood at the rear of the car, giving her space to work on the driver's side. She put Adrienne's lightweight jacket into a plastic bag and lowered it so Robo could sniff. He thrust his nose into the bag, getting full value for his effort.

"Search," she told him.

He quartered the area near the car, nose to the ground, head moving back and forth. He searched for several minutes, covering the area of the pullout, the road next to the car, and up and down the roadside for about thirty feet in each direction. He came back to sniff the area more thoroughly, as if double-checking his work. He trotted to the open door on the driver's side, touched the seat with his mouth, and then sat and looked up at Mattie.

"What's wrong with him?" Brody asked.

Brody could be a butthead at times, and she was used to biting her tongue to keep the peace. But she wouldn't let him criticize her partner. "There's nothing wrong with him. He's telling me that he's picking up her scent on the driver's seat."

"Well, what the fuck? Why isn't he showing us the direction she went from here?"

Mattie felt her patience slip. "It might be because you two tromped around and jacked up the scent trail. Give us a minute."

She stroked Robo's head, smoothing the fur between his ears and telling him he was a good boy. She snapped the leash onto his tracking harness and led him about fifteen feet away from the car, checking wind direction as she went. The area was somewhat sheltered by the surrounding forest and a rock face positioned toward the northwest, but gusts continuously stirred the air from both the west and north as if the rock face split and funneled them.

This trail would probably be forty-eight hours old by now and torn up by the wind. Her only hope would be that epithelial cells left by Adrienne would remain trapped in the forest undergrowth beyond the road. Of one thing she was certain: if a scent trail existed out here, Robo would find it.

She led her dog into the forest and started working upwind, quartering back and forth, offering him the scent article, although she knew he probably didn't need it. Adrienne's scent would be locked in Robo's memory for the rest of his life. When he didn't identify a trail on the upwind side of the car, they started searching downwind.

A dreadful feeling began to build inside Mattie and after an hour, it reached its peak. She paused to reevaluate, knowing that Robo needed a break and some water. Her owns legs had grown tired from following him over the rugged terrain that surrounded the car. As she patted Robo to let him know he was doing his work right, she spotted two riders coming up the logging road. They must have left their truck and trailer down below instead of risking getting stuck up here. Believing that one rider might be Cole, her mood lifted slightly, and she decided to go back to the car.

She needed to tell Brody what she was thinking, and it wouldn't be easy news to share. She reached the car about the same time as the riders. She recognized that one of them *was* Cole. He'd been watching her, and he met her gaze. He wore a serious expression, which she knew matched hers. She wanted to tell him how glad she was to see him, but all she could do was nod. He returned the greeting the same way.

Brody stood next to the other rider whom she could see now was Garrett Hartman. She and Hartman nodded at each other, too.

"Well?" Brody said, his voice gruff and demanding.

"There's no scent trail out here," she told him. "I don't think Adrienne has been in this area. At least not in the last couple of days."

"What do you mean? Her car's here."

"If there was a scent trail leading away from the car, Robo would have found it. There's no hiking trail in this area, so I don't think she came here to go hiking. I think we need to seal this car and get prints off it." Stating her thoughts filled her with trepidation. "I think someone else ditched the car here, Brody."

He stared at her for a moment and then turned away to stare at the storm clouds piled high on top of each other, filling the sky. "The wind must have destroyed the scent trail. She's got to be up here. I just know it. She might be hurt. Johnson, take the cruiser down where you can get contact with the sheriff. Have him go ahead and send the search party. We need hikers that can cover this area."

"Johnson needs to print the car. I don't think we should employ a search party. If Robo can't find a trail, it means she wasn't up here," Mattie said.

"That dog can't smell shit. Get going, Johnson." Brody glared at her. "You print the damn car, Cobb."

Johnson went to the cruiser.

She wished Cole and Mr. Hartman weren't here to witness, but she would speak her piece. "You know what Robo is capable of." She was referring to the day Robo found Grace Hartman's body, and she knew that everyone present realized it.

Johnson started the cruiser's engine and began to maneuver the car to turn it. Mattie glanced at Cole, and he nodded his agreement. Mr. Hartman's face sagged in lines of sorrow. She looked back at Brody, reading desperation in his eyes.

"I won't give up yet, Brody. Let me give Robo a break while I print the car, and then we'll search this area again. Do either of you have tracking skills?" Mattie asked the riders.

"A little," Cole said while Garrett said, "Yes, I do."

"If you'd cover the area behind me and search for signs, maybe you'll see something." She knew it would be wasted effort, but she wanted to be thorough. And Brody wasn't able to give up yet.

"I'll print the car," Brody growled, giving the cloud bank one more baleful glance. "I need you and Robo on the mountain. When I'm done, I'll follow you up."

"All right," Mattie said. When Sheriff McCoy arrived, he would take over command. For now, she would do things Brody's way.

Chapter 7

Saturday

Lying on his side, Cole awakened in total darkness. Muscles that were unused to riding horseback nagged at him to move. Groaning quietly, he rolled onto his back to check the clock. The red digits said 5:47. After returning from the search for Adrienne, he'd opened his clinic to see patients, so he hadn't made it to bed until late. He felt wide-awake now, though, and he doubted he'd be able to go back to sleep.

Hard as everyone searched, they'd found no sign of the missing woman. The volunteer mountain rescue team consisted of about fifteen folks, men and women, all skilled in hunting, tracking, and navigating the wilderness without getting lost. They'd scoured the area the best they could, although the rugged terrain might still hide a hiker who'd fallen from a cliff and been injured. Or worse yet, killed.

He understood Mattie's theory that someone else ditched the car. He also understood what that could mean, even though the law enforcement officers had been pretty tight-lipped. There'd been no discussion in front of the volunteers. But it didn't take a rocket scientist to conclude that Adrienne might be the victim of foul play. It pained him to think of it. It had pained Garrett, too, and he'd noticed his friend's face become more and more grim as the afternoon toiled into evening.

He believed that the strung-out deputy in charge—the one they called Brody—might be too close to the case. He'd taken a moment, when they were far enough away from the car, to ask Mattie about Brody's relationship with Adrienne. She'd forced out the word "boyfriend" as if she hated to give up anything, and he didn't press her for more; she'd tell him what she could, when she could.

He admired the way Mattie handled the situation, working Robo in concentric circles, going farther out from the car each time, trying to pick up a scent trail. He'd been busy at his own task of trying to find a sign, but he'd caught glimpses of her through the trees, she and her dog moving together as if they were one. He'd never watched them work before. He respected her skill as a handler . . . and her stamina. He'd hate to guess how many miles of terrain those two covered before sundown. And thank goodness the sheriff had taken over when he arrived, or they'd probably all still be out there with flashlights, searching for someone that Cole, like Mattie, believed had never been in the area.

He stifled another groan as he moved his sore legs to get out of bed. Might as well get up. Even though it was Saturday, he'd rescheduled clients from yesterday and filled the morning. He showered and shaved and went downstairs at about six thirty. He was surprised to find Mrs. Gibbs in the kitchen.

"You're up early," he said, noticing the coffee pot was full and hot, and he headed that way to pour himself a cup. "You should feel free to sleep in on the weekends. The girls will, and I can fend for myself. They can, too, for that matter."

"Oh, I'm an early riser, I am. And I might as well make myself useful." She was whipping up eggs to pour in a skillet that was warming on the stove.

"I do appreciate a hot breakfast, but I don't want you to feel like you have to be working all the time."

"I'll keep it in mind when I need to take a break."

As far as he could tell, the woman possessed a deep well of energy for someone her age. He popped a couple slices of bread into the toaster. "How many pieces of toast do you want?" he asked.

"I can make me own toast, thank you."

He started to say he didn't mind, and then decided not. No reason to force the issue. They each needed to be able to do what they wanted in the kitchen without pushing at each other.

"I need to talk to you about Angela," she said.

He checked her face and saw her frowning at the eggs she stirred in the skillet. This wasn't going to be good. "All right."

"I'm concerned about her. She was very quiet after we left Mrs. Hartman yesterday afternoon. When I asked if something was bothering her, she told me to mind me own business. Said I weren't her mum so keep me nose to myself, or something like that."

Ugh. "I'll talk to her. She should be more respectful."

"No. No, I don't want that. It's her version of kicking the dog, and I can handle it myself, at least for now. But I'm worried about her. She's been dealt a lot for a youngster to handle. Sophie told me how their mum doesn't want to see them anymore and about losing Angela's friend this summer."

He bet Sophie had; he wondered what else the girl had told her new listener. Cole kept silent, thinking about what he should do.

"She's had a hard time of it," Mrs. Gibbs said.

"Yes, but that doesn't mean she can be disrespectful to people."

Mrs. Gibbs gave him the look a mother gives a child who's said the wrong thing. "It will work itself out between us. I'm just telling you this so you can think about the girl. See if there's a way you can help her work through these things. They're not ready to be brushed under the carpet yet."

Cole waited while she scooped scrambled eggs onto his plate to sit beside the toast. He was glad she had some insight into the behavior of kids. Girls especially. He often felt like a bumbling first-year vet student when it came to trying to figure out his daughters, though he hoped to get better at it as fast as he could. "I'll think about it. And I'll work out a time to talk to her."

"But don't mention we had this conversation. That wouldn't be good."

She must think she has to spell it out for me. Well, maybe she does. "Mum's the word."

He bolted his breakfast in silence, hoping to get out of there before any more troubles could be aired. Saying good-bye, he left to go to his clinic, where he usually could keep things relatively within his control.

★

Mattie woke before the alarm. She peeked at Robo from under the cover she'd drawn over her head to combat the cold of the room. In the gray light that filtered through the window, she saw him curled up on his dog bed, still asleep. Typically, he'd be up, pressing his nose against her, ready to go for his run. Not today. He'd had enough exercise yesterday to curb his energy for a while.

She nestled back under Mama T's handmade quilt, hoping to go back to sleep. But Adrienne came into her mind, and her stomach clenched. This must be how Brody had been feeling all along. She was sure now that the woman hadn't left town willingly, and she doubted if kidnapping was a reasonable option. No one would take the time to dump a car way up in that isolated spot if he was on the run with a kidnapped person.

She was afraid Adrienne had been killed.

Someone was covering up a crime, trying to mislead them. If she didn't trust Robo so much, she might've fallen for it herself. But she knew in her heart, even after the first time around the car, that Adrienne had never been up in that forest. She also knew that she couldn't give up before Brody was thoroughly exhausted with the search. Thank goodness Sheriff McCoy had been there to call it.

She sensed the moment Robo raised his head and then heard his nails against the hardwood floor as he got out of bed. Smiling under the cover, she heard the little squeak he made when he yawned. This time when she peeked out, his nose rested on the edge of the bed and he was watching her. As soon as she lifted her head from the pillow, he grinned and trotted toward the door, stopping to look back and inviting her to follow. *Maybe he didn't get too much exercise yesterday.*

"Do you need to go outside?" she asked, sending him into a tizzy as he rushed through the doorway. One thing about a dog like Robo—you never needed an alarm in the morning.

Mattie pulled on a pair of sweats, shoved her feet into her warmest slippers, and grabbed a coat on her way through the living room. She let Robo out the kitchen door into the backyard and stepped outside onto the porch to watch him, the frigid air pinching her nose. *Still no snow, and the wind's stopped.*

Last summer, a killer had tried to poison Robo. And even though the perp was in prison and the county had installed razor wire above the chain link fence around the yard, Mattie still watched her dog circle it each morning and in the afternoon when they returned from work.

After he did his business, Robo came inside and Mattie fed him. She flipped on the radio for a weather report while she fixed her own breakfast. "This storm seems to have blown itself out, and the snow we were expecting has settled in the northern mountains of our state. The southern mountains can expect some snow activity by tonight, although not as much as previously expected. Probably about three inches above nine thousand feet. Lower elevations may have to wait until the next storm front for the first snow of the season."

She switched off the radio and decided to get dressed and go to work early. She wouldn't be surprised if the others did the same.

At the station, Brody and the sheriff had already parked their vehicles. Inside, she found that Rainbow hadn't yet come on duty. She went to the staff office, grabbed her first cup of coffee, and searched for the others, Robo tagging along beside her. She found them in the briefing room where she thought they'd be.

Sheriff McCoy nodded a greeting. "Glad you came in early. We were discussing what to do next."

Brody sat slumped, and he and the sheriff wore matching steely expressions. Mattie pulled up a chair and sat at the table. Robo sat close to her, and she placed a hand on his shoulders. "Let's talk about our car scene," McCoy said.

Brody stared at Adrienne's picture on the board.

"What did you pick up when you printed the car?" she asked.

Brody looked beaten down. "The steering wheel was clean. There were no prints at all."

"Wiped clean," McCoy said.

"I assume so," Brody said. "The prints on the door handles belong to me and Johnson."

They should've never touched that car with bare hands. At least their prints could easily be eliminated. Well, she guessed she might as well say it again—somebody had to. "I think someone ditched the car, and Adrienne wasn't in it at the time."

McCoy nodded.

"We don't know that for a fact," Brody was quick to say.

"No, we don't," Mattie said, "but let's take a look at the evidence. Prints on the car were wiped. That indicates someone other than Adrienne drove that car up there. And Robo never once indicated picking up her scent outside the car."

Brody stared at Mattie with tortured eyes, and this time when he spoke, his voice had lost its belligerence. "It had probably been forty-eight hours since the car was left. Forty-eight hours in that kind of wind could blow away your scent trail."

"I'll concede that if Adrienne walked only on the harder surface of the road, the scent trail could have deteriorated in that amount of time. But we searched the foliage up and down that road thoroughly. I think epithelials would have blown and caught in nearby plants. If she was there, Robo would have found some trace of her scent."

Brody shook his head, avoiding her eyes. He remained unconvinced.

But McCoy seemed to share at least a little bit of her faith in her partner. "Let's accept your theory and go with it for a minute. What does this mean?" He looked at Mattie.

"If someone else ditched that car, then it either means Adrienne used an accomplice to help her disappear or she's been a victim of foul play. I'd bet my paycheck on the second theory."

"And?" McCoy prompted her.

Mattie couldn't bring herself to say "treat this like a homicide" in front of Brody, so she said, "We need to get that warrant from Judge Taylor and search Adrienne's living quarters. We should do a thorough investigation of her life to determine who might have kidnapped or harmed her."

The door to the briefing room opened, and Rainbow stepped in, her face blanched and anxious. "You guys? I'm sorry to interrupt, but I just took a phone tip that you need to know about right now."

Dismayed by the look on her friend's face, Mattie pushed her chair back from the table causing it to screech as she stood. "What is it?"

"This man on the phone said Adrienne's up near Tucker Peak, just below the lake," Rainbow said, walking across the room to join them.

"Who said it?" McCoy asked.

"That's just it, he wouldn't leave his name. I tried to get him to tell me, but he hung up on me. When he first called, he told me to listen and take notes. He gave directions to where we could find her. I wrote it down." Rainbow reached to give her notes to the sheriff, a tremor in her fingers causing the paper to flutter.

Brody looked as if he'd found new energy. "Did he tell you her condition?"

"No." Rainbow shook her head, eyes wide. "He wouldn't say anything more. He acted like, well, like everything was such a secret or something."

"We need to get up there," Brody said. "Now."

"Wait a minute," McCoy said. "Are you sure this call was legit, Rainbow?"

"I think so."

"Did anything else stand out about it?"

Rainbow paused, thinking. "He had sort of a Spanish accent."

"Did you trace the call?" Mattie asked.

"Not yet. I came right in here."

"Trace that call, Rainbow. See if it's local," McCoy said, as she hurried to follow through. "I'd like to know if this is another attempt to mislead us. It might be, but I don't think we can discount it. What do you think?" McCoy's eyes moved from Brody to Mattie. It was obvious what Brody thought—he looked ready to bolt out the door.

"I think someone tried to mislead us with the car. This could be a wild-goose chase, but we can't ignore it," Mattie said.

"Then you two get ready for a hike up that mountain to see what you can find. Make sure you pack gear to protect yourselves from the storm. It's early, so if this is a false lead, you can get back down before nightfall. In the meantime, I'll put the search and rescue volunteers on standby."

"Let's go," Brody said, heading for the door.

Mattie stayed. "We need to get that warrant to search Adrienne's place."

"Yes, I'll work on that," McCoy said.

She gave the sheriff a short salute and turned to leave.

"Look after Brody," he said. "And be careful up there."

Chapter 8

A merciless headwind battled Mattie's every step as she followed Robo up the mountain. Its icy chill bit at her cheeks. Typically, this type of climb wouldn't have taken much out of her, but today she was worn out. She struggled up the last few steps toward her goal, the leeward side of a massive boulder, treading carefully on the barely visible path. Rocks, exposed tree roots, and tufts of grass all threatened to turn her ankle. Finally, she reached the boulder, leaned against it, and whispered a thank-you for its shelter.

Robo had forged ahead, so she called to him to come back. "It's time to rest," she told him, taking out the GPS tracking unit she'd placed in her utility belt. While she waited for Brody to catch up, she read the data to see how far they'd come. Just under two miles . . . it seemed like twenty.

She spotted Brody, winding his way up the trail not too far below. She guessed he was just about done, the lack of sleep and likely poor nutrition over the past few days taking their toll.

Her watch told her it was half past noon. She shucked off her backpack, took out Robo's collapsible bowl, and drained some water from her supply into it. He slurped it greedily.

When Brody reached her position, their eyes met for a split second before he looked away. He slipped out of his backpack and sank down into the boulder's shelter, looking spent. She could tell he felt bad about her kicking his butt on the climb . . . or maybe he just felt bad. She searched and found a couple energy bars, gave one to him, and peeled open the other one for herself.

"I'm not sure I can eat," he said, taking the bar but not opening it.

"You have to. That's why you're struggling. That and the fact that this is the damnedest trail I've ever had to climb. And that wind. Shit!"

He threw her a look that was almost grateful, one that she'd never seen from Brody. He must have realized she was trying to encourage him.

"Do you think Adrienne would've hiked up here?" she asked.

He shook his head, peeling back the paper on the bar. "Not this time of year. And not alone."

"This trail might be used by a few hunters, but that's about all."

"Yeah." Brody took a bite, staring out across the tops of pine as he chewed.

Mattie might have enjoyed the spectacular view under other conditions. From their boulder, they could look down on miles of pristine forest wilderness, layers rolling away toward the horizon. The wind blew a dust devil from the patchy trail, and she watched it rise upward like a ghost. She shivered.

"The directions say to leave the trail and head due west about a half mile down from the lake. How the hell can we tell when we're a half mile down?" Brody said.

"Yeah. That's a problem. But I've been able to plug the total distance into the GPS from state forest department maps. I set it for a half mile down, so I'll be able to tell when we get there."

"Shit, Cobb. You're quite the techie."

Brody didn't hand out compliments. "And this unit allows Rainbow and the sheriff to track us."

"When did you get this stuff?"

"A few weeks ago. Sheriff McCoy authorized it from the K-9 fund."

"Just in time."

"Yeah."

They both finished their bars, and Mattie stood to pull on her backpack. Brody did the same. Although she doubted Robo needed it, she took the scent article from her utility belt to refresh his memory. As they neared the spot where they would leave the trail, she wanted him to remember the reason they'd come up here was to look for Adrienne.

Robo led the way out from the boulder's shelter, a blast of wind flattening his ears and rippling his fur. Bracing herself, Mattie followed, and Brody brought up the rear. They toiled up the path with Mattie stopping frequently to check the GPS and to allow Brody time to catch his breath.

As they breached another steep rise, Robo came to a sudden stop. He paused with his ears pricked forward, nose up, sniffing the wind. When Mattie drew up beside him, he turned to look into her eyes. He shifted, stood at attention, and looked down into a draw off to the west. She recognized the stance: Full Alert.

Her heart pounded from exertion, but this gave it an extra jolt. She glanced at the GPS and figured they were near the mark. She scanned the draw, realizing it funneled the wind up to their current position. Brody struggled up the last few steps to reach her side.

"Robo's got a hit," she told him, pointing down into the draw. "Wind's coming from there. We'll leave the trail now."

Brody's brow shot upward and the familiar penetrating look came into his icy blue eyes. Mattie realized she'd missed it the last few days when he'd looked so whipped. He nodded, still puffing to catch his breath.

"I'm going to change Robo's gear." She slipped his tracking harness out from a pocket on her utility belt and put it on him, knowing that he would now be in full tracking mode. He'd proven lately that he would match her pace, so she opted not to use the leash.

She looked at Brody, and he nodded. "Let's go," she said. And then to Robo: "Search."

Robo spilled down the steep edge into the draw, sliding part of the way on a small rockslide. Mattie sat and slid on her butt, feet first, digging them in to slow her momentum. Brody followed off to her left, so he wouldn't cover her with rocky debris. They reached the bottom of the draw a little dirty but none the worse for wear. Robo started uphill, nose up, obviously air scenting.

At the bottom of the draw, the footing became tricky, with deadfall and rocks blocking the way. Robo entered a dry streambed made by spring runoff from snowmelt and continued upward, ears moving forward and back as he checked on Mattie behind him.

Brody seemed fueled by newfound energy, and he stayed close to Mattie, sometimes clearing dead branches or fallen timber to let her pass more easily. It was slow going for humans, and Robo paused frequently to let them catch up. One thing the draw provided was more shelter from the wind, although

Mattie could hear it roaring through the boughs up above. They must be downwind from whatever Robo was scenting.

Steep sides eventually flattened out and opened into a wider space filled with boulders, rocky outcroppings, and pine. Robo picked up speed. Mattie rushed to keep up with him, breaking into a jog. Brody fell behind.

Robo darted toward a large pile of rocks. He pinned his ears as he approached—hunkered and slinked up, poking his nose into a crack in the mound. Mattie hurried toward him as he turned. He made eye contact . . . and he sat. Robo's signal to indicate a find.

She felt her chest tighten, unable to catch her breath. She could read Robo's distress in the tightness around his eyes. His two-day search for the missing woman had come to an end.

This must be Adrienne's grave.

Typically Robo would be bumping his nose against the pouch that held his tennis ball, signaling it was time to play. But not this time. He uttered a short whine and lay down, looking up at Mattie for reassurance. She'd heard about dogs feeling depressed when long search missions failed to turn up a living person. She knelt beside him to stroke his head, telling him what a good boy he was.

Brody slowed as he approached, obviously reading the situation. Face stony and grim, he circled the grave, going to the opposite side where there was sign that a scavenger had been digging. Mattie stood and walked around to join him.

An appendage—an arm—flesh torn, bone and muscle exposed. "Come away, Brody."

The pain in his eyes tore at her heart. "I have to see if it's her."

"Robo says it is. Come away. This is a crime scene. We've got to treat it like one."

He looked down at the desecrated grave and moved to where she would guess the head was located. He reached for the stones.

"Brody, wait," Mattie said, taking out her cell phone. She knew she couldn't stop him. "At least let me get pictures and then we'll uncover her face. If you need to make sure."

Brody stepped back while she snapped photos of the site from all directions. He approached when she finished and knelt, gently removing stones and placing them aside. Pine boughs were next, and Mattie photographed those. Blonde hair appeared first and then Brody brushed aside more dirt. He revealed Adrienne's face, stained deep maroon from lividity, marred and swollen from the beginnings of decomposition, jaw gaped, eyes closed. At least the makeshift grave had protected her eyes from the birds.

"That's enough," Mattie said. "We've got to get Detective LoSasso and a crime scene unit up here."

Brody rocked back on his heels, staring at Adrienne's face. He reached out and placed a hand tenderly on her hair, picking up a strand to hold between his fingers. Robo came and nudged Mattie's hand. She squatted down and hugged him close. They stayed together like that for a very long time, giving Brody some space, waiting for him to move.

Chapter 9

Tess had Saturdays off, so Cole worked the morning shift by himself. Around eleven o'clock, he was saying good-bye to his last client when he heard the back door slam shut. He recognized the noisy entry as Sophie's. He peered through the pass-through from the exam room into the office. Both of his daughters, Angela in the lead, came into sight. Angela sat down at the computer while Sophie twirled one of the swivel chairs and jumped into it, trying to catch a spin. As she came around toward him, he waved to catch her eye.

She grinned at him. "Hi, Dad."

"Hey, squirt. I'm glad you guys came up to help."

Angela's expression wasn't so friendly. "We didn't have much choice."

"Oh?"

"Mrs. Gibbs said we needed to go outside for fresh air," Sophie said, losing her grin. From the looks of it, she'd decided she wasn't having fun after all.

"We need to talk, Dad," Angela said.

"I'm done with clients. We can talk now. Come on in here, and we'll talk while we clean up."

Sophie leapt from the chair and scooted through the door into the exam room. Spraying and wiping tables happened to be one of her favorite jobs. Knowing the routine, she grabbed a pair of disposable gloves from the box on the counter and tugged them on. Angela followed more slowly and took a seat.

"What do you want to talk about, Angel?"

"Mrs. Gibbs."

Uh-oh. "Okay. We should touch base on how it's going."

"I hate her."

"Now wait a minute. Those are harsh words, Angie. Why are you so mad?"

"She won't leave me alone. She's snooping in my business."

"What do you mean?"

"She's, like . . ." Angela used a whiny voice unlike Molly Gibbs's but otherwise mimicking the Irish accent spot on. "What's botherin' ye, girl? I won't have ye hole away up here in yer room while I'm on the job, I won't."

"I doubt she used that tone. And Mrs. Gibbs deserves your respect even if you're mad at her. I want you to remember that."

"I knew you'd take her side."

"I'm not taking anyone's side. Have you been in your room all morning?"

"So now I'm not allowed to be in my room?"

Cole took a moment, put some bottled vaccine back in the refrigerator, hooked a rolling stool with his foot, and brought it up to sit close to Angela. "Sure you can be in your room. But you might need some time outside of your room, too. You've come here on Saturdays with me before, and I appreciate your help. Why don't you work with me next weekend?"

Angela shrugged. "I don't want her bossing me around."

"But she's in charge when I'm gone, Angela. We have a lot to work out, and she's been here less than a week. You need to be more respectful. Let's give it some time and keep those communication channels open."

Working on the table closest to him, Sophie echoed his last words as he said them, causing him to think he must sound like a broken record. He reached out a hand and ruffled her brown curls. She smiled.

"How are things going for you with Mrs. Gibbs?" he asked her.

She glanced at Angela, and a frown returned to her face. "I don't like her either."

He had to wonder if this was Sophie's true opinion or if she was imitating her older sister. "What is she doing that you don't like?"

"She made me turn off the TV."

Cole nodded slowly as if considering her complaint. "Now that's a serious offense, isn't it?"

Sophie peered up at him, trying to suppress the twinkle in her eye. When Cole snorted, she laughed along with him. "She's okay, I guess," she said.

Angela scowled. "I don't know what you think is so funny."

"Angel, we've got to keep a sense of humor." He decided to bring up what he believed to be the true issue. "You know we all miss Mom."

Sophie sobered and looked down. Cole drew her close with one arm and she leaned against him.

"I don't miss her," Angela said.

"You might say that because your feelings are hurt. Mine are too, but I know I miss her. And we've got to have someone share in the housework and keep an eye on Sophie. Otherwise that's going to fall on you, Angie. I thought we decided we didn't want that. Right?"

She shrugged, avoiding his gaze.

"I know it's different having someone new in the house. It's hard to take direction from a new person, but I want her to be in charge when I'm gone."

"That's just it, Dad."

"What?"

"Her being here makes it so easy for you to be gone."

A pang of guilt hit him. Why did parenting have to be filled with so many moments of guilt?

"We got home from school yesterday, and you were gone. You didn't get home until late," Angela said.

"I was helping search for Adrienne."

"I thought we were all going to help search for Adrienne."

"You were in school when I got the call, Angel."

She shrugged, evidently conceding that point.

"Look, if you have a concern, take it up with me," Cole said. "Don't fight with Mrs. Gibbs about it."

"But she's so nosy, Dad. She's not my friend, you know. I don't want to talk to her."

Her argumentative tone had begun to irritate him. "That's a poor attitude. She's trying to be friendly, and all you're giving back is disrespect. I thought we raised you better than that."

Angela looked down at the floor, biting her lip.

He tried to rein in his temper. He'd been trying so hard to make a good life for these girls and got little appreciation in return. "Okay, next weekend I'll get you up to come out to work with me instead of letting you sleep in? Would you like that better?"

Angela shrugged, refusing to look at him. Sophie stood within the circle of his arm, playing some game with her fingers. He doubted if she'd been paying attention. He squeezed her. "What do you think?" he asked her.

"About what?" Sophie asked.

Doubt confirmed. "Come help me here next Saturday."

"I want to watch cartoons."

"Well, you can do some of that, too. Let's have you watch TV for an hour first, then come up here."

"Okay."

If only teenagers were as compliant as eight-year-olds. "I have one more phone call to make and then we'll go to the house. Angie, I put my paperwork in the box. Do you want to catch things up on the computer?"

She shrugged again but stood up to go back into the office. She loved the computer work and had taken to it like a horse to green pasture. Maybe that would pacify her.

"Thanks for cleaning tables, Sophie," he said.

"I'm not done yet."

"Okay. You can finish up while I make this call." Cole pulled out his cell phone, checked the number in his records, and dialed Carmen Santiago of Dark Horse Stable.

She answered right away, obviously recognizing his number on caller ID. "Hello, Doctor."

"How's Diablo today?"

"About the same."

"I got the lab results back. They aren't exactly what I expected."

A pause, and he could hear the concern in her voice when she spoke. "Why is that?"

"He's hyperglycemic, and his liver enzymes are elevated, which isn't typical with tying up. On the other hand, the enzymes we measure to detect muscle damage are elevated, which *is* something I'd expect."

"Okay? What does that mean?"

"I'm not sure yet. Is he eating?"

"A little bit of hay. Not much."

"Has he defecated?" Cole asked.

"A small amount."

"That tells us his gut is still working. What's his heart rate?"

"Eighty-five beats per minute. He's still sweating but not quite as much."

Cole thought it over. "Let's give our treatment plan another day. I should come up tomorrow. I'll want to run another blood sample."

"All right. What time?"

"I'll call in the morning and we'll decide," Cole said.

"Late morning will work. Perhaps you can stay for a meal."

He needed a chance to spend time with his kids tomorrow, and he planned to take them with him. "No, thank you anyway. My kids will be with me, and we won't be able to stay. I'll call in the morning around eight to schedule."

"Children? Are you married?"

He thought the question rather personal. "Divorced."

"How many children?"

"Two."

"I love kids. And two more would be fun."

It was nice of her to welcome his children. "Thanks for the offer, but I'm not sure it will work out. I'll check with the girls about their plans and get back to you in the morning. Can we decide then about lunch?"

"Sure. I hope you can join me. I would love to spend time with your daughters."

He ended the call, and Sophie looked up at him from across the room where she'd been busily squirting and wiping the stainless steel exam table over and over. "Who was that?" she asked.

"A lady named Carmen Santiago. She's got a sick horse."

"Do you like her?"

"Sure. I don't know her very well, but she seems nice."

Sophie tilted her head to the side, studying him.

"Why did you tell her you were divorced?"

What is that old saying about little pitchers and big ears? "When I told her I had kids, she asked if I was married."

A sad expression crossed her face as she looked down at the table. "Why did she want to know that?"

Cole wondered about that himself, although he had a notion about it. "Just making conversation, I guess. It's okay, Sophie. I have to tell people about our family some of the time."

She nodded, her eyes downcast, as she continued wiping the table.

He crossed the room, pulled her close with one arm, and hugged her briefly to his side. "You've done a great job helping me clean. Let's go home now and see what we can rustle up to eat."

She tipped up her face, giving him a quivery smile that almost broke his heart. "Mrs. Gibbs is making soup."

"That sounds good on a cold day. Let's help Angie finish up so we can go."

Following Sophie from the room, his mind jumped back to Carmen. She seemed interested in getting to know him better. He supposed someday he might find himself attracted to a woman other than Olivia. If and when that happened, he knew one thing for sure: he had these kids and their needs to consider before he made decisions about adding anyone to their family.

Chapter 10

Brody removed his hand from Adrienne's hair and stood.

"You have to go down and organize a retrieval mission," Mattie said.

"I'll stay with her."

"Sorry, Brody. You can't. You're too close." Besides, the boyfriend was always a suspect. She didn't know what to do with that.

He glared at her. "This is all I have left."

"That's not true. You've got memories, and staying here with her corpse shouldn't be one of them."

He looked down on Adrienne's face, uncovered, reddened, and lifeless.

"I brought a plastic tarp in my backpack. Let's cover her and secure the gravesite. Then you need to head down that trail. I'll give you some flagging tape to mark it on your way down."

He looked at Mattie. "I can find my way back up here."

"Of course. But there may be more than one party needing to get up here later this afternoon. You might not be able to guide them all. We don't want anyone getting lost." She glanced up at the sky, covered with gray snow clouds. He followed her glance and apparently knew what she was thinking.

"And it might snow before I get back," he said.

"Yeah."

"Shit. I'll make sure we can find the trail."

Mattie nodded, trusting him to keep his word. "We need to hurry."

She removed the black plastic sheeting she'd carried up in her backpack and started spreading it out. Brody went to the far side of the grave, keeping his eyes averted from the carnage wrought by some scavenger, and helped her spread it over the site. They secured the sheeting by anchoring the edges with stones. The wind tugged at it, trying to tear it away, but soon the black plastic turned into a taut shield from the elements. It would be up to Mattie and Robo to defend the grave from further desecration by wildlife.

"Robo and I will go back to the trail with you, and I'll mark it with orange tape from there to here on my way back. I think it's probably shorter to head due east instead of coming up the draw like we did to follow the scent trail. I'll build a cairn in the middle of the trail to mark where you should turn off and head back here."

"I've been thinking," Brody said. "What if her killer returns while you're up here alone? What if that anonymous tip was a setup?"

"I suppose anything's possible, but I don't think it's likely."

"You have your service weapon."

"Right. And Robo won't let anyone sneak up on us." She pulled out her GPS and used the compass function to chart a course due east. "It's time to go."

"Wait a minute." Brody looked back at the black plastic sheet that covered Adrienne's grave, his face filled with a mixture of emotion. Hesitation, grief, and concern were all registered there, easy for Mattie to read. She gave him a minute to sort through his thoughts, and then said, "You need to get started, Brody."

She set out, dodging around towering pine and boulders, staying on an easterly course.

After following for several yards, Brody broke his silence. "Are you sure you're going to be okay up here?"

She didn't want to tell him that she'd feared all along that they would find a corpse, and she'd planned for it. "I'll be all right. I brought some food and plenty of warm clothing."

"I'll come back this afternoon. I'll think of things we need as I go down."

Mattie glanced at his haggard face, noting his slumped posture when he typically stood ramrod straight. "Brody," she said, pausing for emphasis, "unless someone can put you on a horse, think twice before you try to make this climb again. You've spent days without food and sleep, and you've covered a lot of territory on little fuel. Mark that trail on your way down so anyone can find it."

"I'll be back."

Stubborn.

It took about ten minutes to connect with the trail. Brody surprised her when he offered a handshake. He gripped hers hard when she took it. "Thank you for all you've done . . . and everything you're going to do," he said.

"Sure, Brody. You'd do the same for me." That wouldn't have been true a few months ago, but things had changed between them.

He turned and started down the trail. Mattie watched him until he trudged out of sight on the far side of the first rise. Brody looked done in, and she worried that it would take him a long time to make it back to the trailhead. Well, there was nothing she could do about that.

She began to build the cairn, stacking rocks smack in the middle of the trail, large ones on the bottom and progressively smaller ones layered up to the top. She built it about two feet high and knew it couldn't be missed. Taking out her GPS again, she and Robo headed due west to return to the gravesite, marking trees with orange flagging tape about every twenty yards as they went.

Once there, Mattie decided to walk a grid with Robo, just in case they could turn up something the killer dropped. She gave him a drink of water and put on his working collar. Snapping a short lead onto his collar, she led him to the start of the grid that she'd already planned mentally, located between the trail and the gravesite.

"Seek," she told him, his command for evidence detection, and she gestured toward the ground.

Robo put his nose down and went to work, quartering the area in short sweeps. Soon he touched the ground with his mouth and sat. At first Mattie couldn't see what he was indicating, but when she brushed aside some pine needles she discovered a flattened cigarette butt. "Good find, Robo."

She bagged it and started searching for footprints. She found several partial cowboy boot prints in the soft ground next to a tree. *He must've leaned here to have a smoke.* She marked them with orange tape on a thin metal spike.

She also found horseshoe prints. She photographed them, but she could barely see them in the photo. Looking up at the heavy sky, she knew she needed to preserve all the prints from the snow, so the CSI technicians could process them with their equipment.

After finishing the grid, she decided to use plastic evidence bags to cover the prints. Splitting them open, she chose the prints that were the most clearly defined, covered them, and then anchored the plastic with sharp bits of tree branch and rocks around the edges, being careful to avoid pressing on the middle. She left the orange flags so that anyone entering the area would know not to disturb them.

Mattie and Robo spent the next hour searching around the gravesite and back toward the trail. She snapped pictures of disturbed greenery, areas where rocks had been removed, and places where the terrain had been altered during the digging of the grave. None of these things would be very useful.

What she didn't find brought images and theories to her mind: Robo didn't indicate finding Adrienne's scent trail on the ground, and Mattie didn't spot smaller hiking-boot prints that Adrienne might have left. She theorized that Adrienne had been killed elsewhere and left face down or head down for several hours, accounting for the lividity observed in her face. She guessed she'd been carried here on horseback and then buried, probably by the anonymous tipster. Maybe he felt guilt or remorse, and that's why he called. The autopsy could confirm the first part of her theory; the rest was guesswork.

Cold air nipped her face, and she realized the temperature had dropped. She'd better pay attention to her own needs before it was too late. She took off Robo's collar and tracking harness to let him know he was now off duty. She headed out into the timber to find firewood, taking along his tennis ball, causing him to frolic beside her. His reward was long overdue. She was relieved to see that he acted like his happy self again, his depression left behind.

But she couldn't erase the image of Adrienne's marred face and gaping mouth from her mind, or the one of Brody kneeling beside the dead woman. It would take longer for her own mood to lighten.

★

Cole was playing a game of Monopoly with his kids when his cell phone rang. One glance told him it was the sheriff's department, and he answered it immediately. The caller was Sheriff McCoy.

"Hello, Sheriff."

"I've got some bad news, Dr. Walker," McCoy said. "Adrienne Howard's body has been found."

"I was afraid that's what you were going to say." Cole checked his kids and saw they were listening to his side of the call. "Excuse me a moment, Sheriff."

He got up from the kitchen table. "Give me a minute, you guys," he said to the girls. "I've got to take this call, but I'll be right back."

"But Dad . . ."

"I'll be right back, Angela, and I'll tell you what's happening. But now, I need some privacy." He walked out of the room and headed upstairs, resuming his conversation with the sheriff as he went. "All right, I'm back."

"She was found about a half mile down from Tucker Peak. Do you know that area?"

"I'm familiar with it. I used to hunt that area with my dad. That's rugged country. How on earth did you find her?"

"Robo. Look, the reason I'm calling is that I need your help organizing a retrieval mission. And we're going to need several extra horses to carry our detective and technicians up to the site."

By now Cole had reached his bedroom and shut the door. The red digits on his alarm clock said 4:51. It was getting late. "How soon do you want us to load up?"

"Can we start at sunrise tomorrow morning?"

"I'm sure that between Garrett and my dad we can organize enough horses by then. You don't think we should go up sooner?"

"That's the other part of my problem," McCoy said. "I've got Deputy Cobb up there securing the site."

"By herself?"

"Yes. I need at least one rider to take supplies up to her for the night. A tent, food, water, dog food for Robo, insulated sleeping bags. We've got the trail marked, but we've also got this snowstorm rolling in. I need someone who can handle himself out in the wilderness during winter weather."

There was no way he would let Mattie spend the night up there alone. "I'm your guy."

"It won't be easy."

"Hey, it doesn't need to be. I'll contact Garrett and ask him to organize things for tomorrow morning. I've got a horse named Mountaineer that can stick to any trail in the dark. I'll be ready to leave within the hour."

"Deputy Brody wants to go with you, but I need him to guide up tomorrow's party."

"I can make it on my own."

"I'll turn the phone over to him so he can give you detailed directions. And thanks, Cole."

Cole took notes from Brody's description, deciding he needed to take a strong flashlight to see the orange tape in the dark. He ended the call and went downstairs to his daughters, his mind making a list of supplies while he went. They both waited at the kitchen table. There was no need to soften the blow with these two. Like it or not, they were experienced in receiving bad news.

"That was the sheriff. They've found Adrienne. I'm sorry to have to tell you this, but she's no longer alive."

Neither spoke. Angie looked down at the table while Sophie's worried brown eyes sought out his. "Did somebody kill her, Dad? Like Grace?" Sophie asked.

"I don't know any details. But I do know that Mattie's up there in the mountains, guarding the site by herself."

Angie looked up at him, a furrow of concern on her brow. "Alone?"

"Yeah, I've volunteered to take supplies up to her so she's not caught out in this storm without food and shelter." Cole realized his action would take him away from the kids for the night, something he'd promised Angie he would try to avoid. He watched her closely for her response.

"Can we help you pack so you can get started?" Angie asked. "We can't leave Mattie up there in the cold."

Her reply would make any parent proud. "Thanks, Angel. I hoped you'd feel that way."

"What about our appointment tomorrow morning with Miss Carmen Sandiego?" Sophie asked, referring to a cartoon character she watched on the Internet.

"Sophie-bug, you're a genius. How did you remember that?"

She looked smug. "I just did."

"I'll call her when I'm on my way and reschedule for tomorrow afternoon. You girls plan to go with me then, okay?"

After getting their agreement, he set off to explain the situation to Mrs. Gibbs and round up his supplies.

Chapter 11

Mattie stacked another stone on the rock wall she was building on the opposite side of her fire pit, its purpose to reflect heat back toward her and Robo. She'd decided to set up shelter in the leeward side of a boulder about forty feet from the grave, close enough to guard without feeling like she was on top of it.

A few hours earlier, the gray skies had opened up to dump snow in the high country, and now several inches covered the ground. White shrouds draped the evergreens, and Mattie's breath fogged the air. She stamped her feet and held her cold hands above the fire for a moment.

After sundown she'd given up hope of someone coming, and she'd resigned herself to a miserable night. Robo had dogged her tracks while she searched for deadfall to build a makeshift lean-to. It wasn't much, but without a hatchet, it was the best she could do. He lay next to the fire watching her work, one of his favorite pastimes.

She raised her face to the sky, feeling icy snowflakes spatter her cheeks. "Looks like it's just you and me tonight, Robo."

She could swear he quirked his eyebrows in agreement.

Protect and serve, she thought. *Even the dead.*

She fed Robo a cup of food, saving the last for morning. Her own stomach rumbled with hunger. Settling into her sparse shelter, she peeled the wrapper off an energy bar, the only food she had left.

Her thoughts went back to Adrienne. Who could have buried her way up here? And how did she die?

Then a terrible scream echoed down the draw. It sounded like a woman. Mattie dropped her food and rose to her feet, drawing her Glock. Robo leapt up barking, the hair rising on his back. She stood beside him, her service weapon in hand.

Gradually, it dawned on her what she'd heard. In all the years she'd lived in Timber Creek, she'd never heard it before. Hunters spoke of the eerie sound: the scream of a mountain lion. And it was close.

"Holy shit," she muttered, shuddering from the adrenaline that shot through her system.

She peered into the darkness outside the ring of her campfire light. Mountain lion attacks weren't frequent in this wilderness, the huge cats preferring to shy away from human contact. But they weren't unheard of. She kept hold of her handgun while she turned a slow circle, completing a visual probe of the surrounding area. Nothing.

Robo stood motionless, staring off to her left. His hackles stood at attention, and he huffed an angry sound from deep in his chest.

"Where is it, Robo?"

She fired one shot into the air, hoping to scare the lion away. Robo glanced at her when the gun fired but turned back to stare into the night. Creeping forward, she stepped outside the firelight and paused to allow her eyes to adjust. The brilliant whiteness of the newly fallen snow cast a ghostly light on the clearing. Adrienne's grave lay undisturbed, the black plastic sheet now blanketed in white.

Robo stayed at her side, quiet and steady, searching with her. He seemed less upset than he'd been before, so maybe her gunshot had done the trick. If the cat stayed near enough, she would probably be able to see firelight reflect in its eyes, and she could see nothing like that.

"Is it gone, Robo?"

Not taking his eyes off the forest, he waved his tail once before standing guard. They waited in place for several minutes; Mattie's heartbeat slowly resumed its normal pace. Robo began to relax somewhat, shifting his eyes between the tree line and her, as if checking to see what to do next. She decided that meant the danger had passed.

Keeping her gun in hand, she went back to the fire and threw another log on the flames. "This fire should help," she said aloud, thinking it might be the best protection she and Robo had from predators. At least the four-legged kind.

A branch snapped behind her. She whirled, taking a shooting stance and pointing out at the darkness. She stepped to the side, slipping away from the firelight, making sure it wouldn't backlight her silhouette. A growl rumbled from Robo as he came with her.

She waited. When Robo settled and there was no further sound, she began to feel silly. The mountain lion's scream had set her on edge. She needed to calm down. Drawing a breath, she turned back to the fire, deciding to build it up to an enormous height for both security and heat.

Robo faced the forest, keeping watch. A gust of wind swirled the falling snow, blurring the boundary between clearing and trees. As the logs in her fire caught and blazed hot, Mattie eyed her dwindling woodpile. She couldn't afford to let the fire die down, but she didn't want to sacrifice the deadfall in her shelter. Soon, she'd be forced to leave the safety of the firelight to gather more wood.

She kept an eye on her dog, knowing he would alert her to danger. While she waited, she warmed her fingers and toes and a layer of white formed on Robo's back. It took a long time, but eventually he let down his guard and returned to her side, looking up at her and waving his tail, apparently seeking warmth and reassurance. "You're a good boy." Mattie squatted beside him and held him close as the fire danced and snapped. They stayed together sharing body heat until it started to wane.

"We have to get some more wood." She hated to go into the forest, but she'd already gathered the small amount of easy fuel she'd found nearby. "Let's go."

Taking her flashlight from her utility belt, she crossed the small clearing and entered a world caught between shadow and luminescence. Robo stayed in front, occasionally stopping to stare off between the snow-covered pines. Then he would dart back to her side before heading off again. Mattie pressed the light on and swept it in widening arcs as she searched for logs and branches that would fit into her fire pit but still provide a prolonged burn.

It was slow going, but she gathered and carried enough wood for two trips back to her campsite. After sizing up her stack, she decided one more trip might fill the quota she needed to keep her fire burning throughout the night. Returning to the forest, Robo alternated between staying close and turning away to scan the area. Mattie trained the flashlight for him but, always seeing nothing, she decided to hurry, gather the wood she needed, and get back to the safety of the fire.

She tugged at some deadfall, searching for logs, and uncovered a strange sight. Focusing her flashlight, she could see bits of fur, hide, and small bones. Probably rabbit. And here . . . hair from a fox?

Robo chuffed a series of short growls from deep in his chest, pressing against her legs. She flicked the light on him; his hackles were raised. Her own neck prickled. She could swear she was being watched.

She followed Robo's stare and directed her flashlight in that direction. Two orbs glowed, reflecting the beam.

She dropped the wood she'd gathered and reached for her Glock. Robo exploded. With a ferocious bark, he rushed the mountain lion. Mattie's light showed her what he was up against: a huge cougar, snarling and hissing, sharp teeth bared, backed up against a boulder.

Robo charged, his hair puffed up, making him look twice his size, vicious. Mattie raised her weapon and sighted in on the cat. Before she could squeeze off the shot, Robo feinted close, snapping his jaws and barking, blocking her shot. The lion swiped bared claws at him. Robo jumped back.

In a split second, Mattie decided to fire into the air. Even as she raised her weapon, the lion attacked. Robo whirled away but hit a tree. The lion went after him and closed in— too close. Robo dodged. The two animals tangled. Fur, snow, and pine needles flew around them.

Mattie screamed and fired her gun into the air. She rushed toward her partner, shouting, hoping she could break up the fight and get a clean shot. The lion broke off and turned away. She could see its tawny color, its long black-tipped tail. The cat was huge . . . six to seven feet from head to tail. Robo charged after it.

"Robo," she screamed. "Out!"

Robo hesitated, poised to launch himself at the lion. Mattie shot into the air, calling Robo back to her at the same time. With her dog out of the way, she could try to shoot the monstrous cat, but she knew that Robo might dart into the line of fire, so she held the shot. She'd almost emptied her gun's magazine, and she needed to preserve the rounds she had left.

The cat slipped out of sight into the forest, its golden fur tarnished by dark patches. Bloody spots where Robo had gotten in his licks. Robo stood guard, growling, each hair on his body at attention. Mattie shone her light on him, searching for wounds. Blood glistened on his shoulder, forming a rivulet that splashed red drops onto the snow. He sank to lie down, still watching the spot where the cat disappeared.

Her gut tightened when she saw the blood. "Robo."

He struggled to sit, staring after the lion. Mattie went to him, realizing he'd chosen his duty to protect her over his own safety.

She knelt at his side, snow chilling her knees through her jeans. "You're hurt."

In the glow of her flashlight, she could see a gaping slash on his shoulder. Bloody patches showed her other wounds on his face and neck. A brief look at these didn't alarm her. They looked superficial. But his poor shoulder.

After sending one last gunshot into the air, Mattie stood and asked Robo to heel. He weighed almost as much as she did, and she feared she couldn't carry him. He stayed by her side, limping, while she gathered the wood she'd dropped and headed back to the campsite, refusing to leave behind their hard-won bounty. She observed him as they went. She prayed the damage wasn't too severe. He continuously stopped, chuffing his displeasure and looking behind. "Robo, come."

Back in the relative security of the campsite, Mattie dumped the wood and threw a log on the fire. Taking an extra magazine from her utility belt, she reloaded and holstered her Glock. She took out her first aid kit, bent to retrieve her water supply from her backpack, and called Robo to her. Sitting on a large log she'd placed near the shelter, she gently cleaned his wounds. Inspecting the shoulder injury, she saw that it was about four inches long. She cleaned it the best she could by sloshing water on it. Blood flowed steadily and it looked horrible. She fought the bile that rose in her throat.

She pressed a gauze pad on the wound and bound it tight with an elasticized bandage. It was a tricky place to wrap, but she alternated between chest and ribcage and was satisfied with the job. The bandage appeared to apply pressure at the shoulder without infringing on his neck and airway. "There."

She hugged him close while she gently applied more pressure on the wound. It was important to stop the bleeding. He could bleed to death from a tear this big. She buried her nose in the fur at his neck, continuing to apply pressure on the bandage with her hand. What should she do? Stay here and guard Adrienne's grave or take Robo down for medical care?

He licked her face, a stolen kiss. She usually didn't allow him to lick, but this time she made an exception. "Be still now. Let me hold you."

Robo started to shiver. Was it from shock? Blood loss? Still holding him close, she leaned back so that she could see his face. He tipped his head to gaze up at her, looking into her eyes. "Are you okay?" He trembled, and she placed her cheek against his.

She realized she was shivering, too. She knew her trembling was from the letdown after the adrenaline had charged her system. Maybe that's what was going on with Robo. She hoped so.

They sat together for a long time, Mattie holding Robo while she pressed directly on the gauze bandage. Shivers that wracked his body gradually subsided as he relaxed against her.

The cat screamed again, this time from farther away. Robo struggled against her, facing the eerie sound and trying to stand. Mattie wouldn't let him and continued to hold him close. "It's okay, boy. I think it's going away. At least for now."

Shining her flashlight on the gauze pad, she saw that blood had saturated through but was no longer dripping. She noted the size of the stain. She would check it again in a half hour to see how much larger the bloodstain had grown.

She couldn't go anywhere while Robo was still bleeding. It was imperative she stop the blood flow, or she could lose her partner. And she wasn't going to let that happen. Covering the wound to hold it tightly, she settled onto the log and hugged her dog. It was going to be a long night.

Chapter 12

Snowflakes gave off tiny hissing sounds as they fell into the fire. The storm didn't show any sign of letting up. She'd checked Robo's bandage a couple times and thought the blood flow was slowing.

"Mattie!" she heard a voice shout off to the east. "Mattie! It's Cole!"

"Cole!" she called to him. "We're over here."

Robo pulled against her to stand, so she let him, not wanting him to struggle and aggravate the bleeding.

"I see your fire," Cole called out. Moments later he materialized through the trees, the shod hooves of the horse he rode creating a muffled click against snow-covered rocks as he approached.

She walked out to greet him as he dismounted, and when he opened his arms, it felt natural for her to step into his embrace to give him a hug. His arms and body were warm; the fabric of his down coat felt smooth against her cheek as she rested it against his chest. He smelled of winter, snow, and pine forest. But it took only a few moments for her to grow uncomfortable with their closeness. She shivered.

"You're cold," he said.

"A bit," she said, pulling away. She avoided his eyes, look-ing at Robo instead. "I can't tell you how glad I am to see you. Robo's been hurt. Mountain lion attack."

Concern filled Cole's face. "Robo, come here. Let me take a look at you."

Cole bent over the dog while Mattie trained the flash-light and regained her composure. Cole's arrival created such a wave of relief; she thought she might melt into the ground.

"I think I've been able to slow the blood flow. But the stain has gotten bigger, so it must still be seeping," she said.

"I'm not going to take the bandage off yet. It's best to keep some pressure on it, and let's make an icepack with some snow to put on it. That ought to stop the bleeding."

"I didn't think of that."

Cole stood up. "You've done a great job. Let me unpack some things and look for a plastic bag to make that pack."

Mattie started toward her own backpack. "I have an evi-dence bag we can use."

"Are you okay, Mattie? The lion didn't get at you, did it?"

"No, I'm fine. Robo got between us."

"He's a brave dog."

She leaned down to scoop snow into the evidence bag. "He is. We were both pretty shaken up afterward."

Cole placed a hand on her shoulder. "I can imagine."

Mattie bent toward Robo to refocus attention on him. Cole took the bag from her, tied the top, and handed it back.

"Hold this against the bandage while I unpack," he said.

Mattie settled down onto the log and pulled Robo in to cradle him against her chest. She pressed the makeshift ice-pack over the gauze pad. "We'd decided we were going to have to stay here by ourselves tonight."

"I couldn't let that happen."

"Thank goodness. Did you hear the lion scream?"

"I did," he said, while he unpacked the panniers. "It's the eeriest sound in the world."

"It scared the bejesus out of me when I first heard it. I decided to build up the fire and went to get wood. That's when it attacked."

"Atypical behavior," Cole said. "But I suppose this time of year, it could have been a female with a cub."

"I saw fur and bones in the area right before it jumped Robo."

"You might have stumbled onto a cache. They often store a kill and come back to it. Especially if they're feeding babies." He paused and looked around, searching outside the ring of light made by the fire. "Where is Adrienne buried?"

"About forty feet over that way." Mattie nodded toward the site. "I also have some evidence marked out between here and there. I camped here to keep anyone who might come from accidentally disturbing it."

"I'll stay away. Poor Adrienne. I feel terrible about this. I didn't know her well, but what I knew was all good."

"That's what I've gathered." Mattie wondered if the dead woman's soul still lingered and was listening in.

"Do you know how she died?"

Cole's participation in the sheriff's posse gave him a semiofficial status. And after he'd ridden up here in the face of a snowstorm to help, she felt like she could give him information—what little she had to share. "Not yet. But she's buried in an unmarked grave. I doubt if it was natural causes."

"Good God, what's happening around here?"

Mattie shrugged. "It's hard to say. I doubt if this is related to last summer's deaths."

Cole had taken off the leather panniers and began to unsaddle his horse. "I'm lucky this fellow has been up here before.

He seemed to know his way. When I started out, I could see the tapes that marked the trail. But once it got dark and started to snow, things got dicey."

"How did you manage?"

"I had a flashlight, and Mountaineer stuck to the trail like a mountain goat. He stopped when he reached the cairn you built."

"I built it where it would mark the place to leave the trail."

"It did the job." Cole was unpacking the panniers. "Here's my kit. I never go hunting without one."

He was holding a rectangular, leather case similar to one men use for travel. Sitting down on the log next to her, he unzipped it and started taking out his supplies. "I've got everything we need right here—lidocaine, antiseptic sponges, antibiotic cream, and skin staples. Okay, Robo, will you let me take a look?"

Mattie held Robo while Cole unwrapped the bandage. She reached for her flashlight and trained it on Robo's shoulder. With a gentle touch, Cole inspected the wound as he frowned with concentration. Although the heavy bleeding had subsided, Mattie's stomach lurched when she saw the gaping slash.

"This doesn't look too bad," Cole said, glancing at her. He gave her a smile of reassurance. "I mean, I know it looks terrible, but the muscle is still intact. It's primarily a skin tear, and it shouldn't slow him down much. He's one lucky dog."

Mattie felt such relief she couldn't respond. She pressed her lips to the top of Robo's head.

"I don't have a muzzle, but I can fashion one out of your leash," Cole said.

"He might be okay without it."

"Yeah, maybe. But he's still pretty pumped up, and I've learned not to take the chance."

"All right." Mattie reached to retrieve a leash from her utility belt. "Let me put it on him. Just tell me how to do it."

"Wrap it around his muzzle, make a tie below his chin, take the ends back behind his ears and secure it there with another tie."

Mattie murmured soothing words while she followed Cole's instructions. Robo's brow furrowed with his disapproval, but he allowed her to finish the process. She pulled him in for a hug and told him he was a good boy. When Cole took out a syringe to fill with the numbing medicine, she decided to look away, choosing instead to hold Robo close and rub his ears.

"A little sting," Cole said as he began blocking the wound.

Robo flinched and then settled while the medicine took effect. At that point, Mattie watched the fire while Cole worked. When he finished, the gash on Robo's shoulder had been cleaned and closed with a series of staples. The blood flow had all but stopped.

Cole leaned back to inspect his work. "When we get down to the truck tomorrow, I'll start him on antibiotics."

"Thank you." It was hard to put into words how good it felt to know Robo was taken care of and he was going to be okay.

"I'm not going to put a bandage on it. It's too far forward on his shoulder for him to irritate it, and I want to leave it where we can check it easily. It should heal just fine open to the air. But let's cover it with gauze so you can apply the ice-pack for a few more minutes."

While Mattie took care of Robo, Cole used one of his antiseptic sponges and some water to wash his hands.

"Are you hungry?"

"I guess I am. Robo might be, too."

"I brought food for both of you."

He turned back to the panniers, indicating the items. "There's food, water, a tent, and some space-age blankets. I couldn't fit sleeping bags in."

"I won't do much sleeping tonight anyway. A blanket sounds like exactly what I need."

Cole set out containers of thick ham sandwiches, apple slices, baby carrots, bottles of water, and what appeared to be homemade brownies.

"You've brought a feast," she said.

"Mrs. Gibbs made it."

"That was nice of her."

Cole came close to check Robo's wound. "I think we can leave that alone for a while and check it later. It looks like it's stopped bleeding."

Mattie cleaned her hands with an antiseptic sponge that Cole gave her. She fed Robo a cup of the food that Cole had brought, but he didn't seem interested. Considering what he'd been through, she wasn't too surprised. She left it so that he could get to it if he should change his mind. She and Cole each selected a sandwich from the container and took seats on opposite ends of the log.

"I hope Mrs. Gibbs is going to work out," he said. "It sure would make things easier at home if she did. But the girls seem to be giving her a tough time. Or at least Angie is, I should say. Sophie's just following suit."

Mattie chewed her sandwich, staring at the fire. She and Cole didn't talk about their personal lives. She really didn't know what to say, and she didn't want to probe.

Cole seemed not to have any problem with the conversation. "Mrs. Gibbs had a talk with me this morning, and it's been bothering me all day."

"Oh?"

"She took the girls to see Leslie Hartman yesterday after school. I guess Angie was real quiet on the way home, and Mrs. Gibbs asked her what was wrong. Angie gave her some lip."

"Maybe she didn't want to talk about what was bothering her with someone she barely knows."

"You're probably right about that," he said, taking a bite and pausing to chew. "What bothers me, though, is that Mrs. Gibbs suggested that Angie has had too much trauma in her life to handle lately."

Mattie swallowed her food. "School counselor."

"What?"

Since Mattie taught the antidrug program at Timber Creek High, she knew the faculty. "There's a counselor at school you could talk to. Her name's Mrs. Willis. Have you met her?"

"No, but I know who she is."

"You could talk to her to get her opinion. She seems nice, and the kids like her. I bet she could help you decide what to do." She was in *this* deep, she might as well go deeper; after all, this was Angie they were talking about. "Have you tried to talk to her about her feelings?"

He appeared to squirm in his seat. "I did. I tend to screw things up. I think I ended up telling her she needs to act more respectful toward Mrs. Gibbs or something like that."

She smiled. "Sounds like a dad."

"Does it?" He looked relieved. "That's what I am. I'll never be able to fill their mom's shoes. Anyway, it's hard for me to talk to her about how she feels right now. We all feel pretty torn up about things."

"Maybe all of you could use some professional help."

"Good Lord. I'm not sure I could go for that. I think we just need a little time."

"Well, start with Angie then."

"Yeah. I'll think about it."

The fire snapped. Mattie stretched her feet out toward it, welcoming the warmth that seeped into the soles of her boots as the snow fell peacefully around them.

"You told me you were raised in foster care. How did that happen? What happened to your parents?"

She studied his face, wondering what made him ask about her past. She rarely shared that part of herself.

"I'm sorry," he said, giving her a searching look. "That might be something you don't want to talk about. I didn't think."

"No, it's okay. But why do you want to know?"

He scrutinized her. "I was thinking about my girls, how hard it is on them to be abandoned by their mom. It made me think of you being raised without either parent. It's none of my business really."

Mattie looked out toward the gravesite. "There's no reason I can't talk about my childhood. I typically don't, so I'm not used to it."

"Then let's talk about something else. How about those Broncos?"

Mattie couldn't help but smile. He did have a way of easing her discomfort. "No, I want to talk about it now."

He placed another log on the fire and settled back into his seat. Robo lay at her feet, and his eyebrows twitched as he fought sleep.

"There were four of us in my family, like yours, but my sibling is a brother. My dad was an alcoholic. A violent drunk.

He hit all of us at one time or another, but most of the time, he beat on my mom."

"What was your mom like?"

"Do you mean, did she drink, too? No, she didn't."

"No, I meant what I said—what was she like?"

"Well, I was only six when our family broke up. But I remember her as being quiet, gentle, loving toward us kids." Mattie forced herself to examine her memories from an adult perspective. "I think she was probably afraid most of the time. I remember her as being very pretty with black hair and dark eyes, Hispanic ancestry. She was small, much smaller than my dad."

She shivered and her chest tightened. Even thinking about it brought back the scary feelings of living in a house where violence reigned.

Cole got up and went to the pannier again, this time bringing back a blanket. He bent over and wrapped it around her, placing a warm hand on her shoulder for a moment before sitting back down.

"One night he beat her worse than he ever had before." Mattie could still remember putting her fingers in her ears to block the sound of the punches, closing her eyes to shut out the sight of blood and the dazed look on her mother's face as she fought to remain conscious. "He reached for a kitchen knife, and I knew he meant to use it on her. So I sneaked to my parent's room and dialed nine-one-one. The cops came, my dad went to prison, and my mom was taken to the hospital."

Cole had crossed his arms over his chest. "What a thing to have to go through. Did your mother die?"

"No. She got out of the hospital, but she didn't want to take care of me and my brother anymore. She turned us over to the county. I haven't seen or heard from her since the night the ambulance came to take her away."

"Is your dad still living?"

"He got killed at the prison by another inmate. Never made it out."

He appeared to be mulling it over. "I hate to say it, but it sounds like he got what he deserved."

Mattie shrugged. "Who's to say? Inmates should be safe in prison. It's hard to justify violence no matter where it is."

"I suppose you're right about that."

"My brother and I were messed-up little kids. He was hard to place—he burned down a haystack at one of our foster homes, so he got taken out of that one. Finally got sent to Colorado Springs to live in a foster home there. I turned into a hellion until the track coach found out I could run, and he funneled all that anger and excess energy into cross-country training. Then I was placed in my last foster home with Teresa Lovato—do you know her?"

"No, can't say as I do. Does she have pets?"

Mattie let out a puff of amusement. "No, no pets per se. Maybe the kids feed a stray now and then, but Mama T has no extra money for pet food. She takes in stray kids mostly."

"Did you have a good experience in her home?"

"The best. Thank goodness for that. She straightened me out." She gave him a pointed look. "But I'm thinking of your kids and how they must feel. Abandonment issues can really mess with your head. You'd be smart to get the girls professional help early before real problems start."

"Case made, Counselor." He gave her a pointed look. "Are you sure you don't have a law degree? You remind me of my sister. She can jump on a subject, shake it around, and shape it any way she wants to make her point."

Mattie laughed, the tightness in her chest loosening. The mountain lion screamed, the sound echoing from a distance. Robo alerted, standing to sniff the air.

"Sounds like it's moved off a ways," she said.

"Just wants us to know we're in its territory."

"I suppose so."

They sat in silence for a few moments.

"Do you think Adrienne was killed up here?" Cole asked.

"No." Mattie knew very little, but of that she was sure. "It wasn't right here."

"I can't imagine her hiking up here on her own."

"Me either."

He sighed. "My kids will be traumatized by this, too. They'd grown fond of her. She was teaching Angie massage techniques for horses."

"Um-hmm."

Cole looked at her, chagrinned. "You don't have to say it. I know what you're thinking."

A gust of wind battered them, and with it came the snow in earnest.

"Let's set up that tent I brought," Cole said.

"All right. No reason you can't stretch out and get some sleep."

"We'll take turns," he said. "You first. Robo needs to get in out of the snow and warm up."

Chapter 13

Sunday

Evidently deciding that two humans and a dog were too much to contend with, the mountain lion stayed away, and the rest of the night passed quickly. The intimacy of the campsite made it easier to tell secrets, and Cole shared his feelings about his wife leaving and about his hopes to pick up the pieces and establish a stable home for his kids. Mattie felt reassured that they knew each other better than ever before, and he didn't judge her for her difficult past.

The snow stopped falling sometime during the wee hours of the night, leaving about four inches. By midmorning, the sun shone bright and the retrieval party arrived. Mattie scanned the riders, looking for Stella LoSasso, a detective she liked and respected after they'd teamed up during their last homicide investigation.

Stella sat atop a brown and white paint toward the middle of the string, holding onto the saddle horn with gloved hands. Wearing white down pants and a parka, she looked more like the Pillsbury Doughboy than the sharply dressed woman Mattie knew her to be. Stella appeared to be looking for her, too, and when their eyes met, her face lit up in greeting.

Brody rode the first horse in the string of six, and he stopped well away from Mattie and Cole's campsite. Mattie recognized the two crime scene technicians she'd worked with last summer and Garrett Hartman as the other riders. Hartman led the sixth horse, which wore a packsaddle to carry out Adrienne's body when they were done with the scene.

Cole and Mattie joined the group. Mattie exchanged nods with Brody, taking a moment to determine how he was holding up. Clean-shaven and not quite so strung out, it looked as if he may have gotten some sleep. Perhaps there'd been some closure in finding Adrienne and knowing that she was not stranded someplace, suffering from injury and nature's elements.

"Hello, Mattie . . . Dr. Walker," Stella said when they approached. "Could one of you help me down from this beast?"

"Sure," Cole said, reaching up to her while Mattie took hold of the reins.

Stella slid off the horse, staggering as she straightened her legs. "My God, I'm not used to that. And the worst thing is, I have to ride back down."

"You can walk out with me," Mattie told her. "It's good to see you again, Stella."

The two women clasped hands while Cole went on to help the others and to greet Hartman.

"I'll stick with the horse, thank you," Stella said, bending down to pet Robo, avoiding the staples on his shoulder. "What happened to your partner? He looks like the son of Frankenstein."

"He tangled with a mountain lion last night."

Astonishment crossed Stella's face. "Good grief! You're kidding me."

"No, I'm not. He was very brave."

"I'm sure he was," Stella said, stroking the fur on Robo's head. "When is he not?"

Robo waved his tail, trotted over to sniff the newcomers, and came back to Mattie's side.

Mattie and Stella watched him. "He's not limping very much," Stella said.

"Cole said it didn't get into the muscle. He's got a four-inch gash in his skin, but he's going to be okay."

"Thank God."

"Yeah."

"How have you been, Mattie Cobb?"

"I've been better. It's hard to believe we need you again so soon." Mattie gestured toward the gravesite. "Before the lion attack, we did a grid search and found some evidence. Robo found a cigarette butt that looks fresh, and I found some tracks that I covered before the storm. The gravesite is covered and protected from the snow, too."

"Good job, you two," Stella said, bending down to pat Robo again. "Well, let's get to it."

Mattie led Stella and the crime scene techs to the grave, pointing out her evidence markers. One of the techs began snapping photos. Brody carried over supplies while Cole and Garrett stayed by the fire.

"We'll open the grave first," Stella said. "Deputy Brody, would you care to join the boys over there?"

"I'll stay."

"Suit yourself, but this might not be the best way to remember your friend, and there isn't anything you can do for her now. Let us take care of her." Stella gave Mattie a pointed look.

"Come on, Brody," Mattie said, touching his arm.

Without protest, he turned away and followed her back to the fire. From that distance, Mattie watched Stella and the techs kneel at the gravesite and slowly strip away the layers of snow, plastic tarp, stones, and pine boughs that covered Brody's sweetheart. In the back of her mind, she wondered if the fact that he truly did seem devastated was enough to give Timber Creek's chief deputy a pass on being a suspect.

★

While exhausted from the relatively sleepless night, Mattie still kept up with the horseback riders on the way down. Robo stayed close, and Cole rode behind her. They'd debated trying to lift Robo up to ride in front of Cole, but an uneasy attempt showed them he wanted nothing to do with it. Mattie decided to let him go down on his own and try again if his limp became worse.

Garrett Hartman rode at the front of the line, leading the packhorse that carried the body. Footing was treacherous in some places with snow and ice on the trail, but about midway down the snowfall had ended, leaving the trail wet but clear. The forecast for snow at only higher elevations above nine thousand feet had been accurate; by the time they reached the trailhead, the ground at the lower elevation was bare. Timber Creek would be, too.

At the parking area, Mattie went with Cole to his pickup and trailer to get the antibiotics. "Thanks for coming up to help last night," she said. "When do you want me to bring him in to get the staples out?"

He popped open the latch at the back of the trailer and swung the door wide. "In about ten days."

"Should I restrict his movement or take him off work?"

"He's moving around fine. He shouldn't have any trouble with it. You can go about your business as usual." Cole clicked his tongue, and Mountaineer stepped into the trailer. He followed him in to exchange his bridle for a halter and to tie him to the trailer's side.

"I'll make an appointment for ten days from now, then." Mattie loaded Robo into her own vehicle, noticing that he was moving freely.

When they entered their home, it felt like she'd been gone for ages instead of one night. Even though she'd fed him that morning up on the mountain, Robo trotted into the kitchen to check out his food bowl. She could hear him slurping water while she stretched her sore calf and thigh muscles. She decided to give him an extra ration, and he gobbled it before joining her in her bedroom, circling on his dog bed, and plopping down with a sigh.

"I bet you're exhausted." Even prior to the lion attack, he'd covered twice the miles she had as he ran ahead and then back on the trail yesterday, and he'd been awake through most of the night. "Get some sleep while I clean up."

Feeling refreshed from her shower, Mattie toweled her hair as she padded into the kitchen in sweats and stocking feet. Robo slept while she made and ate a peanut butter and jelly sandwich and scoured her pantry for anything that might give her some energy. Settling on an apple and a bag of trail mix to take with her, she drank some orange juice and then went to her bedroom to get dressed in her uniform. Although his brow and ears twitched, Robo didn't open his eyes. She decided to leave him at home while she went to her meeting. She could pick him up later after she'd established her plan for the day.

At the station, the first person Mattie met was Rainbow, something she'd been dreading. Noticing the dispatcher's swollen, reddened eyes, she felt somehow responsible. "Rainbow, I thought you had a day off today."

"I had to know, so I traded a day with Sam," she said, referring to Sam Corns, the other dispatcher.

In a gesture of sympathy, Mattie touched the back of her wrist, and Rainbow turned her hand up to grasp Mattie's.

"I'm sorry, Rainbow."

Tears welled, and one spilled over to roll down Rainbow's cheek. "Me too. I really can't believe it. She was such a great person, you know? She loved her new life here and everything about it."

"Do you know anything about her from before she came to Timber Creek? We're going to need to know everything."

"Some. Nothing sinister. I can't think of anything that will help."

"Most of the time, it's hard to know what might help or not. I'm going to mention to Stella that you knew her. She's probably going to want to interview you."

"Okay." Rainbow sniffed and used a tissue to blot her eyes. "But I don't think she likes me."

Mattie knew that to be true, although she believed the detective had judged Rainbow for her flower child–like, ditzy appearance and not for any reason of substance. "That shouldn't make a difference."

She squeezed Rainbow's hand and released it, making a mental note to sit in on that interview. "Are the others here yet?"

"In the briefing room."

"I'd better get in there. We'll talk more later."

When Mattie entered the room, she found Stella, McCoy, and Brody at the front table engaged in discussion. All but Brody turned to see who'd entered. Sheriff McCoy gestured for her to come in and take a seat.

"I was just addressing the elephant in the room," Stella said after Mattie sat.

Mattie swept her eyes across the faces of the others and then settled on Brody. Familiar with his rage, she could tell it was full blown: neck and cheeks crimson, face stony, lips tight.

"I've proposed that Deputy Brody excuse himself from this investigation," Stella said.

I wondered about that myself. Grateful that Stella was the one who'd brought it up, she nodded. Brody locked eyes with Mattie.

Sheriff McCoy asked Brody what he thought about the suggestion. Without taking his eyes off Mattie he said, "I think it's bullshit." His voice was almost a growl.

"I can see how you would. But you know how this investigation will go. We'll look at everyone who knew her. You included."

"Then look."

"You need to go home, Chief Deputy," McCoy said. "Take the rest of the day. Put everything you know into a report, including a detailed list of your time and activities since noon on Wednesday until yesterday morning. I'll take a look at it, verify what I can, and consider your role in the investigation. Get that report to me as quickly as you can. I'll take it under advisement and give you an answer ASAP."

Brody's chair screeched on the linoleum as he shoved back from the table and stood. "You won't shut me out," he said to Stella and turned to leave.

"I'll keep you apprised of what I can," she said to his back.

"Excuse me a moment," Mattie said, hurrying after Brody on a whim. Something begged to be said between them. Perhaps their time together on the mountain required it.

He charged out of the station with her close behind. "Brody," she called to him as he strode toward his cruiser. He stopped and turned, grim-faced and silent.

"I'm sorry for your loss. But you have to think about it. This is standard operating procedure, and you'll be far more help to Adrienne if you keep a level head. Cool off and then put everything you can think of in writing to help us develop some leads."

He shrugged, looking down at the pavement. "I don't know much about her past."

That confession must hurt. "Put some thought into it. And get some rest. Are you back on duty tomorrow?"

"Day off, but I'll be here."

"I'll see you then." She started to turn away, but stayed to say one more thing. "I know you loved her."

His eyes filled, and he turned his back to get into his car. Mattie stayed in place to watch him drive away; she lifted a hand in farewell, though he didn't look her way. She'd once suspected Brody of involvement with Grace Hartman's murder. This time, her gut insisted that he was an innocent man.

When Mattie reentered the briefing room, Stella was cleaning the dry-erase board. She finished and laid the eraser on the metal shelf below it.

"Somebody had to say it, Mattie," Stella said.

Mattie nodded, taking a seat back at the table.

"I'll assume the responsibility for checking Deputy Brody's schedule and clearing his alibi," McCoy said. "He's a fine officer, Detective. I stand behind him."

Stella gave McCoy an unwavering gaze. "I'm sure he is, Sheriff, and I'm willing to bet he had nothing to do with his girlfriend's death. It's not about how fine an officer he is. He's too close to this one. He needs to take a step back and become an officer instead of a boyfriend. If he's able to do that, he might be of assistance. If not, he needs to be at the perimeter of this investigation instead of at the center."

Mattie agreed with Stella and thought she'd expressed the underlying concern well. McCoy nodded and appeared to agree, too.

"Where's your partner?" Stella asked.

"Home asleep."

"Looks like you could use some of that yourself." Stella brushed her hands together. "Let's lay out this case, brainstorm on it, and decide where we're going next."

Stella turned back to the board and wrote *Victim—Adrienne Howard* at the top. "Let's lay out the grid. We'll start with the information you've gleaned over the past few days."

She looked down at her notebook lying open on the table. Evidently she'd copied the board before erasing it. "First—History," she said, writing as she spoke. "Raised in Hightower. Mother—Velda Howard/Hightower/estranged. What else do we know?"

"Not much," Mattie said. "But we should interview our dispatcher, Rainbow, and the massage therapist at Valley Vista, Anya Yamamoto. Both were close friends."

Stella nodded, pursing her lips. Skipping over to the far side of the board, she started a new list titled *Interview* and wrote *Rainbow* beneath it. "What's her last name?"

"Sanderson."

After writing it down, Stella added the name and then recorded Anya Yamamoto. "What about my old buddy Dean Hornsby?"

"I doubt if he knows any personal information, but we now have a warrant, so we can take a look at Adrienne's employment records. A résumé would give us information to fill in the gaps between Hightower and Timber Creek," McCoy said.

Moving her pen slightly to the right of her first category, Stella wrote *Evidence* and started a new list under the word. "We casted the prints at the crime scene: a partial cowboy boot and horseshoes. There appeared to be nothing unique about them, so they may not be too helpful. We'll see if the crime scene unit can give us an estimate on boot size. The cigarette butt Robo found might provide DNA, assuming it was left by the person who buried our victim."

"We traced the phone call on the tip that sent us up there," McCoy said. "It was a TracFone, purchased at a Walmart store in Willow Springs last March."

Willow Springs was one of the larger towns in Timber Creek County and was located about twenty miles beyond Hightower.

Sheriff McCoy continued. "It was paid for with cash, so it was impossible to find out who purchased it. At least we've got the phone number. And I've got a warrant to determine what tower the call pinged from, so we can determine an approximate location of our caller. Though I'm not sure how much help that will be in these mountains."

"That's good, Sheriff. Very good," Stella said. "What else can I add?"

"Her cell phone is also missing," Mattie said. "Purple cover."

"Not missing anymore," Stella said. "It was in her pants pocket, turned off and smashed. We'll see if the lab can lift any prints other than the victim's from it."

"I've initiated a court order for production of records," McCoy said, "so we can access her cell phone records, texts, and her e-mail account. I put a STAT on it."

Stella had been recording everything Mattie and the sheriff said. "We can look to see if that TracFone number ever contacted our victim. The autopsy will take place in Byers County at eight o'clock tomorrow morning. I plan to go home tonight and stay for the autopsy, so I won't be back until later in the morning. We'll have more to add here after that. Anything else?"

After waiting a few moments but getting no response, she moved her pen to the right to write a new category, *Persons of Interest.* She wrote *Kevin Conrad*, something she'd copied from their first grid. "What do we know about this guy?"

"Ex-boyfriend, high school sweetheart," Mattie said.

"He lives in California," McCoy said. "Deputy Brody talked with him first, and I followed up yesterday. Denies knowing where Adrienne lived. He has a tight alibi with his employer who says he was at work this past week. Has a wife and kids."

"Did they part amicably?"

"He says yes," McCoy said. "They haven't been in touch for five years. He says he's moved on."

"Any reason to hire a hit?" Stella asked.

"None that I can turn up," McCoy said.

"Okay," Stella said. "Let's add Adrienne's mother to our list of people to interview."

"And we've got to notify her of the death," Mattie said.

"I've taken care of that already," McCoy said.

Mattie felt relief that family notification of death wouldn't fall to her. It was a task that no one embraced, but one the sheriff was good at. "What about the people at the hot springs?"

"I decided it would be best to take care of that in person, when you go out to search," McCoy said.

It made sense, but Mattie predicted that Anya would be devastated.

"I'll do it," Stella said, looking at Mattie. "Be sure to observe how they react."

"We also need to get a complete list of Adrienne's current massage therapy clients," Mattie said.

"Okay, let's head out to the hot springs now," Stella said, putting down her marking pen. "We have a good investigation started here. Nice job on the lead work. Let's all meet back here tomorrow at eleven so I can brief you on the autopsy. And I do *not* want to include Brody in that meeting, Sheriff, no matter what you find in his report. I'll talk to him separately to brief him on what he needs to know, and then we'll decide his level of participation."

The flinty look in Stella's gaze told Mattie that the detective meant what she said, and there would be no negotiation.

Chapter 14

Mattie drove and Stella rode shotgun on the trip to Valley Vista hot springs. Once they were on the way, Stella leaned back in her seat, and Mattie could feel the detective studying her.

"What?" Mattie asked, giving her a sideways glance while keeping an eye on the road.

Stella gave her a knowing smile. "So you spent the night all alone with the handsome vet."

Mattie snorted, shaking her head. "Not alone exactly. We had a corpse with us."

"Well, I guess there was that."

"Yes, there was that. He patched Robo up, and we stayed up all night guarding the gravesite. Strictly business."

"Hmm. I see." Stella looked out her window, pursing her lips.

Mattie let the silence lengthen. After reaching the turnoff, she turned onto the gravel road that led to the hot springs. It ran straight up into the foothills like a flat, gray ribbon. The health resort sat one-third of the way up the mountain, surrounded by a cluster of white yurts. Both she and Stella had been to it once before, when they were investigating Grace's murder.

She parked beside the bathhouse that had been under construction when she'd first visited, noticing that it now appeared to be finished. They left the vehicle and followed the pathway that led to the office. The flaps at the entryway, which had been open last summer, were now closed tightly against the autumn chill. Mattie couldn't imagine going through a Timber Creek winter with canvas walls. Standing outside the secured doorway, she gave Stella a questioning look, which the detective answered with a shrug. Mattie rapped lightly on one of the yurt's wooden supports.

Anya Yamamoto opened the flap and gestured for them to come inside. Dean Hornsby sat at his desk, working on his computer, its light reflecting off the lenses of his glasses. He stood, slightly stooped, a look of surprise crossing his face. On the other hand, Anya's emotions remained hidden behind her typical, inscrutable expression.

"Detective, Miss Cobb," Hornsby said, looking at each of them in turn, "to what do we owe the pleasure?"

It irritated Mattie that Hornsby refused to address her by her title. She'd corrected him before, but this time she let it go.

"It's about Adrienne," Anya said, her dark eyes riveted on Mattie.

Mattie nodded, meeting her gaze.

"We're here in an official capacity," Stella said. "I regret to have to tell you this, but Adrienne Howard has been found dead."

Pain registered on Anya's face before she turned it downward to stare at her clasped hands.

Hornsby looked stunned. "That can't be."

"I'm sorry," Stella said. She waited a few beats while Hornsby looked helplessly about the room.

Anya raised her eyes to look at Stella. "What happened to her?"

"Her death is under investigation as a homicide," Stella said.

Anya's lips parted as her breath caught. "Someone killed her?"

"Yes."

"Where did you find her?" Anya asked.

"In the mountains. We're not releasing the exact location," Stella said. "I understand you reported Adrienne missing on Thursday. Do either of you have a theory as to where she might have gone when she left here?"

"I have no idea," Hornsby said.

"I thought she went hiking, but I didn't know where," Anya said, her face starting to show the strain of trying to control her emotions. A tear slipped down her cheek, and she swiped it with a finger. "She goes hiking alone quite often."

"Do you know of anyone who might do Adrienne harm?" Stella asked.

Both denied that kind of knowledge.

"That's an important question, and I want you both to take your time thinking about it. You can call me if you come up with ideas," Stella said. "Right now, we need to take a look at Adrienne's employment records, her living quarters, and where she works."

"I can't show you employment records," Hornsby said.

Stella took out the warrant she carried in her case. "Yes, you can, Mr. Hornsby. This is a homicide investigation, and I can show you our search warrant."

He shook his head. "I mean, I don't keep employment records."

"A résumé? An application form?"

Hornsby shrugged, casting a sidelong glance at Anya. "We don't bother with those things. It's hard to attract good therapists to Timber Creek. If one can show her credentials, and if Anya observes a good aura, we hire. Such was the case with Adrienne."

Stella raised a brow. "I see. That's uh . . . rather unorthodox. Do you have any knowledge of Adrienne's past work history or where she lived?"

"She came from Willow Springs," Anya said.

"When did she move here?"

"The end of April, soon after the rest of us."

"Where did she work in Willow Springs?" Mattie asked.

"She worked for a chiropractor." Anya paused to think. "I don't recall her ever mentioning his name."

"Do you know where she worked and lived before Willow Springs?" Mattie asked.

"No, Adrienne didn't like to talk about her past."

Mattie found it hard to believe how little Adrienne's employer and friend seemed to know about her, but then Brody was no better.

"Could you show us Adrienne's living quarters, Ms. Yamamoto?" Stella asked.

"We share a yurt. You're welcome to search the entire room," Anya said, turning to get her coat.

Stella handed a business card to Hornsby. "I'll probably call you again, Mr. Hornsby. But in the meantime, if you think of anything that might help our investigation, please call."

Hornsby nodded, taking the card and looking at it.

Mattie and Stella followed Anya down a pathway between the white canvas buildings. Mattie had seen Anya's treatment area and a guest yurt during her last visit to the spa. They were utilitarian structures, sparsely furnished, and she thought it more likely that leads would be found in the victim's sleeping space rather than her work space.

Anya remained silent while their footsteps crunched along the gravel pathway.

Stella quickened her step to walk beside Anya while Mattie followed. "Were you and Ms. Howard close?"

Anya hunched forward, hands in her coat pockets. "I would say yes."

"Do you know anything about her love life?"

Anya glanced at the detective before continuing to walk with downcast head. "Adrienne was a woman in love who loved her career. She didn't have any enemies that I know of. She had a kind and gentle soul."

"In love with . . . ?"

"Deputy Brody of course. I think you already know that."

Stella nodded, giving the woman a slight smile. Mattie knew what she was after.

"Did she and Deputy Brody seem to be getting along okay?" Stella asked.

"Yes. Their feelings were mutual."

"Could they have had an argument?"

"Not to my knowledge, at least not as of Tuesday night. It would have had to occur Wednesday, and she was with clients all morning."

They came to the doorway of a small yurt. Anya entered, flipping on an overhead electrical bulb to compensate for the lack of natural light through windows. The space was clean and neat with a wooden floor and canvas roof and walls. Twin beds sat across the room from each other covered with maroon comforters. Matching small chests of drawers acted as bedside tables, and a large wardrobe filled the center of the back wall. A space heater glowed, taking the chill off the room.

"That is Adrienne's side of the room," Anya said, gesturing. "But you're welcome to search my space, too, though I'm aware of nothing I have that could be of help."

"Thank you," Stella said. "We'll take a look at both."

Mattie pulled a pair of latex gloves from a pocket on her belt and tugged them on while crossing the room. She inspected the items on top of the small chest. A stack of books sat by a reading light, and she sifted through them, revealing titles on massage therapy techniques for horses as well as humans.

One book stood out as different from the others. *Moving On: Recovery from Childhood Abuse.* Maybe this helped explain Adrienne's estrangement from her mother. Mattie held the book out to show the title.

"For Adrienne or for a client?" Mattie asked Anya while Stella turned from her search to read the title.

"I cannot say."

"Don't know? Or won't say?" Stella asked.

Anya remained silent.

"We're not asking out of idle curiosity. If Adrienne has a history of childhood abuse, that's something we should follow up," Mattie said.

Anya looked down at the floor for a moment and then up at Mattie. "I am her therapist and healer. There is not much I can say."

But her words spoke volumes. "I think we'd better follow up."

"Yes."

"I can get a warrant for her medical records," Stella said.

"There is no written record."

Stella shot a disbelieving glance at Mattie before looking back at Anya. "No record?"

"I'm a body worker. I use many modalities, assessing what the body needs each time I provide a treatment. I didn't ask for payment from Adrienne, and I didn't conduct a form of talk therapy in the traditional sense. There was no need to document our sessions."

"Anya," Mattie said. "It's important we find leads so we can track down the person who killed your friend. You won't be betraying her confidence by answering our questions."

Anya stared at Mattie, her eyes reddened with unshed tears. She nodded in silent agreement.

"Can you confirm that Adrienne was abused as a child?" Mattie asked.

"Yes."

"Was she at a point in her treatment where she might have pressed charges against her abuser?" Stella asked.

"If she was considering it, she didn't tell me."

"What do you know about her abuser?"

"Nothing specific. I believe it was parental."

That struck a chord that resonated with Mattie's own past. "Father? Mother?"

"Perhaps both." Anya paused, her face drawn with sadness. "Adrienne shed her grief over her past in tears during our treatments and seemed to be gaining a new level of happiness. She said she felt better about it now than she'd felt her entire adult life."

Mattie nodded, looking downward to search drawers that contained nothing but clothing while Stella searched the wardrobe.

Anya brushed her hand across an empty space on top of the chest. "There's something missing right here."

"What's that?" Mattie asked.

"Her laptop." Anya pointed to a power cord left plugged into the wall, as if its loose end proved the laptop's absence. "It has a zebra-striped cover. It's gone, and I haven't been able to find it."

"Would she have taken it with her on Wednesday?"

"I've wondered about that. She keeps her own treatment records in it, and she takes it with her when she goes to do massage for horses." Anya looked troubled. "But I thought she went on a hike."

Mattie looked across the room and met Stella's gaze.

"Why did you think she went on a hike?" Stella asked.

"It's what she usually does on her afternoons off."

"Who keeps her horse appointment schedule?"

"She does."

"Do you know where her schedule might be?"

Anya's frown deepened. "On her laptop."

"Did you look for it in these drawers?" Mattie asked, resuming her search.

"Yes. At first, I glanced into the bottom drawer to see if she'd taken her purse. When I saw it was still there, I decided to call the sheriff."

Mattie opened the bottom drawer and found many things, none of which resembled a computer. It seemed to contain a veritable treasure trove: small rocks and crystals, a vial of something, a stack of brochures, a purse, a stack of opened envelopes addressed to Adrienne Howard, a small pair of ankle weights, a photo album.

Mattie picked up the vial and showed it to Anya. "Do you know what this is?"

Anya opened the vial, sniffed. "Peace and Harmony, an essential oil."

She held it out for Mattie to smell. The scent contained a combination of citrus and patchouli. It made her nose twitch, and she suppressed a sneeze. A peaceful response to that odor might depend on the individual.

Mattie opened the purse and poured its contents on Adrienne's bed. It contained the usual items carried by women: hairbrush, sunglasses, makeup bag, checkbook, and wallet. She looked through the wallet, but there was nothing inside other than a small amount of cash, a credit card, and a driver's license. The makeup bag contained only the basics: mascara and several types of lip gloss.

Sorting through the brochures, she saw that most of them advertised massage therapy conferences, including one for horses, all sometime in the future. There were also a few travel brochures on Alaskan cruises and Yellowstone. These seemed to be consistent with what she already knew about the victim.

Stella picked up the photo album and started leafing through it. "Do you know any of these people in the pictures, Ms. Yamamoto?"

"You may call me Anya." She moved near Stella to peer at the photographs. "I don't know any of these people. The pictures look like they were taken some time ago. Before Adrienne moved here."

Stella tapped a salmon-colored nail on a page near the end of the album. "What about this one?"

Mattie leaned near to look. It showed Adrienne and a good-looking man posed against a pine-forest background, their arms wrapped around each other, both smiling. The man had brown hair so dark it was nearly black, eyes the color of chocolate, and skin several shades darker than Adrienne's. His skin tone and coloring reminded Mattie of her own, and she wondered if he was of Hispanic descent.

"I don't know that man," Anya said.

"Did Adrienne ever mention someone who might have fit this description?"

"Not that I recall."

Mattie took the stack of opened envelopes out of the drawer and started looking through them. "We'll need to take these with us. They're probably from people we'll need to contact."

Most were greeting cards, postmarked around the same date in September. Birthday cards. There was also one from Brody, and she tried to ignore the mushy words, focusing instead on the intent of the message. He seemed to be truly in love with Adrienne, and it saddened her.

The last envelope, long and rectangular, appeared to contain a letter, and it didn't have a return address. It had been postmarked in Willow Springs, Colorado. She opened the envelope and removed the letter from inside, scanning it quickly.

And then she went back to the beginning to read it again.

Hair prickled at the base of her neck. It was another love letter, but this one wasn't sappy like Brody's. "Read this, Detective," she said, putting the letter down on top of the chest of drawers.

Anya diverted her gaze while Stella read, pursing her lips in concentration, an expression familiar to Mattie. Stella shared a pointed look with Mattie before turning to Anya.

"Please read this, Anya, and tell me if you know who might have sent it."

Mattie studied the chilling letter again while Anya read.

Adrienne,

It's been a month since you left, and I feel like my chest is hollow. I love you no less today than I did then, and I believe that in your heart, you love me, too.

I don't know why you ran.

Please, call. Please, talk to me. Please, come home. If you don't, I can't be responsible for what I'll do next.

Yours forever

Anya's fingers trembled as she moved them to her throat. She looked at Mattie with tear-brimmed eyes. "There was a boyfriend in Willow Springs, but I don't know his name."

"Was she running from him?"

"I didn't have that impression. Adrienne said she had a relationship with someone in Willow Springs, but they broke up. That's all I know."

"Have you heard the name Kevin Conrad?" Stella asked. "He lives in California."

"Yes, her old high school boyfriend. She speaks of him fondly. The last boyfriend . . . well, she doesn't say much about him."

With gloved fingers, Mattie picked up the letter and placed it in a plastic evidence sleeve to protect it. She put the envelope inside a different transparent sheet. It had been postmarked on May twenty-fifth, about a month after Adrienne moved to Timber Creek.

"If you remember anything at all that would help us trace this man, please call," Stella said, handing Anya one of her cards.

Tears spilled and etched fluid tracks down her cheeks as Anya took the card with one hand and wiped her face with the other. "I will."

"We need a list of Adrienne's clients," Mattie said.

A look of concern crossed Anya's face.

"You can call them to get permission to release their names to us, or we can get a separate search warrant to go through your medical records," Stella said. "Either way, we're going to talk to these people. Your help will let us get to them sooner rather than later."

"I've contacted everyone once to ask if they knew where she went," Anya said. "I'll call each one again and get back to you as soon as I can."

Mattie and Stella finished up in Adrienne's living quarters, and then followed Anya to the yurt where she worked. The peaceful space, set up for optimal client relaxation, clashed with the reason they were there: a homicide. Mattie tried to disturb the furnishings as little as possible while she searched through cabinets that held soft linens, massage oils, and a set of tuning forks of various sizes. It took only a few minutes for Stella and her to decide that the room held no information for them whatsoever.

After saying good-bye to Anya, they went back to Mattie's SUV.

"I'm going to send that letter and envelope back to Byers County by courier to see if the crime scene techs can lift any prints," Stella said as they climbed inside. "We need to track down who sent it. This photo album and Adrienne's mother might be our best sources."

Turning the key to start the engine, Mattie nodded.

"Let's head over to Hightower to talk with her. Maybe she can tell us the names of some of these people. Especially the mystery man there at the end," Stella said.

"Okay," Mattie said. "I need to check in on Robo when we go through town, but we can get to Hightower in under an hour."

They rode in silence for a few minutes, Mattie thinking about the letter. She hoped they could track down the writer; she suspected it would lead them to Adrienne's killer.

Stella interrupted her thoughts. "Mattie? Did Hornsby actually say they select employees by having Anya read their auras?"

"That's what he said," Mattie replied.

"Well . . . I'll be damned."

Chapter 15

Cole headed toward the stable call at Dark Horse with Angela in the passenger seat beside him and Sophie and Belle in back. Belle sat strapped into the seat beside Sophie with a large-dog seatbelt Angela had found on the Internet. Having the dog along as a passenger kept Sophie from squabbling with her older sister over who got to ride shotgun, making Cole consider the belt well worth the investment.

Talk about his night away in the mountains, the mountain lion, and Sophie's camping stories dominated the conversation all the way up to the stable. Everyone avoided speaking about the reason for the night's stay: guarding Adrienne's corpse. Angela seemed quieter than usual, but maybe she just couldn't get a word in edgewise around her chatty little sister.

"Sophie," Cole said as they drove toward the red metal barn. "I need you to keep your mouth zipped while we're inside, sweetheart. Too much talking spooks the horses."

"Okay, Dad," Sophie said, not appearing to mind. Being told to keep quiet was a common enough occurrence.

At the front of the barn, the Doberman lunged against a chain.

"Oh, yeah," Cole said. "I forgot to tell you about the guard dog. I want you girls to keep your distance."

Angela got out of the truck and started to help her sister out of the backseat while Cole retrieved supplies from the vet box in back.

Sophie had unfastened Belle's seatbelt, and the dog jumped up to await her turn at the door. "Belle needs to stay here," Cole warned the kids, not wanting to infuriate the guard dog even more.

Belle's ears flattened and she hung her head.

"Poor Belle," Sophie said. "I'll come out and check on her later"

"Don't come out here by yourself, Sophie," Cole said. "I think that chain will hold the dog, but I don't want to take any chances."

"I won't," Sophie said, looking at the Doberman fascinated. When they passed by, she spoke to him using baby talk. "It's okay, doggie. We're not going to hurt you."

The Doberman stopped barking and stood stock-still, staring hard at Sophie. Then he dropped into a "let's play" position before rising up to bark again.

"I wonder if he was raised around a little girl," Angela said.

Cole placed a hand on Sophie's head and smiled. "Either that or this one's a dog whisperer. I still don't want you coming out here by yourself though, Sophie. You understand."

"Okay," she replied, looking disappointed.

Carmen met them inside the barn. She wore snug riding breeches and a sweater that accentuated her slender shape, and her long, black hair had been woven into a braid that trailed down her back. She leaned forward with a soft smile as Cole introduced his children. "I'm so happy to meet you girls," she said. And then to Cole: "You have gorgeous daughters."

Cole knew that to be true. "What do you say, girls?"

They both echoed "thank you" while Cole glowed in his proud moment.

"What's your doggie's name?" Sophie asked as she shook hands with the woman.

"Bruno. He's very fierce, don't you think?"

A serious expression consumed the girl's face. "Maybe. But I think he might be nice, too."

Carmen shook her head. "I don't think so. I want you to be careful around him. Don't go near."

"That's what Dad said."

"Your father is right," Carmen said, smiling at Cole. She extended her free hand toward Angela who took it. "And you're a beautiful young woman. Do you resemble your mother?"

Frowning, Angela looked down at the ground. Cole could tell the comparison disturbed her. He jumped in before she could answer. "She does look like her mother, but she's her own person, that's for sure," he said before changing the subject. "How is Diablo today?"

"I'll let you see for yourself." Carmen turned and led them to his box stall.

The kids stood at the half-door to watch while Cole and Carmen went inside. He was shocked by the horse's condition. Diablo stood hunched in pain with tremors coursing through his muscles in waves. Sweat stained his black coat, and he looked gaunt, his eyes hollow and haunted. The stallion had lost ground since he'd last seen him.

He approached the horse, murmuring soothing sounds and running his hands over tight muscles, palpating around the spine and down the legs. He took his temperature while Carmen held him still.

"Is he eating anything?" Cole asked in a quiet tone.

"A little. Not much today."

"I brought some insulin, and we're going to get him started on that. I'll draw another blood sample so we can see if we're making any progress. I would have expected him to feel better than this by now."

He drew the blood sample from the IV that was taped to the horse's neck and injected the insulin. He'd finished discussing dosages for the other medications when his fatherly instinct made him notice that the kids were no longer watching at the doorway.

"Excuse me a minute," he said, stepping to the door.

He saw that the two girls had made their way down the alleyway, evidently wanting to see other horses, and they were looking into a stall at the far end. The groom that Cole had spoken to during his previous visit was rushing toward them, making shooing gestures with his hands and saying, "Go. *Escapado.*"

Cole hurried down the alley. "What's wrong?" he asked the man.

He answered with a string of Spanish that Cole couldn't comprehend, but he could tell the man looked concerned. He must be telling the kids to leave.

"Come away from the stall, girls," Cole told his daughters, turning his attention back to the man. His eyes were hooded and downcast. He wore jeans, a worn denim jacket, and cowboy boots; and here in the closeness of the barn, he smelled of stale cigarettes.

Carmen came up from behind. "Juan!" she said, following up the man's name with a sentence in Spanish that sounded like a question.

"It's okay, Carmen," Cole said. "I think he was just warning the kids to stay away from the horse in the box stall."

"This horse *is* dangerous." She and the groom exchanged a few words before she dismissed him and turned back to Cole. "Yes, that's what he says he was doing."

"*Gracias*," Cole said to the man's retreating back. Juan hurried away, not acknowledging the expression of appreciation. It appeared that he couldn't get away fast enough.

Sophie was looking worried, so Cole placed a hand on her shoulder and exchanged glances with Angela while they followed Carmen back to Diablo. Angela merely shrugged, apparently unconcerned.

Outside Diablo's stall, Carmen stopped and studied each of his daughters, offering them a smile that softened her aristocratic features and crinkled the small lines at the corners of her eyes. Cole noticed her deep brown irises were edged with long, thick lashes. He couldn't help but think that she was truly a beautiful woman.

"I hope Juan didn't frighten you," Carmen said, giving Sophie's hand a squeeze.

"I'm okay," Sophie said, looking up at the woman with an expression that resembled adoration.

Cole glanced at Angela, who was watching Carmen with narrowed eyes. When Angela caught him looking, she quickly adjusted her features into a neutral mask. He decided to finish up so they could get back in the truck and debrief. He'd like to know what his eldest was thinking.

"Carmen, I'll call you with the results of this blood work as soon as it comes in, but I'll need to come back to check Diablo tomorrow. Do you have any questions about what to do until then?"

"No, I understand his care."

He gathered his supplies, and Carmen went with them out to the truck, past the barking Bruno. She shouted at the dog to be quiet, but he paused for only a few seconds and then started up again. Belle had moved to the front seat and stood watching them eagerly out the windshield. Cole moved to the back of the truck to put away his things but could still hear Carmen conversing with his daughters.

"I see you have a lovely dog there."

"She's Belle," Sophie piped up, grabbing Carmen's hand to lead her close. "She's friendly."

Angela opened the truck door, telling Belle to get into the backseat.

"Let Miss Carmen pet her," Sophie said in a plaintive tone.

"I can pet her in the backseat, Sophie," Carmen said.

Cole appreciated a quick glance as the woman leaned forward into the back of the truck to pet the dog. A little embarrassed by his interest in the woman's backside, he averted his eyes, finished up, and went to open his own door. From across the front seats, Carmen smiled at him as she helped Sophie climb into the truck and then stepped aside to let Angela get in.

"It's been a pleasure to meet you, Sophie and Angela," Carmen said. "I hope you'll all come back and have dinner with me some evening."

While Sophie expressed her delight, Cole said their good-byes and drove out of the barnyard. Sophie bounced around in the back seat to wave at Carmen, making Cole tell her to sit still and put on her seatbelt.

"She's nice," Sophie proclaimed.

When Cole glanced back to toss her a smile of agreement, he saw Angela roll her eyes.

"What?" he said.

"She's a little too eager, Dad."

No further need to debrief; those few words said it all. He decided not to get into it and remained silent while he steered the truck down the lane.

When they passed by the racetrack, Angela asked, "Are these high quality horses?"

"I'd say yes, based on the few I've seen so far," he said.

"Did you see that one down on the end?"

"I'm not sure. I saw a bay and a big, red chestnut out on the racetrack last time I was here. The chestnut looked like a handful."

"That one on the end is big, and he's a chestnut," Angie said. "He was sweating and pacing around in circles. I wondered if he was getting sick like Diablo."

"Diablo's illness isn't contagious."

"Well, this horse didn't look right."

Cole slipped her a teasing grin. "Maybe you'll grow up to be a vet," he said. "Follow in your dad's footsteps."

She ignored him and turned to Sophie. "Did that horse act dangerous to you? Did he try to bite at you or anything?"

"No, he just acted nervous."

"Any horse can be dangerous," Cole said. "I don't want you guys walking away from where I'm working when you go on calls with me. I've told you this before, and I want you to listen this time. I don't want you to get hurt."

"We hear you," Angela said. "You can end the lecture."

"I'm just saying, Angie. It's not good to approach a strange animal by yourself."

"That horse didn't look mean. He looked sick."

"He was probably overheated after his workout. Besides, you can't tell if a horse is mean or not by looking at him, Angela. The one I saw the other day was trying to strike his handler. You never know. That's why you have to be careful."

Cole looked in the rearview mirror to check on Sophie who huddled in her seat, shoulders hitched, looking under siege. He'd noticed that she often zoned out when he and Angie bickered. He needed to try to put a stop to it and change the subject. "What did you think of Bruno, Sophie?"

"I think he's nice."

"We don't know that, Sophie," Cole said, almost going off about safety issues again but catching himself in time. "Carmen said she imported Bruno from Germany, but she's disappointed in his obedience."

"Maybe he talks German," Sophie said.

Cole paused, realizing the child could be right. "That might be the problem, squirt. I think she's been giving him commands in Spanish."

"I wonder what dog commands sound like in German," Angela said.

"I took German in high school," Cole said. "Some of the words sound a lot like English. Like *sitz*."

"That's 'sit'!" Sophie said, delighted with the new game.

Cole caught her eye in the rearview. "What do you think you'd say for down?"

Her brow gathered in concentration. "*Downz?*"

Cole grinned. "That's close. It's *platz*."

Sophie giggled. "*Platz* down. Sounds like plops down."

"You ought to take German, Angel," Cole said. "I don't remember much of it, but I do remember how to say 'you are a dumbhead.'"

Sophie's laughter pealed, filling the truck and Cole's heart with joy.

"Tell us how to say it, Dad," Angela said.

Finally—a topic they could all enjoy.

Chapter 16

Mattie steered around the last curve above Hightower and headed down into the valley where the small town nestled. She'd turned up the heater at the top of the pass, and Robo appeared to be cozy and warm, curled up asleep in his compartment. She'd once thought Stella's silence meant she was dozing too, but a quick check revealed her to be deep in thought. Stella was like that—a thinker.

Armed with Velda Howard's address programmed into her GPS, Mattie drove right to her destination. She parked in front of the small clapboard house, gray boards exposed beneath peeling white paint, yard turned to weeds overgrown to midcalf. Robo stood up, yawned, and stretched, shoulders down and haunches raised.

"You're going to stay here," she told him.

His expectant expression turned to one of resignation as he plopped down into a sit.

"You ruined his day," Stella observed, picking up her briefcase from the floorboard.

Mattie reached through the heavy steel mesh at the front of his cage to give him a pat. She picked up her notebook, and the two of them headed up the cracked sidewalk that led to the front door.

Ringing the bell, Mattie heard an obnoxious buzz on the other side rather than the pleasant dingdong she'd expected. They waited.

The door caught, screeched, and then burst open as the woman behind it tugged. Average height, she wore a thin flannel robe wrapped around her skinny frame. She had mousy blonde hair turned mostly gray, worn loose and frizzy around her face. Wrinkles lined her mouth and her red-rimmed eyes; smoke wafted from the cigarette she held between two fingers, the nails painted with chipped red polish. "Who are you?"

Mattie introduced herself and then Stella. "Are you Velda Howard, ma'am?"

"Yeah. I suppose you're here about Adrienne."

"Yes, ma'am. We're sorry for your loss," Mattie said. "Could we come in and have a word with you?"

Velda looked past her to where Robo sat in the patrol vehicle. "You're not going to bring that dog in, are you?"

"No, ma'am. He'll wait in the car."

The woman gave a heavy sigh and turned away, leaving the door open for them to enter. "That dog looks like a monster with those great big teeth," she muttered, her back turned.

And here Robo was giving you his best smile.

Mattie tried to reserve judgment and stifled her instant dislike. After last summer's murder case, she'd promised herself to not jump to conclusions, especially about families. She struggled to close the sticky door after Stella entered the room, but she had to settle on leaving it slightly cracked open.

She took in her surroundings. Shabby avocado-green carpet, brown recliner and sofa with worn upholstery, cheap-looking end table by the recliner, and coffee table in front of the sofa, everything covered in a layer of grime. The place and the woman both shouted "run-down."

Sinking into the recliner, Velda raised a jelly jar half-filled with amber liquid as if offering a toast while she eyed them both. "Care for a drink?"

"No, thank you," Stella said.

"I didn't suppose you would," Velda said, taking a sip that ended with another long sigh, this one sounding satisfied rather than put out. "What can I do ya for?"

Mattie caught the whiff of whiskey that rode on the sigh. She wondered if it was the alcohol that left the mother so detached about her daughter's death or something else.

"We're working your daughter's homicide," Stella said. "We hope we can get some information from you that can help us solve her case."

"I told that fella that called me, I don't know anything about Adrienne these days."

"When was the last time you heard from her?"

"You make it sound so . . . homey. Like she might think of her mother once in a while. Like she might actually pick up the phone and call." She sniffed, and with a cigarette posed between two fingers, she used the back of her wrist to wipe an indiscernible tear from her eye. Smoke settled around her head.

Mattie followed Stella's lead and waited.

Velda peered at them, adjusted the flap of robe at her neck. "Adrienne left the summer after she graduated from high school. Five, six years ago. I haven't heard from her since."

"We've found her high school boyfriend, Kevin Conrad. Do you know him?" Stella asked.

Velda gave a derisive snort. "That's why she left. The no good SOB made her go."

"Why do you say that?"

"He poisoned her against us."

"Who is 'us'? You and . . ."

"Me and her father. Her family."

"Is her father available for us to talk to?"

"He died a few years ago. Adrienne broke his heart."

"Does Adrienne have siblings?"

Velda narrowed her eyes, looked at her dwindling cigarette, took a puff. "One brother."

"I'd like to contact him," Stella said.

"Good luck. If you find him, tell him his poor old mother
says hello." Velda stubbed out her cigarette with a vengeance
in an overfilled ashtray, took out another, and lit up. "He left
home before Adrienne."

"What's his name?" Mattie asked.

"Roger."

"Same last name . . . Howard?"

"Um-hum." Velda lifted her glass, swirled the whiskey,
and took a sip.

"Why do you say Kevin Conrad poisoned Adrienne against
you?" Mattie asked.

"He made her turn her back on us when we needed
her most."

Another pause. "What do you mean?"

Velda brushed at the nap on her robe. "She graduated high
school. Had a good job. We could have used some help."

"Financial help?" Mattie asked.

"Help around the house, help paying the bills."

"Were you and your husband unemployed at that time?"

A trace of belligerence came into the woman's face.
"What? You think we didn't work hard? David hurt his back,
couldn't work for a while. But what does that have to do
with anything?"

"We're trying to get a picture of the circumstances surrounding Adrienne's departure, see if it ties into anything involving her death," Mattie said. "We need to know more about her."

Velda's lips puckered and turned downward. "She ran. She ran away when things didn't go her way. She was a spoiled brat. That's what she was."

The venom behind her words shocked Mattie. She looked at Stella, turning the lead back over to her.

"We found a photo album in Adrienne's room," Stella said, taking it out of her briefcase. "Could you look at these pictures and see if you recognize anyone?"

Velda perked up, looking like she actually might take an interest. Stella rose from the sofa and moved over to stand beside Velda's chair, offering her the album. Taking it readily, she flipped open the front cover. Mattie had looked through the photos several times and knew that many of them were snapshots of tourist spots and landscapes, but several of them also contained people. She watched as Velda flipped through pages, stopping here and there to search faces.

"Here's Kevin, right here," she said, using the pinkie on the hand that held her cigarette to tap the page. "Smug son of a bitch."

Mattie decided to move over beside Velda's chair where she could see which person the woman was tapping. Posing by the mound of mineral deposit beside the Pagosa Springs, Colorado, sign, Kevin grimaced, pinching his nose with thumb and index finger. Mattie had been there before, and she knew the odiferous water from the hot springs tainted the air throughout the town. He looked young, probably in his late teens at the time of the photo. Sandy hair, ruddy complexion, good-looking. He wore that devil-may-care, bad-boy persona that mothers dread.

Velda turned the page and tapped the photo that showed Adrienne posing with the mystery man. "This looks like Bubba."

"Bubba?" Mattie asked.

Velda's eyes turned bleary as she peered up at Mattie. "Roger."

Adrienne's brother? From the way the twosome cuddled together in the photo, she'd thought they were lovers. "Can you tell where that picture was taken?"

"How the hell should I know? You've seen one forest, you've seen them all."

Pine trees surrounded the couple as they posed with arms around each other and smiles on their faces. Adrienne and the handsome man with the dark features both looked happy. *She reunited with her brother.* Mattie grew uneasy as she studied the photo. Had the happy reunion turned into a bad thing? Something that ended in Adrienne's death?

"It looks like the two of them were reunited recently. Do you have any idea where Roger might be?" Mattie asked.

Velda shook her head slowly, looking down at the photos. She turned the last page and reached the end. "Like I told you, that horse done left the barn." She handed the album to Stella, her face taking on a wistful expression. "Looks like the two of them couldn't be more pleased with themselves."

"They do look happy," Mattie said, going back to sit on the couch where she could observe Velda more easily.

"They have no right."

"No right?"

"To be happy. The two of them, leaving me here alone. Adrienne, right over there in Timber Creek, and she didn't come check on her mama."

Mattie wondered about that, too. "Why do you think Adrienne didn't come see you?"

Anger flared in Velda's bloodshot eyes. "She always blamed me."

"For what?"

"For everything. She was a very unhappy child."

From what Mattie knew of her, she'd turned into a happy woman. From all appearances, she seemed like a person who'd built a satisfying life and career. "Why do you say she was unhappy?"

Velda stared at Mattie for a moment, as if sensing a trap. She glanced furtively toward the front door. "Who knows? Some children are just born unhappy. I'm getting tired now. I need to ask you to leave so I can rest."

Mattie sensed the interview was almost over.

"We appreciate your time, Mrs. Howard. I have only a couple more questions," Stella said, settling back into the couch.

Velda heaved another sigh.

"We have evidence that Adrienne was a victim of child-hood abuse."

Velda's eyes opened wide. "Are you accusing me of that?"

"What do you know about it?" Stella asked.

Tight lipped, Velda rubbed out the ember on her cigarette until she ground it down to the filter. "You need to leave."

Stella remained seated. "I think you know something."

Velda anchored her hands on the arms of her chair and tried to push herself to her feet. It took a couple tries, but she rose, swaying slightly. Mattie feared she might fall, so she stood and reached to steady her. Velda brushed her hand away. "Get out."

"Mrs. Howard, we need to determine if Adrienne's abuser could be the one who killed her," Mattie said, trying to reason with the woman.

"I've said all I'm going to say." Velda walked toward the door, drifting sideways like a ship with a broken sail.

Mattie hurried to assist her, relieved when the woman allowed her to take her arm. "We'll leave here in a minute, Mrs. Howard. Let me help you back to your chair."

Stella stood and hovered near to help if needed. "I suspect some things happened in the past that were out of your control—not your fault," she said in a soothing voice.

"You might show some respect." Velda settled back in her recliner, wrapping her robe tightly, gathering her dignity. "For your information, Adrienne was a difficult child. She demanded a great deal of guidance."

"Yes, ma'am," Mattie murmured, picking up a ragged crocheted afghan from a chair and tucking it around the woman.

Her temper appeased, Velda's eyes drooped, looking as if a nap was imminent. "Spare the rod and spoil the child, her daddy used to say."

A chilly finger traced down Mattie's spine as she stepped back. "Did your husband use the rod on Adrienne?"

Velda's eyes popped open, and she stared hard at Mattie. "None of your damn business."

Stella came forward. "We'll leave now, Mrs. Howard. Thank you for your time."

Velda looked at Stella as if trying to remember who she was. "You come back and see me sometime, dear."

"Thank you," Stella said. "Our condolences for your loss."

They stepped outside onto the porch. Mattie twisted the lock on the knob and tugged the door tight, despite its screech of protest.

"I don't think she gives a rat's ass about her daughter's death," Stella muttered as they walked to the SUV.

Robo's head popped up inside the window. He looked sleepy but gave Mattie one of his toothy grins, soothing her uneasiness. She climbed inside, settled into the bucket seat, and turned to stroke Robo's silky fur. He nosed her hand, encouraging her to stroke his face.

Stella settled into the passenger seat beside her. "If Daddy was the abuser, he's not around to be a suspect anymore."

"And if Mom was, she doesn't look like she's in any condition to be a threat to anyone but herself."

"Unless she took out a hit, but that theory has some holes in it. She might have the motive, but she lacks money and the brainpower for planning. That leads us to Roger Howard, the star discovery of our interview," Stella said while she fastened her seat belt. "Brothers as perpetrators of abuse aren't unheard of."

Mattie nodded and stared out the windshield, thinking while she left a hand on Robo's back. Her mind had darted to her own brother, but she quickly brought it back to Adrienne's case. "It appears that both Roger and Adrienne left home and never looked back," she mused. "I think they were raised in an abusive environment with at least one alcoholic parent, maybe two."

Her uneasy stomach testified as to how much this type of childhood resonated with her. She could write a chapter in the book about alcoholic parents. She thought Adrienne could have, too.

"Let's see if we can find Roger Howard here in Colorado," Mattie said as she started plugging Roger Howard's name into her mobile data terminal. "I'll see if he has a current driver's license."

"Search for criminal records, too," Stella said. She pulled a notebook from her briefcase and began writing in it. Presumably notes from the interview.

A quick search through the Colorado DMV revealed four Roger Howards. The Colorado and National Crime Information Center databases revealed nothing.

Mattie shared the news with Stella. "No criminal history, but four potential driver's licenses."

Stella pursed her lips, absently tapping her notebook with her pen. "We'll have to dig deeper back at the station."

"We should put Brody on it," Mattie said. "He's our expert on the net."

Stella shrugged. "We'll see. I'm not so bad myself."

Mattie could tell Stella wasn't going to bring Brody into the investigation until she was sure he should be there. "We also have the letter. Maybe your lab will pull a print from it."

"That would rock my world."

Chapter 17

Back at the station, Stella went to use the computer in the office that the sheriff assigned to her. Robo followed Mattie to the staff office, seeking his dog cushion that she kept near her desk. He plopped down and sighed, and she knelt beside him to check his wound. It looked clean and there was no seepage.

She stroked his head before moving to her chair. "You're tired today, aren't you? Getting attacked by a lion would set anyone back."

He put his head between his paws and his brow puckered and twitched.

"You can go back to sleep. We'll be here for a while."

Mattie worked on reports until Sam Corns came in to relieve Rainbow. Leaving her dog asleep on his bed, Mattie led Rainbow to one of the cold and sterile interrogation rooms. She pulled out a metal-frame chair with plastic upholstery to sit in, gesturing for Rainbow to take a seat on the other side of the table.

Rainbow made a slight sound of dismay. "Am I a suspect?"

"No, of course not. I just don't want us to get interrupted," Mattie said. "Do you want a cup of tea or something?" She knew Rainbow didn't drink coffee.

"No, nothing. I don't know if I can help or not, but I've remembered some things this afternoon that might give you some leads."

"Sounds great. Tell me what you've remembered."

Rainbow paused, apparently collecting her thoughts. "Adrienne talked about a boyfriend in Willow Springs that she must have had a tough breakup with. I don't think she ever said his last name, but if I remember right, she called him Jim."

"That's good, Rainbow." Mattie wrote the name in her notepad.

"Adrienne never talked much about her past. She seemed to want to concentrate mostly on the here and now. She always said she wanted to live in the present moment and not dwell on the past or obsess about the future."

"What did she say about this man named Jim?"

"I don't think I can remember word for word."

"It's okay to say it like you remember it. Don't worry."

"Well . . . we were talking about old boyfriends, you know, girl talk."

Mattie nodded, though she'd never participated in such a thing.

"Adrienne was mostly listening, and I was going on about a boyfriend I had when I was in massage school. I asked her to tell me about her last boyfriend, and she said, 'Jim isn't one I'd like to remember. Let's just say it didn't end well.' Or something like that. At least that's the gist of it."

"Did she give any details about how it ended?"

"She said something about different expectations or goals or something. Adrienne didn't really call it goals . . . maybe she said future plans."

"Did she talk about him being violent or rough, anything like that?"

"No. That would have made an impression on me. It was more like they couldn't agree about their future."

"Okay. I just wondered why she said the relationship didn't end well. Did you get any impressions about that?"

"I think they were pretty close, you know. Then they realized they wanted different things in their future. I think it was painful but not violent, if you know what I mean."

"Yeah. Anything else you can tell me about Jim?"

Rainbow shook her head.

"Anything else that you've remembered?"

"Yes. She worked for a chiropractor that owned his own business when she was in Willow Springs. I think she called him Scott."

"Great, Rainbow. We should be able to track that down. How many chiropractors named Scott can there be in Willow Springs?"

"Right. I can follow up on that if you want me to."

"No, one of us should do it. Do you remember anything else about him? Were there any negative feelings when she left?"

Rainbow shook her head. "Not that I know of. She never mentioned anything like that. She just said she learned a lot while she was working there."

"Do you know any other places that Adrienne worked? Places she lived?"

"No. She only mentioned Willow Springs."

"Let's switch focus for a minute," Mattie said. "Did Adrienne ever talk about her family in Hightower?"

"I knew she grew up there. She said both of her parents were alcoholics, and she didn't want to talk about her childhood."

Mattie could relate to that. "Did she mention her brother?"

"Yes. Roger. She said they were close, but he left her there alone when he graduated. It made her sad."

"Did she say where he moved to?"

"Willow Springs. She said she met with him there before she moved here."

"That's good. We should check in with him, too, and this could help us find him."

Rainbow's reddened eyes crinkled slightly at the corners as she smiled briefly before resuming her sad expression. "I'm glad. I didn't think her family had anything to do with this. She seemed to have cut ties with all of them."

"Even Roger?"

"Yes. She said she loved her brother, but she didn't want to be around him anymore."

"Why not?"

"We didn't really discuss it." Rainbow's brow puckered with concentration. "But I think I remember her saying something about her brother going off the deep end or something like that."

This lit Mattie's radar. "Did she feel threatened by him?"

Rainbow released a sigh of frustration as she searched her memory. "I don't remember having that impression. It was more like a bad experience. Something to be avoided."

But still, it made Mattie wonder. She asked a few more questions but soon decided that she'd gleaned all that she could for now.

"Let's call it a day. You've been a lot of help, and if you remember anything else, let me know. You need to go home for the night. I know you're tired."

"You look tired, too. I hope you can go home and get some sleep."

"I need to talk to Stella but then I'll clock out."

They gave each other a quick hug before leaving the interrogation room. Mattie found Stella in her office getting ready to leave. She brought her up to speed, telling her about the boyfriend named Jim, the chiropractor named Scott, and the rather ominous bit about Roger Howard.

Stella slipped on her coat. Looking thoughtful, she said, "This gives us more to consider. I have to observe that autopsy at eight in the morning. Can you follow up and try to locate the chiropractor? Maybe he'll know something about Adrienne's personal life and lead you to more information, maybe something about the ex-boyfriend or the brother."

"Will do."

"I have something else that will make your day," Stella said. "The lab lifted a thumb print off the stamp on that letter. Not a real clear one, but it wasn't too smudged."

"That's great news."

"We're running it through IAFIS now."

The Integrated Automated Fingerprint Identification System could find a match if the subject was already in the system. If a print was distorted, it often came back with several similar prints that a technician would then compare with the original. So even though this system didn't always get a hit, it promised the possibility of some movement in the case.

"You're right. Day made," Mattie said.

Stella smiled in a grim way. "It's late and I'm going home now. I hope to be here tomorrow by eleven."

"I'll see you then. Maybe I'll have some leads in Willow Springs by the time you get back."

After saying good-bye, Mattie went to the staff office to get Robo. As he stood up and stretched, he yawned until his throat squeaked, making her yawn with him. Dead on her feet, she clocked out and headed home.

Chapter 18

Mattie had settled into bed with a book, thinking she would distract herself from the events of the past few days and relax, when her cell phone rang. Caller ID told her it was an unfamiliar number, even an unfamiliar area code. She answered it.

"This is Deputy Cobb."

"That sounds pretty damn official." It was a man's voice, also unfamiliar. "Last time we talked, it was just plain old Mattie Lu."

Her heart stumbled and then kicked into overdrive. "Who is this?"

"Your big brother. Weren't you expecting me to call?"

His voice was so deep, grown up. "Willie—hey. I've been hoping you'd call for weeks. You surprised me."

"Sorry about that. Took a while to get up the nerve." He cleared his throat. "I was glad to hear you were willing to talk."

A lump in her own throat kept her from responding. She nodded, holding the phone clamped to her ear.

"How are you?" Her brother's voice was rough and throaty, like a two-pack-a-day smoker.

"I'm good. How are you, Willie?"

"I'm okay. Better than I was a few months ago."

"Were you sick?"

"We can talk about that later. I want to know about you. What's your life like? Teresa says you're a deputy in the sheriff's department."

"Yeah. Seven years. You live in Los Angeles?"

"Yeah, in Hollywood actually. I'm a mechanic in a garage near Sunset Boulevard."

"Wow, sounds fancy."

Willie gave a little laugh. "There's lots of places in Hollywood that aren't all that fancy. But it's good enough for me."

"Do you like your job?"

"It's steady work and it occupies my days, sometimes my nights. I need it that way. So you stayed in Timber Creek? I can't hardly believe that."

It felt like a hand was tightening around Mattie's throat, choking her. "Yeah, well . . ."

"How are you doing, Mattie Lu? You're not married?"

"No."

"Got someone special?"

"No. How about you?"

"I met a girl a few months ago. We're pretty serious. She's changing my life."

"Oh, yeah?"

"Yeah." That little laugh again. "She must see something in me. She's helping me put things back together."

That meant things must've fallen apart before. "Have you had a bad time of it?"

"You might say so. How's everything with you?"

Mattie focused hard on not choking up. "Pretty good. I like my work. I'm doing K-9 now, that's something new."

"Do you have one of those big, badass dogs?"

Mattie looked at Robo lying patiently on his own bed watching her. His ears pricked and his mouth opened slightly in a pant. She'd learned that his mouth seemed to be the barometer for his stress level. He must be picking up on *her* anxiety at the moment. "Robo's a pussycat most of the time. Unless I tell him to be otherwise."

Robo cocked his head at her when he heard his name.

"Otherwise, he's a badass."

"You got that right." Mattie smiled, her lips close to the phone.

"Seems strange, my little sis ordering around bad guys, siccing a real police dog on 'em."

"It's mostly patrol and narcotics detection, some public-relations work. Here in Timber Creek, there's very little action like you see on that *Cops* TV show."

"I guess it's really not so hard to imagine you as a cop after all."

An awkward silence followed. Was he thinking about that night, about her phone call, the one she made that broke up their family? To divert the subject, she asked, "What's your girlfriend's name?"

"Tamara."

"What does she do?"

"Well, here's the deal. She works in the kitchen of a drug rehab center. That's where we met."

"Oh?"

"Yeah . . . Oh?" Willie seemed to be teasing her. "I was there by court order. My last chance to clean up my act."

"I hope it's working for you."

"Seems to be. Every day's a struggle. I'm working the twelve steps."

Now it all became clear. His twelve-step program dictated contacting his sister. He had to make amends or at least try. She told herself it was silly to feel disappointed; no matter what made him call, she'd take it.

"Yeah, she has a kid, a four-year-old boy," Willie said. "She says I've got to be a good role model for him, though God knows my own was a real fuck-up. So I just ask myself, what would my old man do? Then I do the opposite."

"That would make for a pretty good start."

"Do you ever see the old man?" Willie asked.

"No one told you?"

"What?"

"He died while he was in prison. One of the other inmates killed him."

The line went silent. "I can't say I'm sorry," he said after a long pause.

She didn't know how to respond.

"Hell, Mattie—what makes you stay in Timber Creek? It can't have anything but bad memories."

Mattie placed her hand on the base of her throat. Finally, she managed to speak. "I stayed here so you or Mom could find me—if you wanted to."

There was a long silence while Willie seemed to be wrestling with his response. When he spoke, he sounded sort of choked up, too. "Have you heard from Mom?"

"No. Have you?"

"Naw. She wouldn't have any idea where I am."

"I tried to trace you both a few times—on our department computer—but I didn't have any luck."

"I wish I'd known you would talk to me. Maybe I'd have called sooner."

"Why would you think I wouldn't talk to you?"

"Well . . . I didn't exactly protect you like a big brother should, did I?"

Mattie was dumbfounded. "Protect me? You took the shit, Willie. It was you and Mom who took most of the blows."

"I should've stopped him from hurting you, Mattie Lu. I should've figured out a way to stop him."

A cold thread was starting to knot in Mattie's stomach. "He didn't hurt me that bad."

"How can you say that? I know how he'd visit you at night. I saw how shell-shocked you looked in the morning."

Mattie's stomach clenched, and she fought a wave of nausea. "I—" Her throat closed, and she couldn't utter a sound.

"I'm sorry, Mattie Lu." Willie sounded like he was struggling to speak, too. "I'm sorry that I had to bring that up, and I'm sorry I didn't take better care of you."

"You—" Mattie cleared her throat and forced the words out. "You have nothing to apologize to me for."

Willie sniffed, and in the silence that followed, Mattie could tell he was crying. She pressed the phone hard against her ear, her other hand pressed to her stomach. Holding on, she rocked forward and back.

"Can I see you sometime?" Willie said. "I mean, would you come out to L.A. and see me? I don't think I could ever come back to Timber Creek. But I'd like you to meet Tamara and her kid, Elliot."

"Maybe." Mattie swallowed hard. "I don't get much time off, but I'll look into it."

"You can call me any time. On this number."

"Yeah." She needed to get off the phone. Now.

"Well, then . . . bye."

"Good-bye, Willie." She disconnected the call. A sob from somewhere deep inside jolted her, making her body jump. She clamped a hand over her mouth and bent forward. An icy fist had delivered a sucker-punch to her belly. Robo rose from his bed and padded over to nudge her arm with his wet nose.

Hoarse with pent-up tears, she said, "Let's go for a run."

She put on sweats, gloves, and running shoes. Stooped like an old woman, she walked to the hook where she'd left Robo's leash. Over and over, she told herself, *Don't think, just run. Don't think, just run.*

★

Mattie sat on a rocky outcropping at the top of T-hill with Robo sitting next to her, panting like crazy and blowing a cloud of steam into the cold air. She'd run with him matching her step for step until she'd decided to quit for his sake. The sky had cleared and a nearly full moon lit the landscape. Below her, lights from houses and streetlights defined the boundaries of Timber Creek.

She and Robo had climbed the sloping backside of a sheer stone wall, and now she sat with her legs dangling over the edge. She picked up a rock that filled her palm and threw it as far as she could. It clattered as it hit the rocky terrain of the hill, and then rolled down, creating a small avalanche of clattering stones that rolled with it.

A chill breeze blew from the northwest, and Mattie shivered. As was typical, Robo bobbed his head and sniffed, examining whatever scent the wind carried. She took off her glove and buried her cold fingers in the soft fur at his throat.

"Thanks for coming with me," she said softly. "I guess you didn't have much of a choice, did you?"

Robo continued to sniff the air for a few seconds, and then lay still and alert, head up, paws out front. Mattie stroked one of his paws, picked it up and held it for a while in her hand, the connection warm and comforting. He touched her hand with his mouth—one quick, wet touch—and then he lifted his face to the wind again.

She didn't know what visits Willie was talking about, but while she ran, vague memories had come in flashes. One so sharp, it cut her to the core. "If you tell, I'll kill your mother."

Shame washed over her in waves. She struggled to remember exactly what happened, but all she could imagine was a frightened little girl. Someone else? *No—me.*

Willie's words, meant only to heal, had ignited an awful tumult inside her. What was she supposed to do with this pain? She bent forward and wrapped her arms across her middle, quaking like an aspen leaf.

Suck it up, Cobb. Coach's words from her days of cross-country training came back to her. *Ignore the pain. Keep running. Go farther and faster than you ever believed you could.* Each footfall drummed that into her head, year after year.

In her job, she worked with victims; she didn't consider herself one. She wouldn't allow herself to become one. Willie's words didn't have to change her life. She'd sealed off these memories before; she could do it again.

Mattie threw another rock out into the air, listening to it clatter down below in the shadows where it was too dark to see what kind of following it gathered. She could hear the stones clacking against each other.

"We'd better go home, Robo. It's way too cold to sit up here." She stroked his velvety muzzle while he played with her fingertips, the contact making him sneeze. "We'll have to walk. I don't think I could run one more step."

Mattie picked her way down off the backside of the outcropping, letting Robo lead. She figured he could see the rocky path better than she could. On her way down, she thought about her father being killed in prison. And for the first time, it made her glad.

Chapter 19

Monday

After tossing and turning most of the night, Mattie finally fell asleep sometime during the early hours of the morning. At six o'clock, Robo nudged her awake, eager for his morning run. Never mind that they'd returned from running their legs off only a few hours before.

"Let's sleep in," she told him. "Go back to bed."

She watched him circle before lying down and cradling his head on his front paws. He noticed her watching him, and when their eyes met, he raised his head to stare, ears pricked forward. She didn't know if she had the energy to deal with him, so she pulled her quilt up over her face to escape the chill in the room as well as his laser-beam gaze.

The radio alarm went off, broadcasting the six o'clock weather report. "This storm has passed through and milder temperatures will return for a few days. But by Thursday, another front will organize from the north, bringing snow to the lower elevations. Stay tuned for details on what you can expect."

She hit the off button and tried to settle down under the cover again. Thoughts of her conversation with Willie circled in her mind, picking up where she'd left off during the night.

Her cell phone rang. It was no good; she might as well get up. Snaking one arm out from under the warm quilt, she picked up the phone and checked the caller ID. Mama T. She connected the call.

"Good morning, *mijita*. Did I catch you sleeping?"

Their little joke warmed Mattie's heart. "You won't catch me sleeping, Mama. How are you this morning?"

"Fat and sassy. Will you come for breakfast?"

She pictured herself sitting at the table discussing Willie's phone call, and her spirits sank. "No thank you, I can't make it today. I have to go into work early."

"I have your favorite. Breakfast burrito with green chili."

Despite her typical appetite for anything generated in Mama T's kitchen, this morning the very thought of food nauseated her. "Everything you cook is my favorite. You know that."

"Won't you come?"

"Sorry, Mama. I can't. Another time."

"Okay," Mama T said. "Did your brother call?"

It had been their major topic for weeks. Mattie needed to be honest, or her foster mom would never forgive her. "He called last night. I was just going to tell you."

"*Mi cielo!* Why didn't you call me?"

The call had taken her mama by surprise, just as it had Mattie. Enough to warrant her favorite expletive: "my heavens." "It was late, Mama. You would've been in bed. I figured it could wait until this morning, so I'm telling you now."

"What did he say?"

"Well, let's see." There was only so much she could say. "He's working in Hollywood as a car mechanic."

"That is wonderful. Does he know any movie stars?"

Despite the strain of withholding secrets from the woman who had always shown her nothing but love, Mattie smiled. "I didn't ask. But I bet he does, don't you?"

"Ask him next time. What else did he say?"

Mattie told her about Willie having a girlfriend, going through rehab, and now a twelve-step program.

"That should help him, don't you think?" Mama said.

"Yes, I agree."

"When will you see each other again?"

Mama seemed to think it a foregone conclusion. "I don't know. Willie doesn't want to come back to Timber Creek."

"You go to California."

"It's hard to take time off, Mama."

"Hmm."

It was time to get off the phone. "I've got to go, Mama. Robo needs his run, and I've got to shower. I don't want to be late." The punctuality card always worked with her foster mother.

"All right. But try to arrange some time off to go see your brother. He's family."

"You're my family, Mama."

"*Si*. I am, *mijita*. Don't you forget that."

"I won't." Her throat was beginning to swell and tears threatened. "Have a good day."

"You too."

Mattie ended the call and collapsed onto her pillow, exhausted. Robo stood and approached the bed, this time placing his muzzle on the edge to stare at her. She turned to her side and stroked his head, thinking of the word *family* and all its meanings. Her mind skipped around, touching on Cole and his daughters, the Hartmans and their dead child, her broken and dysfunctional kin. And Robo. He was her family now. She needed to get up and take care of him.

She sat, swinging her legs outside the quilt. The cold hardwood floor shocked her bare feet, and she got up to close the window, understanding now why she always needed it open during the night. Escape.

★

The first person Mattie met at the station was Brody, and his
mood had not improved. She took one look at the darkness in
his face and didn't bother with a greeting. "Did you talk with
the sheriff this morning?" she asked him.

"I did." He turned away and started toward his office. "He
wants to see you first thing."

Rainbow winced at her desk where she'd apparently
watched Mattie and Brody's brief interchange. Mattie raised a
hand in greeting and went over to say good morning.

"Are you okay?" Rainbow asked.

Mattie searched her friend's face, noting her swollen eyes
and reddened nose. "I'm fine. You?"

Rainbow nodded—a small, quick movement of her head.
"Sheriff McCoy said for you to join him in his office as soon
as you check in." She scrutinized Mattie. "Are you sure
you're okay?"

Would the whole world be able to tell that she'd changed?
She would have to try harder. "Yeah, I'm just tired. I'll clock
in and meet with the sheriff."

"I'll let him know you're here."

When Mattie tapped at the door of his office, McCoy said,
"Come in, Deputy."

After glancing at her, he did a double take and a slight
frown creased his brow. "Have a seat."

Mattie sat in one of the two chairs in front of his desk, and
Robo sat on the floor next to her without needing direction.

McCoy gave her a searching look while he spoke. "I've
read your report from your interview with Rainbow. I understand you're following up on that this morning."

"Yes, sir."

"Deputies Brody and Johnson will share patrol this morning. Deputy Brody will handle briefing for shift change, but you don't need to attend. You should have the staff office to yourself most of the morning. Any questions?" He gave her a probing look.

"No, I'll get started," Mattie said, hoping he wouldn't ask her how she felt and all that stuff. She pushed up out of her chair and headed toward the door with Robo at heel, relieved that McCoy remained silent.

She found the staff office empty. After logging on to the computer, she searched a business directory for chiropractors in Willow Springs. Although much larger than Timber Creek, Willow Springs was by far smaller than Denver. There were about five chiropractors in the town, and it took only a second to hit on one who had the first name Scott. Dr. Scott Stroud—Willow Springs Family Chiropractic.

Mattie glanced at the clock. Stella was due in at eleven, which gave her four hours to drive to Willow Springs to interview Scott Stroud, plenty of time. Taking Robo with her, she cleared her plan with the sheriff, checked out with Rainbow, and set off toward her destination. In shortly under an hour, she reached the chiropractor's office, a squatty, blond brick building that looked like it had been built in the sixties, and she parked out front.

Leaving Robo in the SUV, she went inside and introduced herself to the receptionist. After showing her badge, she convinced the woman that her business was important enough to interrupt the doctor. The receptionist ushered her into a small office where Mattie took a seat in front of the desk and waited for only a few minutes.

Scott Stroud entered the room, giving Mattie a friendly smile as he introduced himself and shook hands. His grip was firm, and he wore an open expression on his round face. With his sandy hair, blue eyes, and athletic build, he might have been a model for a wholesome-living magazine. "How can I help you, Officer?" he asked, taking a seat on the other side of his desk.

Mattie told him that she was investigating a crime in Timber Creek, but she withheld further details. "Did a massage therapist named Adrienne Howard once work for you?"

"Yes." He stretched out the syllable as if hesitant to acknowledge it.

"How long was she employed?"

"Maybe six months, but I'm guessing."

"Why did she leave?" She hoped to find out if something—or someone—drove Adrienne away from Willow Springs.

"She accepted a job offer there in Timber Creek. I can't tell you the name of her new place of employment, but it was some kind of health spa. I suspect you know the place."

"Did you speak with Adrienne or have any type of correspondence with her after she moved away?"

"No."

"Did you and Adrienne have a friendship or any type of relationship outside of working hours?"

"Well . . ." He paused, a worried frown clouding his face. "Yes and no. I need to know why we're having this conversation."

"I'm sorry to have to inform you, but I'm investigating Adrienne Howard's death."

"Good grief!" He pushed his chair back from his desk. "How did she die?"

"I can't share details, but I need information about her personal life. What type of relationship did you and Adrienne have?"

"Adrienne was dating one of my best friends. I introduced the two of them. God—I can't believe she's dead."

His disbelief seemed genuine, and Mattie had no reason yet to think of him as a suspect. But she needed to know more about this friend. "What's your friend's name?"

"Jim Cameron. He's a real estate agent here. I've known him for years. They only dated for a short time, but . . . he's going to be shocked."

"What agency is he with?"

"His own. Cameron Realty and Associates."

It would be easy to retrieve an address; she didn't need to waste time asking for it. She already knew the breakup wasn't easy. She decided to fish for general information. "Why did Adrienne decide to change jobs and move from Willow Springs?"

"She said she needed new scenery, and she liked the idea of helping set up a health resort. She seemed unhappy after she and Jim broke things off, although from what he said, the decision was mutual."

"Oh?" Mattie hoped he would keep talking.

"He didn't seem as torn up about it as she was. But Jim doesn't let much of anything get him down."

She waited, but this time he didn't fill the silence. "Did he want to patch things up?"

"No, not at all. He was dating someone else by the next weekend. She didn't want to patch things up either. Instead, she just wanted to move away. Start again. I hate to say this, but that seemed to be her pattern. As I recall, she didn't stay very long at any of the jobs she'd had previously. But it's hard to find well-qualified candidates like Adrienne here, so I decided not to let that influence my decision to hire her. She was good at her work and a pleasant person to be around. Very professional. Smart."

"Did she work somewhere else in Willow Springs before you hired her?"

"No, she had just moved here from California. I don't mind sharing her past employment information with you, but I need you to get that from my office manager. May I introduce you to her now? I really should get back to my patients."

"Just a couple more questions. Do you know a man named Roger Howard?"

"No. Is he related to Adrienne?"

"Her brother. Did she ever mention a brother?"

"No, I don't think so. She didn't talk about her family. But we didn't spend much time together after hours. She spent most of that with Jim. I suppose you'll be wanting to talk to him, too."

"I will. I'd appreciate it if you'd let me break the news to him rather than you calling him right now."

"Like I said, I need to get back to work."

"Just one more question, Dr. Stroud. Where were you Wednesday afternoon?"

"Is that when Adrienne died? Wait a minute—are you telling me someone killed her?"

"Her death is being investigated as a homicide."

"My God . . . I wish you'd told me that earlier. What happened to her?"

"I can't say. Getting back to my question: can you tell me where you were last Wednesday afternoon?"

"You can't suspect that I had anything to do with this."

"Just a routine question. I try to eliminate anyone I talk to as soon as I can. Keeps me from having to circle around and waste both of our time."

"Well, thank God I can put your mind at ease." A hint of sarcasm crept into his voice. "I was here at the office all day on Wednesday. My office manager and a whole schedule full of patients can vouch for that."

"Thank you for your time and the information, Dr. Stroud. I appreciate it. I'll let you take me to your office manager now so you can get back to work."

It took only a few more minutes to verify the information from Stroud's office manager and check out his alibi. Mattie left the office with a copy of Adrienne's résumé in hand.

Although it was always wise to keep an open mind, Mattie decided to eliminate Scott Stroud as a suspect unless further information changed his status. Using her mobile data terminal, she quickly located Jim Cameron's business listing under "Real Estate Agents" and plugged his address into her GPS. She followed its guidance to an office building made of stone and cedar siding with a peaked roof and large picture windows. Once again, she parked out front and left Robo in the car.

After introducing herself to Cameron's secretary, she was escorted at once into a conference room dominated by a long, shiny walnut table surrounded with plush chairs. The woman acted as if she'd expected her.

Cameron entered the room, extending his hand to introduce himself and getting right down to business. "I just got off the phone with Scott Stroud, so I'm up to speed, Detective. How can I help?"

So much for allowing me to break the news. She wasn't too surprised actually; the good ol' boy network would dictate Stroud calling to alert his friend. She recognized him from a picture in Adrienne's album: handsome with brown hair and eyes, medium height and build, fit. She decided not to correct his misunderstanding of her title. "I need information about Adrienne's personal life. Who were her friends while she was living here in Willow Springs?"

"Adrienne lived here only about six months and didn't seem to make a lot of close friends. I mean, we had my group of friends we associated with, but she didn't really connect with anyone in my crowd. She was a different kind of gal from the ones I usually date."

"What do you mean?"

"Did you know Adrienne?" he asked.

"I'd met her."

"Adrienne was a free spirit, would have thrived in the sixties. I think that's what attracted me to her, not to mention the fact that she was gorgeous. But her being a free spirit ultimately broke us apart."

"Oh?"

"Well, you know the old saying 'Opposites attract'? We were good examples of that. I'm focused on business; she was focused on health. I'm goal driven; she was laid back. She wanted to let things evolve. Those were her words—'let things evolve.'"

Mattie was getting a clearer picture of the two of them. "So who decided to end your relationship?"

"We both did. I know you may be skeptical, but it's the truth. We talked things over like adults and decided to break things off."

"I understand she was pretty broken up about it."

He let out his breath in a soft sigh of frustration. "I'm sorry to say, she was. We loved each other, but she was becoming more committed than I was. So I guess it was me that initiated the conversation. But she seemed to be in full agreement by the time it was over."

Mattie imagined a confrontation between a goal-driven businessman and a flower child. It would be easy to predict the outcome of that one. "I appreciate your candor. Let's get back to the question of friends. Is there anyone that you remember her talking about who might have known her personally?"

"She spent most of her time off at an organic farm just outside of town. Green Thumb Organics. Maybe she made friends with someone out there, but she never introduced me to anyone. Do you want that number?"

Apparently bending over backward to be helpful, he pulled out his cell phone and tapped the screen. Mattie wrote down the phone number he gave her. "Did you meet Adrienne's brother, Roger Howard?"

"Adrienne never mentioned a brother. Don't know him."

"Can you tell me where you were last Wednesday afternoon?"

"Scott told me you would ask that question, so I've already looked at my calendar. I usually take Wednesdays off. I played golf early that morning with a friend who can vouch for it. We ended our game around eleven. I had lunch at home by myself, did some yard work, and worked in my home office the rest of the afternoon. I had dinner with clients that evening at seven."

Mattie did the math. Eight hours with no alibi. It would take about sixty minutes to get from Willow Springs to Timber Creek. Plenty of time to drive over, kill Adrienne, and drive back. But someone else would have had to take her body up into the wilderness. Unless . . . "All right. And where were you on Thursday?"

He let out a puff of pent up breath. He'd probably anticipated an accusation regarding his lack of alibi. "Just one moment, let me look it up." He consulted his cell phone again. "Here in the office by eight, with a couple showing them houses most of the morning, lunch with a different client, several different appointments in the afternoon, dinner with my girlfriend."

So no time to move the body on Thursday. "Do you own a horse, Mr. Cameron?"

"Call me Jim. No, I really don't know anything at all about horses. Don't ride. Uh . . . why do you ask?"

"I'll let you get back to work now. I might need to call you back later for more details or confirmation of this information, but I believe that's all I need right now. Thank you for your time."

"Sure, sure. Anything I can do to help, just let me know. Call me anytime."

He seemed like the eager Boy Scout type. Too eager? Hard to say.

Chapter 20

Mattie was finishing a written summary of her two interviews when Rainbow came to the office door to tell her that Stella had arrived. She and the sheriff wanted Mattie to join them in the briefing room.

"Tell them I'll be right there." She sent the two reports to the printer, picking them up on her way. Stella liked to keep a hard copy murder book in addition to a digital record. Mattie didn't mind; she could organize her thoughts better with printed pages herself.

The grim expressions on her colleagues' faces told her that they'd already been discussing the autopsy. She joined them at the front table, choosing a seat near the end on the sheriff's side while Robo settled beside her.

Mattie noticed the detective studying her as she sat, locking eyes until Mattie grew uncomfortable and looked away. She knew from experience that Stella had a way of performing a mind probe, and she didn't want to participate. She also knew from Rainbow's and the sheriff's reactions that she must look like shit this morning. Thankfully, Stella didn't mention it.

Instead, she launched into summarizing the autopsy. "I was just telling the sheriff about the manner and cause of death."

Mattie met Stella's gaze again, raising her brows in question.

"Cause of death: exsanguination from a penetrating wound through the victim's chest that nicked the left chamber of her heart."

Bled out. "Shot, then," Mattie said.

"Yes," Stella said. "Shot from the back and exiting through the front. The projectile went clear through her. But it wasn't a bullet."

"What?"

"The medical examiner says it must have been an arrow."

Stella paused for a moment for Mattie to digest this image. An arrow shot cleanly through the victim's chest entering through her back. That must have been a powerful bow, or a powerful shooter. Or both. All kinds of questions raced through her mind.

Was it an accident? Was Adrienne running away? Or worse yet, was she being hunted?

"The ME has some experience with hunting and is familiar with mammal wounds," Stella continued. "Bullets typically expand and create all kinds of damage as they traverse the flesh, leaving a much larger exit wound than entry. An arrow with a broadhead point that has two steel cutting edges slices through the flesh. Injured animals usually bleed out; the amount of time it takes depends on which organs are damaged on the way through."

No wonder the two of them looked so grim. "It's hunting season," Mattie said. "She could have been killed accidentally and then hidden to cover it up."

"It's possible. Another important finding is that she had horsehair on her clothing—quite a bit of it and several different colors. She also had an oily residue on her fingertips, the kind you get when you've been rubbing down a horse."

"She'd been working," Mattie said.

"Apparently. We need to find out who she had an appointment with," Stella said. "Where are we with the client list from the vet?"

"Completed," McCoy said. "No one on that list has admitted to an appointment. Now that fact seems suspect."

"Let's review the list for client location. We need to take another look at people who live near the area where the body was buried. And where is the gravesite in relation to the place you found her car?" Stella asked.

Mattie stood and crossed over to a map she'd pinned on the wall. She'd marked the car's location earlier, and she saw that someone else had drawn an "X" marking the gravesite. Stella came and stood beside her.

"Here we are," Mattie said, pointing to Timber Creek and then tracing the routes in question. "These sites are both west of here, but you can see they're only connected by the highway. Each place is accessible by a county road, both roads intersecting the highway about five miles apart. The sites aren't connected directly."

"Then we'll need to take a look at horse clients who live near the car site, too," Stella said.

"All right. I'll get the addresses and screen them," McCoy said. "Where are we on locating Roger Howard?"

"Nowhere," Stella said with a frown. "None of the ones I've turned up are the guy we're looking for. I found record of him back in high school in Hightower. Then he seemed to drop off the face of the earth."

McCoy looked at Mattie. "What did you find out this morning?"

She summarized her findings, giving Stella the interview printouts. "We can't eliminate Jim Cameron as a suspect, and

I plan to follow up with Green Thumb Organics. I hope Adrienne had a friend she confided in while she lived in Willow Springs. A best friend could provide insight into our victim's relationship with her ex-boyfriend. And maybe give us information about her brother."

Stella had been recording the new leads on the board while Mattie spoke. She'd also summarized the autopsy results. "As you know, our victim was fully clothed, and examination revealed no indication of sexual assault. Our crime scene unit gathered what trace evidence they could from her clothing, and now we're sending her clothes to a lab in Denver to see if they can find touch DNA on it. Whoever took her up that mountain had to have handled her body a lot. Testing will take some time, but I think we have a good chance of gathering some powerful evidence. That and matching horse-hair samples when we can. The animal DNA labs in the state don't seem to be as backed up as the human labs. As soon as we have a suspect client, we need to collect a hair sample from his horse, or maybe I should say from his horses."

"I'll talk to Dr. Walker again about his client list. See if he's willing to go out on a limb and suggest someone we might focus on. And we can run everyone through the system to see if we've got someone on the list with a criminal background," Mattie said.

Stella gave her a wicked smile. "I like the way you're thinking. Also, I've got Adrienne's telephone records on the way this morning. They're probably in my e-mail as we speak. I'll start looking at them as soon as we're done here. It's supposed to include copies of her texts, too."

Mattie felt a spark of excitement beneath her dense layer of exhaustion. This investigation was beginning to roll. "I'll make phone calls to Green Thumb Organics and Dr. Walker."

"Okay. One last thing, Sheriff. Where are we with Brody?" Stella asked.

A look of frustration had taken up residence on her boss's face. Mattie could tell how important he deemed Brody's involvement. "He's cooperating. He gave me the report that I asked for. We can confirm his presence here in the office and out on patrol Wednesday afternoon. He checked in regularly. By Thursday, he was searching for Ms. Howard. He gave me his patrol log, which includes an extensive list of all the places he went. He worked alone but continued to check in, so it would've been impossible for him to be up at the gravesite."

Mattie felt she needed to weigh in. "You can count on knowing where Brody stands, and I've never known him to hold back. His reaction when we discovered Adrienne's gravesite was no exception. He appeared to be devastated."

Stella nodded, looking thoughtful. "Let's talk to him together, Sheriff, before we decide. But I have to say, I know him to be sort of a hothead, and I'm not sure it's best to allow him to play a central role in our investigation. Even if we can confirm his innocence."

Stella's cell phone pinged, making her look at the screen. "This is a message from one of my techs," she said. "We got a hit on the print we took from the stamp and sent to IAFIS."

Mattie felt a surge of adrenaline. "That's fantastic!"

Stella continued to read her message aloud. "Ramon Vasquez. Has one charge of misdemeanor possession of narcotics: marijuana possession back in the day. No current warrants for his arrest."

"Did they search for an address yet?" McCoy asked, his face alive with excitement.

"Sure did. Vasquez has a Colorado driver's license with an address listed on a county road outside of Willow Springs."

The town where the letter had been postmarked. Mattie looked at Stella. "Can we bring him in?"

Stella gave her a grim smile. "You might be jumping the gun, Deputy. Let's go question him first and then decide."

As Mattie stood, Robo got up and hurried toward the door. "Hold on a minute, Robo," Mattie said, looking back and forth between her colleagues. "This feels like a big break. Too important for us to screw up. I want Brody in as backup, just in case this guy decides to run."

Stella exchanged a look with McCoy. "All right, let's talk to him now, Sheriff." And then to Mattie: "Be ready to roll in twenty minutes. I'll ride with you and your partner."

★

As she drove down a lane that marked the entrance to Ramon Vasquez's place, Mattie checked her rear view mirror and saw Brody making the turn behind her. They'd driven the highway toward Willow Springs with flashing lights but no sirens, and they'd made excellent time. Stella shifted in her seat on the passenger side, easing her handgun from her shoulder holster under her jacket and then replacing it. As if sensing their amped-up adrenaline, Robo stood to look out the windshield as they approached the house.

Sitting inside a copse of evergreens with several dilapidated outbuildings, the small clapboard farmhouse looked like it might be abandoned. Mattie parked in front of the cracker-box one-story, a coat of fresh paint long overdue, its windows blocked by curtains from the inside. She turned off the engine as Brody pulled up alongside. A ragged, gray picket fence enclosed the yard, its gate hanging askew. They exited their vehicles, Mattie making the decision to leave Robo inside his compartment, at least for the time being.

"I'll go to the door," Stella said. "Mattie, you stay with me. Brody, you go around back."

After going inside the yard, Brody split off to circle around the house. Mattie followed Stella as she stepped up on the porch and knocked on the door.

No answer. No sign of activity. Stella rang the bell. Mattie heard the soft echo of the bell inside, but still no one answered the door.

Mattie was wondering if they were wasting their time when a loud crash resonated through the house. She and Stella exchanged a quick glance the very moment they heard a roar coming from Brody on the other side of the house.

"We've got a runner!" Stella shouted, as she jumped off the porch and headed around the building.

Mattie hit the door-popper button on her utility belt, and the driver's side door of her SUV sprang open, the door to Robo's cage opening automatically. Mattie shouted for him to come. He leaped through the cage door, over the driver's seat, and out the door, hitting his stride as he fell in beside her. She ran around the building taking the side opposite from Stella.

"Heel!" Stopping at the corner of the building with Robo at her side, she eased forward to take a peek. Stella was heading away from her toward a broken-down building that looked like it had once been a garage.

With Robo at heel, Mattie sprinted after her, catching up within seconds. "Where are they?" She kept her tone low, searching the buildings for sign of Brody.

Stella had pulled her handgun. "I don't know. Haven't got a visual."

"Stay behind us," Mattie told her. "Let Robo take the lead. He'll find them."

Not knowing if the fugitive was armed or not, Mattie decided to put Robo on a leash. Taking one from her utility belt, she snapped it on his collar. "Search. Let's find the bad guy."

She encouraged him with her voice while she let him go out in front the full length of the leash. She was relying on a physical response people have when experiencing fear. Endocrine sweat. Patrol dogs were taught to track it in lieu of a scent article. She hoped Vasquez was afraid and that's why he ran.

Robo quartered the area, nose to ground, and picked up a scent trail within a few seconds. He surged forward to the end of the leash, taking Mattie with him. They ran toward the line of spruce that marked the edge of the wooded area surrounding the property. Stella fell behind as Mattie and Robo outdistanced her.

Hackles rose on her dog's neck as he ran. Trees limited her view. *Where's Brody?*

Robo started to bark. Pulling at the end of the leash, he broke through the trees with Mattie close behind. She saw Brody ahead of her. He tackled a guy that was running in front of him, bringing him down and falling on top of him.

Mattie struggled to hold Robo, not wanting him to bite the fugitive if he was under Brody's control. And she certainly didn't want him to bite Brody by accident.

Brody must have outweighed the man by thirty pounds. It looked like he didn't need assistance, so she stood back for a moment. Robo continued to bark and pull against her. Brody straddled the guy and turned him face up.

Then Brody reared back, his right hand raised in a fist, and he punched the guy square in the face.

Shocked, Mattie commanded Robo to guard. He settled and crouched into guard mode as she dropped his leash and leaped onto Brody's back. His elbow came at her and popped her in the eye.

Seeing stars, Mattie grabbed Brody's arm and held on. She heard Stella shout, "Stand down, Deputy!"

Robo rushed in, snarling at Brody. "Out, Robo!" she shouted, hoping to divert an attack. Brody tried to throw her off, but Mattie hung on.

"Vasquez, freeze!" Stella shouted. "That's enough, Deputy."

Something got through to Brody, and Mattie felt the fight go out of him. Releasing his arm, she told Robo to guard and moved away. "Ramon Vasquez, don't move," she said, her voice gruff. "Don't move or this dog will attack."

Robo hovered as if on springs, growling. Any movement might set him off.

Remaining still, the man on the ground shielded his face with his arms. "Jesus," he muttered, "don't let him bite me."

"Stay still, Vasquez, and I'll call off the dog." After making sure that the man complied, she called Robo off.

Robo remained crouched and alert, suspicious glances darting between Vasquez and Brody.

Vasquez lowered his hands and looked up at Mattie. "What the hell's going on?"

Stunned speechless, Mattie couldn't give him an answer.

The man on the ground was a dead ringer for Roger Howard.

Chapter 21

Cole said good-bye to his last morning client, glancing at the clock as he held open the door. The girls would get home from school around three. He'd better whip and spur if he was going to make it up to Dark Horse and get back home to greet them.

"Tess, did we get those lab results on Diablo?" he called through the pass through as he cleaned up.

"Yes, I printed them for you." She handed them to him through the opening.

He paused his cleaning and scanned the results. No improvement from the initial blood-work. "I'm going to leave now for Dark Horse Stable. Did you get the schedule set up for me?"

"Yes, but I'm afraid I had to schedule several appointments starting at four o'clock this afternoon. I've got you booked until six, and you'll have to start at seven thirty in the morning."

This isolated stable was wreaking havoc with his schedule. "That's fine. I just need a little time with the kids when they get home from school. I can make the rest of it work."

Cole grabbed some medications out of the refrigerator and headed out the back door to his truck. After putting the meds inside the fridge in his mobile vet unit, he climbed into the cab and fired up the engine. When he drove past his house, he wished he could stop and grab a sandwich. But he didn't have time for a conversation with Mrs. Gibbs about Angela. Or maybe he just didn't want to take the time. He'd rather stop at the grocery store and pick up something on his way out of town.

After stopping at Crane's Market to do exactly that, he unwrapped his store-bought ham and cheese sandwich, opened his bag of chips, and ate while he drove. The morning breakfast routine hadn't gone as well as he would have liked. When he'd come downstairs, everything seemed normal. Mrs. Gibbs was at the stove cooking scrambled eggs, and Sophie was perched at the table with her hair braided and drinking orange juice. Belle sat beside Sophie patiently waiting for her to drop a bite of something to eat.

"Where's your sister?" he'd asked.

Sophie shrugged as she raised her toast to her mouth to take a bite and then followed up by poising her juice glass in front of her lips while she chewed. Clearly she didn't want to reply.

"Has Angie been down yet?" he asked Mrs. Gibbs.

"No, sir. I haven't seen the young lady yet this mornin'." She set a plate filled with toast and eggs on the table for him while he poured his own coffee.

Carrying his coffee with him, he went to the bottom of the staircase and called up. "Angela. Come on down and have some breakfast."

"I'll be there in a minute, Dad," she called back.

Believing that she would be down soon, Cole went back to the kitchen, thanked Mrs. Gibbs for his breakfast, and dove in. Things went smoothly for the next ten minutes.

"I'm afraid the bus will be coming soon," Mrs. Gibbs said. "Angela is going to miss her breakfast. Sophie, you need to go get on your coat and hat, and be sure to put on your mittens. It's frightful cold out this morning."

When Cole went to see what was taking Angela so long, she barreled down the stairway, planting a kiss on his cheek as she passed by on her way out the front door. She was already wearing her coat and had it zipped up to her chin.

"Angie, slow down for a minute. I don't like you missing breakfast. You need to grab some fruit or something to eat," he said.

"Don't worry, Dad. I've got a granola bar and apple in my backpack. I'll be fine. C'mon, Sophie, we'd better run or we'll miss the bus."

He watched the flurry of Angela helping her sister with hat and backpack as she pushed her out the door, and it dawned on him that this had all been planned. He might be slow, but he wasn't stupid. His daughter's eyelids had been darkened with more makeup than usual, and he wondered what she was wearing under that coat.

He'd turned to find Mrs. Gibbs standing in the kitchen doorway, holding a small paper bag and wearing a frown of disapproval.

"I packed some food for Angela to take, but she was in fine hurry this morning, she was."

"I'm afraid so," he said. "She'll be all right without it."

The frown on Mrs. Gibbs's face deepened. "I wonder why she had such a bee in her bustle."

"I'd hate to guess. I'll talk to her about it when she gets home from school."

He'd pick a tussle with a longhorn bull over that conversation any day.

He turned his thoughts from his kids to the horse that he was headed up to treat, hoping that he'd find it better after starting insulin yesterday. He finished his lunch about the same time he turned off the highway, and he headed up the rough county road toward his destination with both hands free to steer around the potholes.

When he pulled into the stable yard, he saw the red chestnut horse out on the racetrack, streaking around the turn with Carmen on its back. He left his truck and walked over to join the groom named Juan at the guardrail. Juan tipped his head in greeting, shielding his eyes with his cowboy hat for a second. When he raised his eyes, Cole smiled at him, but the man's dour expression didn't change.

"He's fast," Cole observed aloud.

Juan shrugged with a slight shake of his head, signaling that he didn't comprehend.

With a hard tug on the reins, Carmen tried to slow the horse as it pounded past. When she finally got it under control, she turned to come back to them, the horse snorting and tossing its head as it pulled on the bit. Juan ducked under the rail to take the horse's reins, allowing Carmen to slip off. From the looks of it, she must have given the horse quite a workout. Sweat saturated its red coat and it was all lathered up. Still, the big animal danced at the end of its reins as Juan led it down the track to cool off.

Carmen pulled off her riding gloves. "Thank you for coming," she said. "I'm afraid Diablo is losing ground."

Not the news he wanted to hear. After passing the Doberman, who kicked up his usual vicious fuss, Cole followed her inside the barn to look at the stallion, dreading what he might find. The horse was lying down, stretched out flat, his black coat dull and lifeless. He looked thinner even than yesterday. Cole could count every rib.

Pulling his stethoscope from his pocket, he let himself into the stall and squatted next to the sick horse. Cole listened to his heart, counting the beats—not as rapid as it had been the day before, but still faster than it should be. He examined the mucous membrane in his mouth, pressing the gum above the top teeth. Delayed capillary refill time.

He crabbed his way toward the horse's back end, palpating the muscles of his back, haunch, and stifle as he went. As his hand traveled down the leg near the rear hoof, he could feel heat radiate from the hoof wall. He placed his palm flat on the bottom of it, well aware of what this level of warmth meant. Inflammation.

"I think his muscles are less bound up, but now he's got laminitis," he told Carmen. "He's down because his hooves are too sore for him to stand on."

"How can that be?"

Cole knew what she meant. This horse was barely eating anything, and the typical cause of laminitis was overeating rich foodstuffs, like grain or lush green grass. "I'm not sure I know the answer to that. You stopped the grain, right?"

"We did."

"How much is he eating?"

"A few bites of hay per day. We give him more than that, but he doesn't want it."

Cole took a thermometer from his pocket and took Diablo's temperature. The horse didn't budge. He appeared to have reached a level of discomfort that couldn't be surpassed; he would allow this human to do whatever he wanted. Even though it made it much easier to work on these high-strung thoroughbreds, Cole hated to see a horse reach this point. It was usually just one step away from the animal giving up altogether. And once a horse gave up, death often followed.

"His temp is elevated slightly today. Probably a result of the laminitis," Cole said.

"What can we do to help him?" Her distress was evident.

Cole rocked back on his heels and studied Diablo. *What the hell is wrong with this horse?* Well . . . in lieu of a diagnosis, support the horse and treat the symptoms.

"Do you have a set of easy boots?" he asked, referring to padded hoof covers that could be placed on a horse's hooves if its feet were sore.

"I do."

"Let's put those on him and see if we can get him to stand up and move around. His blood work from yesterday still shows the elevated blood sugar, but that was before we started the insulin. We need to take another blood sample today to see if we've improved any on that. Otherwise, we're still getting the elevated readings that show liver and muscle damage. This isn't like any other case of tying up I've seen. I'm afraid we're dealing with something different, but I'm just not sure what it is." Cole hated to admit that he didn't know Diablo's diagnosis, but in his years of practice he'd found it best to come clean when he didn't know the answers.

Carmen frowned, telling Cole he'd not boosted her confidence any.

"Was Diablo getting any other type of supplement?" he asked. "Before this all started?"

"Hay and grain, that's all."

"All right. Go get the easy boots and we'll put them on him."

Cole observed Diablo while the trainer was gone. He lay quiet and still; the muscle tremors had stopped. Respirations were shallow and rapid. When Carmen opened the door to reenter, Diablo didn't move or look up.

He helped Carmen strap on the boots. It took maximum effort combined with pushing, pulling, and cajoling on both their parts to get the horse to stand, but eventually they had him back on his feet. "See if he'll take a few steps for you," Cole said.

The horse picked his way gingerly across the stall.

"That's enough," Cole said, moving forward to palpate the horse's back and leg muscles while he was standing. "We do seem to have made some slight progress on the muscle spasm. Let's continue the insulin and IV hydration with electrolytes like we did yesterday. You'll need to watch him closely. It's okay if he lies down, but we shouldn't let him do that for more than a couple hours without getting him up to move around a little."

"Why do you think this is happening? Is it sugar diabetes?"

Cole studied Diablo for a few moments. "That's not likely the cause. I think his blood sugar is elevated because of some inflammatory process going on."

"What process?"

"I'm not sure. But for now, we'll treat the symptoms and run the blood work to see if his enzymes are coming back into line. I'll do some research and see if there's anything else I should test for."

Carmen was searching his face while he spoke, her eyes dark with concern. "But it looks like he's starting to get better?"

"I'm going to increase the anti-inflammatory to counter-act the laminitis. Our main concern with that—as you probably know—is to keep the third phalanx from rotating and coming through the sole of the hoof. That shouldn't happen, since he doesn't have a lot of calories in his system, and he's already been on the right feed." At this point, Cole was wing-ing it and he knew it.

He reviewed the treatment plan one more time with Car-men and took a last look at Diablo. The horse stood with his head lowered and his eyes seemingly focused on something within himself. He was clearly miserable but hanging in there. "I don't think we have to put him down yet," Cole said, need-ing to express the worst to his client. He wouldn't want Dia-blo to suffer unnecessarily if there was no hope of saving him. "Even with this new symptom, we've made a little progress. Maybe we'll get him turned around soon."

"I don't want him put down," Carmen said, using an ada-mant tone.

Cole took in the hard set of her jaw and decided not to argue the point—yet. "I'll need to see him again tomorrow, but I have to work you into the schedule. It will probably be later in the afternoon before I can get up here."

She walked with him toward his truck. "Stay for dinner with me tomorrow?"

"Thanks, but no. I'll need to get home to have dinner with the kids."

"You're quite the family man."

Cole noticed her face had softened, and she was giving him a teasing smile. He offered a small one in return, wanting to keep it light. "I am that. Being a good dad is my main goal these days."

"And your daughters are special, I can see that." Carmen tilted her head and gave him a sidelong gaze. "But how do they say it? 'All work and no play makes Jack a dull boy'?"

"I think it just keeps Jack out of trouble." They'd arrived at the truck. "Call me if Diablo gets worse or if you have any questions. Otherwise, I'll have Tess give you a call to let you know what time to expect me tomorrow. It might be morning before we get the schedule worked out."

She placed a hand on his arm as he opened the truck door, keeping him from climbing inside. "I'm interested."

"Interested?"

"Yes, interested . . . in you." She'd moved close enough that Cole could feel the heat from her body. Embarrassment made him step up into his truck. But then he felt foolish and knew he needed to exit this situation with more grace than that. "Ms. Carmen, I'm flattered that you're interested. But my life is pretty complicated right now, and I don't want to add a new relationship with anyone into the mix. Let's keep our friendship purely professional."

Her smile reminded him of a cat toying with a mouse. "Just think about it." She stepped back, lifted one hand in farewell, and turned to stride back toward the barn, her movements lithe and feline. She glanced back over her shoulder to throw him a sly smile and caught him watching.

His face warmed as he started his truck. When he put it into gear, the click of the automatic door locks reassured him, making him feel silly.

Thinking about it, he started driving down the lane toward the county road. He'd married Olivia right before starting vet school, and Angela had been born about a year later. His married-with-children status had seemed to shield him from flirtations in the past. Everyone knew he was a one-woman man; no client had ever made a pass at him before.

He squirmed in his seat and stopped the truck so he could pull off his jacket. He found himself grinning as he took his foot off the brake and started driving again. *Sheesh!* This would make one hell of a bar story, but he'd grown up and away from that scene and didn't really have a friend he could tell it to.

Maybe Mattie? Nah—she usually took things too seriously. She probably wouldn't see the humor in it.

Then he thought of one of his classmates from vet school, Trace Dempsey. Trace had been a great friend to both Cole and Olivia. She'd cooked a spaghetti dinner every Friday night, and they'd invited Trace over so the three of them could celebrate getting through another tough week.

Trace had moved to New Mexico after graduation and established an equine practice near Albuquerque, and he had several racing stables among his clientele. Maybe it was time to give Trace a call. Not to tell his bar story but to see if he had any ideas about Diablo. He decided to try to reach out to his old friend that very evening—after he spent some time with the kids.

What was it that Carmen Santiago said? "Quite the family man." He grimaced and allowed himself a sheepish smile. He guessed that would be the best way to describe himself. Even so, a man couldn't help but wonder where the interest of a pretty woman like Carmen might lead.

Chapter 22

Mattie and Stella were conferring in the staff office while Mattie held an icepack against her eye. Sheriff McCoy was meeting with Brody in his office, and Ramon Vasquez waited in the interrogation room. Mattie had taken an icepack to him earlier to use on his own face.

Stella and Mattie had prepared a file that contained the photo of Roger Howard with Adrienne and the threatening letter Vasquez had written to her. Things were convoluted right now with this confusion over the Howard versus Vasquez identity issue, and they hoped to get to the bottom of it. Not to mention what role he played in Adrienne's death.

"Let's go talk to him," Stella said. "Do you have a soda or something you could take in there? And you know, be nice to him."

"Don't tell me we're going to play good cop, bad cop."

Stella grinned and gave a little shrug. "Stay in there with me when I join you. We'll play it by ear."

Mattie shrugged. "Okay, I'll see what we have in the staff fridge. I might have to borrow a can of something from somebody."

"Do what you have to do."

Mattie left the ice pack on her desk and told Robo to stay on his dog bed. Soda in hand, she went to the interrogation room, tapping on the door as she entered. Vasquez gave her a hard look.

"I brought you a drink, Mr. Vasquez," she said. "Do you want it?" She hoped she was being nice enough.

"Has it been opened yet?"

"No."

"I'll take it then."

She set the can down in front of him.

"No telling what you people might put into it," he said, popping the top. It released with a fizz.

Mattie pasted a pleasant look on her face.

"I want to talk with the guy in charge. This was police brutality," he said, indicating his swollen jaw.

"Why did you run?" She figured she already knew the answer. Sheriff McCoy had obtained a search warrant, and Robo had found a stash of drug paraphernalia in his home. No drugs, but the equipment to use them. They'd bagged two pairs of cowboy boots and an ashtray full of cigarette butts. Even more important, they'd found a rifle and a compound bow with a supply of arrows and ammo.

Vasquez glowered at her.

Mattie pulled out a chair opposite from him and sat, fanning her hands on the tabletop. "Sheriff McCoy will join us later."

Stella entered the room and pulled up a chair on Mattie's side of the table. She placed the file in front of her but didn't open it. "Sorry to keep you waiting, Mr. Vasquez. I had a few things to straighten out."

He fixed his glare on Stella, so she gave him one of her too-sweet smiles that were so familiar. Mattie turned her attention to Vasquez, studying him while Stella made small talk. He was a handsome man with high cheekbones, a patrician nose, and dark brown hair. He took a sip of his cola, keeping his eyes on Stella over the top of the can.

Moving on, Stella started the interview. "Please tell me how you're related to Adrienne Howard," she said. Her demeanor told Mattie that—for now, at least—they were playing good cop, good cop.

"I'm her brother."

Stella nodded. "We have a photograph of you and Adrienne that Velda Howard identified you in. She told us your name was Roger Howard."

Vasquez gave a snort of disgust. "That's the name they gave me."

Stella paused, but he offered no other information.

"You knew about Adrienne's death?"

"I found out this morning."

Stella became very serious. "Who told you?"

"Jack Kelly, a friend of mine. Adrienne's too."

"Where does he live?"

"Willow Springs."

"Where is he employed?"

"Green Thumb Organics."

Bingo. The place Mattie intended to contact next. She withdrew a note pad from her pocket and recorded the man's name.

"How did he find out about her death?" Stella asked.

"Hell if I know. You'd have to ask him. Is it true that Adrienne was killed?"

"Yes, it's true. Her death is under investigation."

His gaze dropped to the table, and he made a hissing sound, tongue against teeth, as he released his breath. "Shit, man."

Mattie watched him close his eyes and remain silent, head lowered, for a full minute. When he raised his face, there were no tears and no semblance of surprise. "How can I help you?" he asked.

"You can help by explaining your family to us. How did you come to live with the Howards? This name-change business and so forth," Stella said.

He grimaced. "It's a long story, but I'll keep it short. The family secret." He drew an audible breath. "In the beginning, I was told that my mother and Velda Howard were best friends, and that when I was a baby, my mother gave me to Velda to raise. I was told that my mother couldn't afford to keep me, and the Howards took me in out of the goodness of their hearts. They adopted me and named me Roger Howard. Had a birth certificate to prove it. But a few months ago, I learned it was all a lie."

When his silence lengthened, Stella prompted him. "And what's the truth?"

"Velda Howard is my birth mother." His disappointment in that fact was palpable.

Mattie wondered if Vasquez had written the letter to Adrienne before or after the truth came out. "When did you discover this?"

"June tenth. I'll remember that date until the day I die."

So it was after the letter. "Did Adrienne know the truth?"

"Oh, yes." He frowned. "She's the one who told me. It changed my life completely."

"I bet it was a shock," Stella said. "How did the truth come out?"

The frown deepened. "I, uh, sort of lost my way for a while. Adrienne moved from Willow Springs without telling me. She didn't tell me she was leaving, and she didn't tell me where she was going. I was, uh, pretty upset."

"Why?" Stella asked. "What upset you about it?"

He gave Stella an incredulous look. "Wouldn't you be upset if your sister packed up in the middle of the night and moved away without a word?"

Stella nodded slowly, evidently conceding the point. "Why would Velda Howard lie to you about being your birth mother?"

Pain flickered across Ramon's face before it hardened again. "I don't know, I haven't asked her. Maybe because she considered me her bastard child."

"Let's back up for a minute," Stella said. "Tell me what happened when you graduated from high school. Why did you leave home, and where did you go?"

"The Howards were both alcoholics, and David could be a mean drunk. We never knew what would piss him off or who he was going to hit. He liked to point out that I was Mexican. Called me 'spick,' and when he was really drunk, he'd laugh at me and call me Ramon Vasquez. I grew up being taunted with it, but I felt certain that it was my real birth name." He shrugged and looked down at the table again. "I decided to go to California to look for my birth parents. I knew that Velda lived there before moving to Colorado and marrying David Howard."

"Did you find your father?" Mattie asked.

"No, but I changed my name legally to Ramon Vasquez, believing that was my real name and my parents might search for me someday. Eventually I moved to Denver and worked there for a few years. Then I moved to Willow Springs."

"Is that where you reunited with Adrienne?" Stella asked.

"Yes."

"How did that happen?"

"I worked for Jack Kelly. He knew that my name had once been Roger Howard and that I grew up in Hightower. When Adrienne came in as a customer, he asked her if she was local. After she told him she'd grown up in Hightower, he asked her if we could possibly be related. He put us in touch."

Stella nodded, encouraging him to continue.

"It seemed like a miracle that we found each other." Vasquez's face turned despondent and his eyes grew damp. "She was happy to see me again, too."

Stella took a plastic sheet that contained the photo of Adrienne and Vasquez from the folder she'd prepared. "When was this picture taken?"

He picked up the photo and stared at it. "Where did you get this?"

"Adrienne's photo album."

"Can I have a copy of it?"

"We'll see. When was it taken?"

"In April, right before she left Willow Springs. We went on a picnic and saw the ruins at Mesa Verde. We asked another tourist to take it for us." Vasquez appeared to be lost in the memory.

"And Adrienne left Willow Springs shortly after that picture was taken?" Stella asked. "Why?"

He shrugged, still looking at the picture as if he couldn't take his eyes off it. "She'd broken up with a guy there, a realtor. She was unhappy and decided a change would do her good. But I didn't find this out until we talked again in June, so I wasn't exactly sure what was going on at the time."

"Were you afraid she'd become a victim of foul play?"

"Nah. She packed her things, took her car. I found out she'd given notice to her landlord. I figured she'd decided to move away and start over."

"So you traced Adrienne to Timber Creek," Stella said. "What happened then?"

"I wrote her a letter, asking her if we could see each other." He shifted in his seat.

Stella slipped another plastic sheet out of her folder, this one containing the letter. "Is this the letter you sent?"

His face flushed and he hung his head. "Oh God . . ."

Mattie and Stella both waited, observing Vasquez's response.

Finally, he raised his head, looking from Stella to Mattie. His face had lost its redness, leaving it pinched with sorrow. "This is what I meant when I said I lost my way."

"Explain it to me, Mr. Vasquez," Stella said in a quiet voice.

He raised a hand slightly in a gesture of helplessness. "What's to explain? It's pretty clear. I fell in love with her, and I asked her to marry me. This was before I knew we were half siblings. I still thought we had no blood relationship."

"That must have been hard when you found out."

"I was devastated."

"How did you find out?"

"Like I said, Adrienne told me."

"How did she know?"

"She discovered it when she was about to leave home. She searched for her birth certificate so that she could take it with her. She found my original birth certificate, the one that was issued before David Howard adopted me. When you're adopted, they reissue a birth certificate with your new name and parents. According to Adrienne, my original birth certificate listed Velda Jane Miller as my birth mother—Miller being Velda Howard's maiden name. She realized that we shared a birth mother. The line for my father's name had been left blank."

"Why didn't she tell you all this when you were first reunited?" Mattie asked.

"I asked her that very question. She said she didn't want to bring me any pain or reopen old wounds. She hated that I had no biological father listed on the document. Thought it would hurt my feelings." He bowed his head, shaking it sadly. "If only she'd known the pain she could've spared me by telling me then."

"What was your original birth name?" Mattie asked.

Ramon gave a shrug of resignation. "That's the crazy part. Velda named me Ramon Miller. So I was right about Ramon being my birth name, but I still don't know why David chose the name Vasquez to tease me with. I should ask her . . . if I can ever stomach seeing her again."

"When did you see Adrienne last?" Stella asked.

"On June tenth." He locked eyes with Stella. "She called me as soon as she received this letter and arranged for us to meet. That's when she broke the news to me."

"I would have been pretty mad if someone had withheld such important information from me," Stella said.

He shrugged. "Adrienne thought she was doing the right thing."

"So you saw her on June tenth. Did you continue to communicate with each other?"

"We talked on the phone once in a while."

"Were you aware that she'd developed a new relationship here in Timber Creek?"

Vasquez raised his brows and touched his jaw. "That cop that hit me?"

Mattie felt certain that Vasquez must have known Adrienne was involved with someone else. "What did you know about her beginning a new relationship?"

"She said she had a boyfriend. I didn't know who it was."

"How did you feel about her having a boyfriend?" Stella asked.

"It hurt. But I knew it was for the best. I worked at being happy for her."

"And you? Have you moved on?"

"The best I can." He stared at Stella, daring her to pursue it further.

She did. "Where were you last week on Wednesday and Thursday?"

"I was home."

She waited, but when he didn't offer anything else, she continued. "Working?"

"No."

"Were you with someone who can confirm your whereabouts?"

"No."

"Give me more details, Mr. Vasquez. I need a picture of what you were doing on those two days last week."

He paused. "I was home, taking some time off. Alone."

"Can you prove you were there? Can anyone vouch that they saw you?"

He hunched forward, shoulders rounded. "I holed up last week and didn't go out much."

"Were you using that crack pipe we found?" Mattie asked.

He looked from Stella to Mattie. "It's a relic from my past. A friend gave it to me. It has nothing to do with anything."

"You wrote this letter a few short months ago. Not long after, your world turned upside down. You were aware that Adrienne was moving on. You say that you were moving on, too, but I don't believe you," Stella said.

He clamped his lips shut.

"You've been very forthcoming, Mr. Vasquez," Stella said. "Now you need to think hard and tell me what you can prove about where you were and what you were doing last week."

"Am I a suspect?" Vasquez said, acting incredulous.

"I think you know more than you're saying."

"You think I know more than you do? I can't believe that."

"What do you know about your sister's death?" Stella asked.

"Nothing!" He squirmed in his chair.

"Can you prove where you were last Wednesday?"

"I can't."

"Have you ever gone hunting up in the mountains, Mr. Vasquez?" Stella asked, going a different direction.

Mattie kept her eyes on Vasquez.

"Of course. What does that have to do with anything?"

"Rifle or bow hunting?"

"Both."

"Did you know that your sister liked to hike?" Stella asked.

"We both do. We've hiked together many times."

"Did she like to hunt? Did you ever go hunting together?"

"No. Adrienne had no interest in hunting."

"Do you think Adrienne might have gone along on a hunting trip with someone, just to enjoy being outdoors?"

He reacted without pause. "Never. She wouldn't want to be in a hunting camp. She might like to go hiking and camping, but she wouldn't have anything to do with shooting or killing animals of any kind."

"Do you own a horse?"

"No." His tone reflected his impatience.

"Do you have a friend in Willow Springs or Hightower that owns a horse?"

He shook his head in disbelief. "Why are you asking me all these things?"

"Please answer the question, Mr. Vasquez," Stella said, her tone mirroring his level of impatience.

"Yes, I have several friends in both places who own horses. What of it?"

"Do you know how your sister died?" Stella asked.

"I don't. How many times do I have to tell you?"

Stella leaned back in her seat and paused for a moment. "She was shot."

Vasquez appeared to take it hard. He bent forward, closing in on himself. Mattie noticed that the detective had withheld the exact cause of death: shot by an arrow.

"Wuh . . . was it an accident?" he asked with a slight stammer.

"That's under investigation," Stella said.

He bowed his head for a moment and then looked back at Stella. "Did she go hunting or something? Is that why you asked all those questions?"

"I can't say at this time. Do you think it could be a possibility?"

"I don't. But I can't believe someone would shoot Adrienne on purpose. It must've been an accident." He searched Stella's face, his eyes turning fierce. "Is that what happened here? Did someone shoot her on purpose?"

"Like I said before, Mr. Vasquez, her death is under investigation." Stella gave him a penetrating look. "Did you kill your sister?"

"My God! Absolutely not!"

"Would you be willing to take a polygraph?"

"If that would eliminate me as a suspect, yes. You should be finding the person who shot Adrienne, not wasting time on me."

"I believe we can arrange for a polygraph by tomorrow. We're holding you for possession of drug paraphernalia tonight. We've got a nice, clean cell you can sleep in."

Belligerence came back into his face. "You're making a mistake. Between this and police brutality, you're gonna be sorry."

"I'll get Deputy Johnson to book him," Mattie said, standing to leave the room.

After Johnson took Vasquez to the back, Stella looked at Mattie. "What do you think?" she asked.

"Convincing reactions," Mattie said. "I'm not positive that he killed her."

"Twisted story," Stella said. "I'm not yet convinced that he didn't."

Chapter 23

Cole drove through town in time to follow the school bus to his lane. He stopped his truck behind it, waiting for his kids to unload. After it pulled away, he turned in behind them, making Sophie hop with excitement when she saw him. Angie's reaction was much less exuberant, but at least she gave a smile to her old dad.

He hit the button to roll down the window. "You girls want a ride?"

"Not supposed to ride with strangers," Sophie said with a grin.

"I'm friends with your sister here," he said, giving a nod to Angie.

"I can vouch for him," Angie said, opening the passenger-side door. She boosted her sister up to help her clamber into the seat, Sophie's backpack looking huge on her small frame, and then climbed up to join her. They settled into the bucket seat on the passenger side with Angie's arms around Sophie while Cole drove slowly down the lane toward the house. It did Cole's heart good to see them be playful with each other and to include him. He wished he didn't have to do what he planned, but he decided he couldn't avoid it. Why did parenting have to be so hard?

Cole parked under the cottonwood tree out front, and they all unloaded and trooped inside. While Cole and Sophie paused to strip off their coats, Angie headed toward the staircase. His suspicion somewhat confirmed, Cole decided to follow her rather than confront her in front of Mrs. Gibbs and Sophie.

"Go see if Mrs. Gibbs can help you get a snack in the kitchen," he said to Sophie.

He took the stairs two at a time, hurrying to catch up to Angie before she could shut herself away in her bedroom. "Hold up, Angel," he called after her retreating back. "I want to talk to you."

She paused at her bedroom doorway, facing him with a frown. "Can it wait a minute, so I can put down my things?"

"Sure," he said, coming close to the door so she'd be hard-pressed to shut it in his face.

Making an exasperated sound, she walked in and put her backpack on the bed. With her coat still on, she crossed her arms and faced him. "What do you want, Dad?" Her face and tone said she was none too pleased.

"Go ahead and take off your coat. I can wait a second."

"Dad! What do you want?" If she'd been a few years younger, she would have stamped a foot.

Cole decided on the direct approach; it usually served him best. "Okay, Angela. No more games. I want to see what you wore to school today."

She hugged her coat tightly closed. "Geez, Dad! What's your problem?"

"Angela, let's not quibble about this. I want to know if you wore the shirt that we told you not to wear."

"What makes you think I did?"

"I don't need to explain myself. Did you wear it?"

If possible, she clutched her coat even tighter. "What if I did?"

Her defiance was maddening. "From the way you're acting, I'm going to assume that's the case. It's not acceptable for you to sneak around and disobey me."

"Since when have you even cared what I wear, Dad? Why are you so interested all of a sudden?" Her eyes shot daggers at him.

"I care about you, Angela. And I don't want others to think badly of you."

"You never gave it a second thought until Mrs. Gibbs brought it up."

She had him there. "Maybe so, but cut me some slack. Your mother always took care of your clothing. I'm not used to needing to do it."

She raised her chin, showing the flushed skin on her neck. "Well, I don't need your help. Go back to ignoring me like you're used to."

"I don't want boys to get the wrong idea."

"Maybe one of *them* will pay attention to me."

Cole stopped his next angry retort and drew a breath. "Angela, why do you say things like that? What is it that makes you believe I don't care about you?"

Tears filled her eyes and threatened to spill over. "It's what you do, Dad."

"I'm doing the best I can here. I had Tess schedule this hour so that I could be home to spend time with you kids after school."

"Oh, good. Work us into your schedule."

"Angela! That's enough. It's my work. It's how I pay the bills."

Her breath caught in a sob, tearing at Cole's heart. He wanted to move toward her but stood rooted in the doorway. Would comforting her reinforce her misbehavior? What would Olivia do?

"Maybe I'll go away like Mom. Or die like Grace and Adrienne. Then you won't have to worry about trying to spend time with me," Angela said.

Her words snatched his breath away. "You know that's not what I want. Don't even talk like that."

She unzipped her coat, shrugged it off, and threw it on the bed. She wasn't wearing the forbidden shirt, but the one she had on was just a scrap of a thing—low-cut, tight, and high enough to show glimpses of her belly.

"Where did you get that?" Cole said, stunned but thoroughly aware that she'd never worn this shirt before; he wouldn't have missed it even during his most unconscious days last summer.

The tears had stopped, and she faced him with all the defiance she could gather. "I borrowed it from a friend."

"Exactly which friend loaned it to you?"

She clamped her jaw, thinning her lips.

Cole felt his anger build. "Tomorrow morning, you're going to show me what you have on before you leave this house." He turned to go but stopped when another thought struck him. "And I'll want to inspect your backpack, too."

"Fine," she said. "You've spent some time with us; you can go back to work now."

"I don't want any back talk either, Angela. Show some respect."

Cole escaped from her bedroom before she could retort. Mrs. Gibbs looked up at him from the bottom of the staircase with a frown of concern on her face, not even trying to hide that she'd been eavesdropping. Belle waited there beside her, giving him one slight tail wag before stopping altogether and standing rooted in confusion.

"I didn't know you were upstairs with Angela just now, so I was going to ask her if she wanted a snack," Mrs. Gibbs said.

Cole stomped down the stairway, brushing past her. "I'll be back around six," he said as he grabbed his coat and left the house. He climbed into his truck and slammed it into gear.

What the hell? What was going on with Angela? Why was she acting like this all of a sudden? What was all this running away or dying talk about? He thought of the conversation he'd had with Mattie during their night up on the mountain. Maybe she had a good point after all. Maybe he needed to enlist the help of a good counselor.

He drove to the clinic where he greeted Tess and kept himself busy until his first late-afternoon client arrived. Sometime during his final hour of office visits, Cole took a call from Mattie between patients.

"I was thinking of you earlier," he said as a greeting.

There was silence for a few seconds before she spoke. "Oh?"

"Yeah, I had a fight with Angela. She's saying things I just don't get. Maybe I should talk to that school counselor after all."

"I recommend it . . . for sure. I hope you will."

He paused, thinking her voice sounded tired. "Well, you didn't call to listen to my problems. What can I do for you?"

"We have some information that tells us Adrienne might have been working with horses shortly before she was killed. We're looking at your list of horse clients to see if any of them are close to the trailheads that led to her gravesite or the car site. Could you take a look at the list, too, and tell me if any of them have ever crossed your radar as either violent or cruel with animals?"

"I can tell you right now, I'm sure none of them have. The very fact that they were willing to have Adrienne do massage on their horses tips them into the kind and caring category. But I'll have Tess call you with those located close to the trailheads."

"Okay." She paused. "You're working late."

"I am. I have a client up in a remote area, Dark Horse Stable, and it's wreaking havoc with my schedule." He had a thought. "It's not even close to the areas you're looking at. This woman is a new client, so I didn't refer her to Adrienne. She's just a very nice lady with a real sick horse."

This time the pause was so long that Cole began to wonder if Mattie was still on the line. Finally, she spoke. "I appreciate your time."

"Mattie . . . is everything all right?"

"Why do you ask?"

"I don't know. You sound tired or something."

"Everything's fine. And I *am* tired. I'll try to get some sleep tonight."

"Didn't you get a chance to catch up last night?"

Again, there was a pause. "Something came up. Look, I've gotta go. Thanks for your help."

Her voice sounded strained, and if Cole didn't know her better, he'd think she was fighting tears. But the Mattie he knew didn't cry. He was able to slip in a good-bye just as she disconnected the call.

★

Mattie sat at her desk, struggling with the pain in her chest. She placed a hand over her heart.

Cole's words about his new client had set up a wave of emotion she didn't know how to deal with, but they couldn't be what caused this turmoil. Could it have been what her brother had said? Why was she such a mess?

Soon Tess called, giving her a list of three stables, none of which were owned by people she knew. Tess vouched for all of them, saying these clients were the "salt of the earth," but Mattie still thought they should follow up. Since Adrienne's clothing indicated she'd been working with horses the afternoon she'd been killed, she didn't want to drop all the leads and focus only on Ramon Vasquez. Even though the evidence was stacking up against him, it was too early in the investigation to do that.

She went to join Stella in the office that Sheriff McCoy had assigned her. The detective was going over phone records, texts, and e-mails that they'd received from Adrienne's service providers. Although Mattie's shift had ended an hour earlier, she wanted to see if Stella thought she should follow up with the list of stables tonight.

Tapping on the door, she entered Stella's office, Robo padding behind her.

Stella's brow shot up when she looked up from her work. Nudging her reading glasses down on her nose, she peered over them and focused on Mattie's face. "Your little scuffle this morning earned you a pretty good shiner."

Mattie touched her bruised cheekbone gingerly. "I've had worse."

"Sheriff McCoy said he sent Brody home, but he can't afford to suspend him. He's too short handed."

"We have a lean team here. We need every man we've got." Mattie felt that Brody's behavior was out of line, but there was a small part of her that understood how upset he was. "I have three stables that are near the trailheads we're looking at. Both Dr. Walker and Tess say these owners don't classify as people you'd suspect as killers, but we might still want to follow up. Do you think I should do that tonight?"

Stella frowned, glancing back down at the pile of papers in front of her. "No, I want to talk to them myself. I have a few more phone numbers that I need to cross match and connect with names. Do you have phone numbers assigned to that list of clients?"

"I do."

"Great. I can use that," Stella said, taking the list from her. "The TracFone number that our anonymous tipster called in on doesn't appear on her phone call history. But there are still a lot of numbers here that I'm trying to assign names to."

"Do you want some help?"

"No, not yet. If I need another set of eyes, I'll keep yours in mind." She squinted one eye. "That is, if you can still see out of that one."

Mattie shook her head and offered a thin smile. "The call to Green Thumb Organics didn't net anything. Jack Kelly wasn't working today. I tried a home phone number, but no answer."

"Will he be in tomorrow?"

"Supposed to be."

"Try again in the morning," Stella said.

"All right. If you don't need me for anything else, I should clock out."

"Yeah, that's fine. But I have a favor to ask. I'll be here at least another hour. Could I crash on your sofa for the night? I need to be back here early in the morning."

Typically, Mattie wouldn't want a house guest, but Stella had stayed one night during their last investigation, and tonight the distraction might be the thing she needed to stay out of her own head. "Sure. Just come when you're done."

"Can I pick up some food? Maybe a pizza from that little hut beside the road?"

"The Pizza Palace. Whatever you want. I don't usually keep a lot of food at my house."

"I'll bring enough for two."

"Sounds good. I'll see you when you're finished."

Rainbow was still at her post when Mattie passed through the lobby, so she stopped to say good-night. "What did you think of Ramon Vasquez's voice?" Mattie asked her. "Could he be the one who called in the anonymous tip?"

"It's hard to say, but I remember a voice that wasn't quite so deep, more of a Spanish accent."

"I suppose he could have disguised his voice on the phone," Mattie said. "In fact, I assume that anyone would."

"Yeah, that's probably true." Rainbow looked distressed. "I wish I could be more help."

"Don't worry. If he's the one who called, we'll figure it out."

After saying good-bye, Mattie clocked out, went outside to her SUV, and loaded Robo into the back. She settled into the driver's seat but hesitated before twisting the key to start the engine. She hated to go home where she'd be alone with her thoughts. She decided to go check in on Brody. She wanted to replace Robo's last memory of him with something better than the violent scuffle he'd had with Mattie. A patrol dog with a grudge didn't make for a very good team player.

She turned the key and drove to Brody's house, a small, clapboard two-story on the edge of town. The windows were dark. His cruiser was parked in front, so she pulled up beside it. She exited the car, taking Robo with her. After stepping up on the small, concrete porch, she knocked on the door. When there was no answer, she turned and studied his cruiser, wondering if he'd gone somewhere on foot. Deciding to check around back, she told Robo to heel and went around the side of the house. In the well-lit backyard, she found an old vintage car—from the thirties or forties?—propped up on cement blocks. A pair of legs clad in grease-stained jeans were poking out from under it, and she assumed they belonged to Brody. A small space heater glowed, sending radiant heat under the car.

"Hey, Brody," she said as she approached the car, not wanting to startle him. "Nice car."

Robo sniffed one of Brody's boots, curious but not vengeful. Glad to see it, Mattie signaled with her hand for him to come to her and then sit. He responded like a champ.

The clanking under the vehicle stopped, but Brody stayed under it. "What are you doing here, Cobb?"

"Thought I'd check in."

"Do you have Vasquez under arrest?"

"We're holding him on possession of drug paraphernalia."

"Why not murder one?"

"Not enough evidence for that."

He rolled out from under the car, his body appearing a few inches at a time. He wore a blue western shirt with the sleeves torn out, revealing well-tanned arms etched with thick, ropy muscle and a variety of tattoos: flames, cars, and all kinds of barbed wire. When his face appeared, also streaked with grease, it took on a pained grimace.

"Damn, Cobb. Did I do that?"

Wanting to keep it light, Mattie wiggled her jaw with one hand as if testing it. "It was an accident. I think I got in your way."

He shook his head, looking disgusted. "Sorry."

She'd never had an apology from Brody before, not that she could recall. "Shit happens. I just wanted to make sure

Robo doesn't bear a grudge." She pulled a dog treat out of her pocket. "Do you want to give him this?"

"Sure." He wiped his hand on his shirt, took the treat, and squatted. "Here, Robo."

"Go get it," Mattie said, releasing her dog from his sit. In an instant Robo took the treat, signaling that her mission had been accomplished. He stood, waving his tail, as Brody patted his side.

"I'm not sure that Vasquez killed her, Brody. Unless we can get more evidence, we shouldn't rush to judgment."

He frowned, and she could see his jaw muscle flex as he clamped it.

"He's the same guy as Roger Howard," she told him. "He's her half brother."

"What? What are you saying?"

Mattie explained the relationship and gave him the details about why and when the letter was written. "He says they reconciled the situation between them. We're not going to quit looking at him, but I don't like him as much for it as I should. We need to keep an open mind."

Brody squinted at her for a long moment, evidently turning things over in his own mind. "You got a minute?" he asked.

"Yeah."

"I need someone to pump the brakes while I bleed the line."

"Okay."

Brody opened the door for her, and Mattie grabbed the steering wheel and hoisted herself up and in. The tan leather upholstery looked new, definitely not the original. She'd learned recently that Brody restored old cars, but she didn't know he was working on something so impressive.

Lying down on the creeper, he rolled himself back under the car. "Okay, start pumping until I tell you to stop."

Mattie did as told, pumping the brake repeatedly until she heard him call a halt. She climbed out of the car and joined Robo on the sidelines where he was watching. Brody reappeared from under the vehicle, stood, and picked up a rag to start wiping his hands.

"Thanks. You came just at the right time." Head lowered over his task, he turned his eyes up toward her and shrugged one shoulder, looking sheepish. "I tinker with these old things when I'm trying to relax."

"You've got reason to be stressed, but you've got to hold it together when you're on duty. We can't afford to lose you, Brody."

He shook his head, looking down at his hands again. Noncommittal.

Surprised that he'd not bitten her head off, Mattie decided that was all she'd better say. "I've gotta go home. Do you need any more help?"

He looked up from his hands and paused his cleaning. "Probably." His eyes glinted with pain and repressed anger. "But not with the car. Thanks for stopping by, Cobb. I appreciate the information."

"We'll find her killer, Brody. And we'll need your help."

He nodded and went back to cleaning his hands.

Chapter 24

By the time the last client went out the door, it was well after six. Once again, Cole found himself falling short of his goal for family time. He and Tess locked up, and he followed her as he drove down the lane to his house while she traveled on to the highway. He sighed, wishing he could keep right on driving tonight, too.

Sophie and Mrs. Gibbs sat at the kitchen table eating dinner. Mrs. Gibbs popped up from her chair as he came through the door from the garage.

"I kept things warm here on the stove," she said. "I'll fix you a plate."

"No, keep your seat. I'll fix my own here in a minute. Where's Angela?"

"She says she isn't hungry. She doesn't want to come down to eat, so I fixed her a tray and took it to her in her room."

Wondering if pandering to his daughter's tantrum was the right thing to do, he exchanged pointed looks with his housekeeper. As if reading his mind, she shrugged and turned back to the stove. Perhaps she was at a loss as much as he was.

"A little extra attention won't hurt," she murmured while she picked up a spoon and started to stir something in a pot. "Maybe she'll feel more like talking after dinner."

Cole took that as a message that he should reach out to his daughter again, and it irritated him unreasonably. For a moment, he could relate to Angela's desire for their new housekeeper to mind her own business. But he took a breath, pulled off his boots, and went to the half-bath under the stairwell to wash his hands. When he came out, he had his irritation under control.

He visited with Sophie while they finished their meal, helped Mrs. Gibbs clear the table, and then followed his youngest into the great room to watch television when the housekeeper shooed them out of her kitchen. Sophie snuggled in under his arm while they watched a show, and then he told her it was time to go upstairs to take a bath before bed. Deciding he could face the lion's den again, he followed Sophie up the staircase and tapped on Angela's door.

"Who is it?" she called.

"It's Dad. Can I come in for a minute?"

"I guess so."

Fortifying himself, he cracked open the door to let himself in. Angela sat on the bed with paper and textbooks spread around, presumably doing homework. The tray of food sat on her desk, looking like she hadn't eaten much. He gestured toward it. "Not hungry?"

Her expression stony, she refused to look at him. "No."

"You're not getting sick, are you?"

Her breath escaped in an exasperated puff. "I'm fine."

"Do you want to talk?"

"Not really."

Cole went into the bedroom anyway and sat on the desk chair, not quite sure how to proceed. "Well, I guess I can't force you to talk, but I've got something I want to say, so maybe you could just listen. I mean . . . feel free to talk if you feel like it . . . you know what I mean."

Angela threw him a look. She probably thought her father had turned into a blithering idiot. Well, he might as well tackle this full on.

"I'm worried about you, Angel. You're not acting like yourself. I know things have been tough, and hard times have piled up higher than good times here lately. But we've got to hang tough. You know, hang together."

Silent, she started gathering up her papers.

"I don't want us to be mad at each other, but I do want you to have some self-respect and to do as I say."

She glared at him, narrowing her eyes. "Yes, Dad."

He didn't really know what to say next, so he decided to muddle through. "I hope you'll think about it and truly agree. In the meantime, I can't promise that I'll spend more time here at home, but I'll do the best I can. I'd like for us to work together at the clinic sometimes and have fun together when we're not working. Like we were doing until just lately. I can't believe we're feuding over something as silly as clothes."

She looked away and began putting textbooks into her backpack.

"Maybe this isn't about clothes. What is it about, Angel?"

She shrugged.

"Let's cool off and think about it. And let's talk again after dinner tomorrow night. I've always trusted you to do what's right. I'm putting you on the honor system for tomorrow morning, and I trust you to pick something appropriate to wear. You don't have to show me your backpack, but I do want you downstairs for breakfast like always. Trying to be together when we can goes both ways, and it's your responsibility, too."

Silence.

"I'll see you after school. And I *will* promise you this—if I can't make it home when I say I will, I'll call to let you know. And I'll expect you to do the same for me. Okay?"

"Okay."

It sounded begrudging, but at least it was a reply. Cole decided to take it, and he stood up to leave. "Let's talk again tomorrow. Good night, Angel."

No reply. Cole quietly closed the door behind him on his way out.

By the time he read a story to Sophie and got her tucked into bed, it was shortly after nine. Not too late to call his vet school friend, Trace Dempsey. Though he felt exhausted from the long day, he needed to see if his friend could help him with a diagnosis for Diablo.

Trace answered the phone, sounding happy to hear from him. "How you doing, Cole? It's been a while."

"It has. Been busy. You?"

"Busy enough. How are Olivia and the kids?"

Cole should have realized his friend would ask about his family, but he hadn't stopped to think about it, and it caught him off guard. "Well . . . Olivia moved out last May and our divorce was final in August. The kids are with me, and they're doing fine." The words tasted bitter in his mouth—half-truths.

There was a pause. "I'm sorry to hear that, Cole."

"We'll survive. How are Helen and your kids?"

"Everyone's healthy and the kids keep us hopping."

Cole chuckled, thoughts of Trace's triplets giving him much-needed levity. "I'll bet that's a fact. How old are they now?"

"Twelve. We've got puberty rearing its ugly head. Times three."

"I hear ya."

There was an awkward silence, and Cole decided to get to business. "Do you have a minute to talk about an equine case that's got me stumped?"

"Sure. What've you got?"

"A racehorse. Stud. I thought he was tying up when I first saw him. Had all the classic symptoms. But he hasn't responded to treatment, and the blood work isn't quite matching the picture."

"Sweating, agitation, muscle tremor, tachycardia, hyperglycemic, elevated bilirubin?"

"Yeah." Seemed odd that Trace could summarize the clinical findings like that.

"Frog juice."

"What?"

"Never heard of it?" Trace asked.

"No."

"It's a highly concentrated form of Clenbuterol that some misguided trainers believe enhances performance in racehorses. They think it enhances aerobic capacity, but it can actually damage the heart muscle in high dosages," Trace said. "It also breaks down fat tissue, so they're using it to develop lean muscle mass."

"There's not an ounce of fat on this horse," Cole said. "I asked the trainer if she had this horse on any supplements, and she denied it."

"She probably would. It's illegal. The racing commission would take away her license and ban her horses from the track."

"Good Lord."

"It's a common problem down here, and we're all on the lookout for it. The illegal form is smuggled in from Mexico in gallon jugs. Some of these horses get so hopped up, they'd run through a brick wall if you put them in front of one."

"This is the first time I've had a racing stable in my case-load. I had no idea."

"Sounds like your stud horse got too much of it."

"How many days will it stay in the bloodstream?" Cole asked.

"Oh, about one to two weeks. Hair sample will pick it up for about six months."

"I have a blood sample I drew today. I'll call the lab and have them run a test for it tomorrow morning," Cole said. "I started this horse on insulin yesterday, and today it's got laminitis. So far, I'm treating the symptoms as they pop up."

"Yeah, he's toxic all right. You'll be lucky if you can save him. If your test turns up positive, you gotta get him started on a beta-adrenergic antagonist." Trace told him which drug he preferred.

"Thanks for the info, Trace. I'll do some more research on it. I owe you one."

"Hey, the next time one of my kids' dogs is sick, I'll give you a call."

"I hope you will."

Cole wrapped up the call and disconnected. He swiped to his contacts list and left a message with his lab saying they should add the screen for Clenbuterol to Diablo's sample and that he would e-mail the order to them first thing in the morning. After that, he was pretty well done in for the day, so he got ready for bed.

Once there, he tossed and turned, unable to shut his mind off and go to sleep. Thoughts of Carmen's pass at him made him analyze her motives. She must be worried that he would detect the Clenbuterol before it passed out of Diablo's system, and losing her license would most likely end her career and break her business. Did she think that a relationship would keep him from reporting her?

And here he'd been thinking she was actually interested in him.

Then his mind jumped to Angela and his concerns about her. Was the presence of Mrs. Gibbs truly the catalyst for the change in his daughter's behavior? Or was it something more serious? Whatever it was, he'd better get to the bottom of it soon. He didn't want anything to drive a wedge between them like the one that had been driven between him and her mother.

★

It was late by the time Stella pulled into the yard. Mattie had already taken sheets and blankets out of the closet and laid them on the coffee table. She kept busy—picking up her house, washing some dishes she had in the sink, feeding Robo—doing anything to keep her mind from going back to her brother's words. She'd been fighting a low-grade sense of nausea all day and hadn't eaten anything since yesterday. But when she met Stella at the door, the scent of the pizza actually tempted her appetite.

Robo started his happy dance when Stella came to the door.

"Smells good," Mattie said, holding the door wide for her guest to enter.

"You've looked peaked all day, Mattie. You're not getting sick from spending the night out in that snowstorm, are you?"

"Nah, it takes more than that to get me down."

"Good. Get out of the way, Robo. Let me set this box down and I'll give you the attention you deserve." Stella carried the pizza through to the kitchen, set it on the counter, and then leaned down to pat Robo. He was ecstatic.

"There, that makes you happy now, doesn't it?" she cooed, looking around the kitchen. "I like your place, Mattie. It's better than mine."

"Thanks."

Stella waved at the ancient refrigerator that huddled against the far wall. "That's got to be an antique. Cute. Say, it wouldn't have a beer in there for me, would it?"

"Sure. Help yourself." Mattie took out paper plates and plastic forks and laid them on top of the pizza box while Stella unscrewed the cap on her bottle. The tangy scent of the brewed drink wafted out, making her stomach lurch.

"Want one?" Stella asked.

"Not tonight. I'll fix some peppermint tea."

Stella raised a brow, looking surprised. "You're off your game, girl. There *is* something wrong with you, and I plan to find out what it is."

Christ. Nothing like having a detective for a friend. "Let's take this into the living room," Mattie said, pointing to the pizza box and the disposable dishware she'd placed on top of it. "I'll heat some water and be right with you."

After a few minutes, she joined Stella and Robo in the living room. Robo was lying on his cushion with his head up and ears pricked, watching everything but looking completely at ease. Stella had kicked off her shoes and leaned back into the sofa cushions, her feet up on the coffee table, a slice of pepperoni pizza filling a plate on her lap. She was taking a pull on her beer when Mattie entered the room.

"Ah . . ." she said, taking the bottle from her lips. "That's good. I needed that."

Mattie sat her tea on her end of the coffee table, chose a pizza slice, and then settled down on the sofa, bending one leg under her. She hoped she could eat. Her body needed fuel if she was going to keep up with Robo.

She turned to the one subject she was always comfortable with: work. "Did you find anything in the phone records and e-mails?"

"Yes and no. It seems crazy in this day and age, but our victim didn't use her cell phone or her e-mail all that much. So I was able to trace back to last May pretty easily. I thought I should take a look at the time she received that letter from Vasquez."

"What did you find?" Mattie asked, taking her first bite of the pizza.

"I found his phone number. I compared dates, and it looked like she called him a few days after that letter was posted, which appears to confirm his statement that she contacted him soon after. There were no e-mails, no texts, but there *were* around ten phone calls back and forth. Some that she initiated, some from him that she answered, and many that lasted for close to an hour. They were talking all right. He didn't lie about that."

"How about close to the time she was killed?"

"No. The back-and-forth phone calls ended in late June. There are a few texts, but they seem to be updates. Normal brother and sister chitchat."

"What about the client list? What did you find there?"

"It looks like she used phone calls and texts to schedule her appointments. There were some phone calls that matched up with the clients on our short list but nothing within the past two weeks. I called them before leaving the station. Everyone denies an appointment on Wednesday, and there were no texts that would contradict them."

"And there were no calls from that TracFone number?"

"I know what you're thinking," Stella said. "We've gotta think that the tipster might also be our killer."

"Rainbow's not sure that Vasquez's voice matches the tipster's, and he doesn't have an accent."

"Yeah. But easy to disguise," Stella said.

"True."

Stella pursed her lips, thinking. Then she took another drink of beer. "Thank God that Adrienne knew the two of them were half-siblings. Incest would have been a tough mistake to get over. What if Vasquez lied about that, and the two of them really did sleep together?"

Mattie gagged as she tried to swallow the bite of pizza she had in her mouth. She put her slice back on her plate.

From her end of the couch, Stella studied her reaction. "You look like someone poisoned your pizza, Mattie. What's bothering you?"

Mattie shook her head, not sure what to say, not sure if she could even talk.

"You've looked sick off and on all day."

She shrugged and picked up her tea to take a sip.

"Did you get in touch with your brother?"

Stricken, Mattie stared at Stella, wondering how she could guess.

"You look like you did the night you told me about your family. What's going on?"

Mattie curled her hands around the tea mug and held on tightly. "I'm not sure I can talk about it."

"Something's eating you up inside. It might do some good to talk. Maybe I can help you put it into perspective."

She took a deep breath and let it out slowly. "Willie called last night. Turns out he's working a twelve-step program.

Drug rehab. He's at the stage of wanting to apologize for his transgressions."

"Okay?"

"I didn't get it when he apologized to me. Didn't know how he might have hurt me. I mean, we were just kids. It was our dad that hurt us."

Stella nodded, her eyes sending encouragement.

"He said he should have stopped our dad from coming into my bedroom . . . at night." Mattie choked, and a wave of nausea hit her.

"Excuse me," she said, getting up and heading toward the bathroom. Robo jumped up to follow her and wouldn't stay outside the door. She had to let him come inside with her, so she leaned against the cool tile on the wall taking huge gulps of air while he pressed against her legs. After a few minutes, her stomach settled, and she tentatively bent to pat him on the head to reassure him. She splashed cold water on her face and returned to the living room with Robo at heel.

Stella remained on the sofa, and she searched Mattie's face as she took her seat. "Do you want me to fix you some more tea?"

Mattie shook her head. "I'll be all right."

Stella sat in silence, her lips pursed.

"I don't know whether to believe it. If he molested me, I don't remember it. But . . ."

Stella raised her brows. "But?"

Mattie took another deep breath. "I get these flashbacks. Just a bit here and there, nothing clear. I don't know what to believe."

"What do you remember?"

"Something he said. Not to tell or he'd kill my mother."

Mattie fixed her eyes on Stella's as if grasping for a lifeline. Stella didn't let her down; her gaze remained true and didn't waver.

"I don't know whether it's my imagination or not," Mattie said. "I don't know what to believe."

"You know that some victims of childhood abuse dissociate while it's happening, right?"

Mattie nodded.

"Could that be the case with you?"

Mattie shrugged, not sure if she wanted to admit to the possibility.

Stella paused, still holding eye contact. Finally, Mattie looked away.

"Mattie, I'm not an expert in these things, but I'll tell you this. Don't waste a lot of time denying it. The sooner you accept that it could be true, the sooner you can get some help."

"I don't even want to think about it." Robo had settled on the floor at her feet, and she leaned forward to stroke the fur on his head.

"I understand. But I don't think it's healthy to bury it, do you?"

She couldn't disagree, so she said nothing.

"You should work with someone, Mattie. Someone who can help you."

Exhaustion pressed down on her; she wanted to curl up on the sofa and go to sleep. "I can't talk about this anymore tonight. I've got to go to bed."

She stood and turned away, Robo dogging her tracks as she headed for her room.

"Sleep well, Mattie," Stella called after her. "Things will get better in time."

Mattie entered her bedroom, closing the door behind her and her dog. She opened her window an inch, climbed into bed fully clothed, and turned out the light. The last thing she heard upon closing her eyes was Robo's sigh as he settled.

Chapter 25

Tuesday

When Mattie returned from taking Robo on his morning run, Stella had already left, leaving folded blankets and sheets on the sofa. She fed Robo and grabbed an energy bar for herself, grateful that the nausea from yesterday seemed to have let up. The sleep of exhaustion apparently had done some good. She hurried to shower so she wouldn't arrive at the office too far behind Stella. Dressed in a khaki coverall with a Timber Creek County Sheriff Department emblem on the sleeve, she left the house well before the usual time, Robo cheerfully running ahead, eager to jump into their vehicle.

As she clocked in, Brody approached her. Apparently he'd come in before his shift started, too, not unusual for him. He frequently came in early and stayed late even though he clocked in and out when he was supposed to.

"You're with the sheriff and detective today," he said by way of turning over her duty assignment. "They're already in the briefing room."

"And you?"

He locked eyes with her. "I'm out."

So they'd decided to leave him out of the inner circle of the investigation. Probably the right move after the incident with Vasquez. "We'll touch base later," she said.

He nodded, giving her another long stare before turning away. What did that mean? She'd had enough experience with Brody sending her angry and resentful looks that she knew this one didn't fall into those categories. Was he asking for her to pass on information to him?

She walked past Rainbow, exchanging greetings with her.

"There's coffee and donuts in the briefing room already," Rainbow said. "I'm supposed to tell you to go in as soon as you can."

"Thanks."

When she entered the briefing room, Stella studied her and then nodded, as if she'd passed muster.

"Come have a seat, Deputy," McCoy said, pouring himself a cup of coffee from an insulated carafe and grabbing a donut. He waved toward the food and drink. "Help yourself."

"I was going over these phone records with Sheriff McCoy. I showed him the patterns I mentioned to you last night," Stella said, moving her finger across the top page in a stack. "Here, you can see what I'm talking about. I have the numbers that we're interested in highlighted in different colors, and this is the key for whom each number belongs to." She picked up a separate page and set it beside the stack for reference.

Mattie scanned the page, glancing at the reference list for orientation, noting the frequent calling back and forth between Adrienne and Vasquez. She removed the top page to expose the one below. "Did you find phone calls to or from Adrienne's old boyfriend, Jim Cameron, or her past employer, Scott Stroud?"

"No. Neither one of them had any contact with her by phone or e-mail. I think we can set them aside, at least for now." Stella tapped a set of three numbers she'd highlighted in yellow on the list of Adrienne's phone calls. "This number is worth our attention. It started showing up about four weeks ago. I used the cross directory to match the number with a name. It belongs to a landline assigned to a place called Dark Horse Stable. It isn't on our list of horse clients that we got from Dr. Walker."

Mattie remembered the name. *The nice lady with the sick horse.* "He mentioned the place to me yesterday afternoon. Said it's a new client, not near the trailheads we're looking at. It's still in a remote mountain location though. Adrienne didn't get a referral from him, and he thought the owner wouldn't have known her."

Stella nodded, thoughtful. "The only reason I think it's worth looking at is because she had horsehair on her clothing. These calls are spaced out, like they might have been setting up appointments weekly. And the last one was the Monday before our victim disappeared."

McCoy nodded. "I agree that it's worth following up. Do you plan to call them?" he asked Stella.

"I will. As soon as we finish up here."

Mattie felt the urge to meet this woman, go visit the property in person. "I'd like to go there, interview the owner face to face."

McCoy looked at Stella, as if deferring to her while Stella seemed to be thinking it over.

She raised an eyebrow. "That's an awfully long drive."

Her comment forced Mattie to think it through. She knew her need was more than idle curiosity. "Cole Walker has been going up the past few days to treat a sick horse for the owner, and she has yet to tell him that she'd been working with Adrienne. Surely she would have brought that up. And if she set up an appointment during that phone call last Monday, I think we need to know what day it was for. I feel better about doing this interview while we can read her face and her body language."

"You've got a point," Stella said. "We've got good circumstantial evidence against Vasquez at the moment, but it's best if we still look at everyone. I've got an examiner bringing a polygraph machine over this morning to interview him, and I've already drafted the questions I want to use. Can we get back here by eleven?"

"That should be no problem," Mattie said.

"Then I'll go with you."

They ended the meeting, and Stella followed Mattie and Robo to their SUV. Once they were buckled in, Stella gave Mattie one of her piercing looks. "Are you feeling better this morning?"

"I am, but I don't want to talk about it."

Stella looked out the window while Mattie fired up the engine and recorded the time in her trip log. In silence, they drove out of Timber Creek toward Dark Horse Stable.

Putting on her sunglasses, Mattie glanced at Stella. "Someone's going to have to keep Deputy Brody in the loop."

Stella nodded. "I'll take care of it."

And that appeared to be all they had to say to each other. The silence deepened as Mattie followed GPS guidance and turned the Explorer onto the county road that led into the mountains. When it came to not talking, she could outlast anyone, and she felt more comfortable with stillness than conversation.

After driving another forty-five minutes and following the road ever upward, they breached the final hill before going down into a draw that sheltered the stable. Forest surrounded them, making it impossible to catch more than a glimpse of the barn roof through the trees. Stella finally spoke. "This place is way the hell out of the way, isn't it?"

"It is."

"Where is the spot you found Adrienne's car in relationship to this place?"

"About twenty miles away and on a different county road south of here. No road connecting this place and that. You have to go back to the main highway and then south."

Mattie turned into the lane, taking the fork that led toward the barn.

"Someone's got money," Stella observed as they drove past the huge log house.

"I'd say so."

Stella frowned. "Let's take Robo when we go inside."

Mattie parked next to the barn's entrance. A Doberman lunged against a chain, barking and looking like something she didn't want Robo to tangle with. "All right. But let's get past that guard dog as quick as we can."

Mattie gave Robo a drink of water, put him into his working collar, and unloaded him. They weren't on an official sweep, so she refrained from revving him up with her voice. The guard dog went crazy, snarling and snapping, and she kept one eye on him to make sure his chain held while she led Robo into the barn. Robo darted glances at him, too, but for the most part did what he was trained to do: ignore other dogs. Mattie couldn't fault him for watching his own back.

When they reached the dim alleyway, Mattie let Robo's leash go slack, but he stayed close by her side at heel. *Either he's getting too well trained to search without command, or there's nothing here that sparks his interest.*

A man of Hispanic descent was mucking out a stall. He stopped and stared, his eyes taking in Mattie and Stella with a glance, fastening on Robo for a few seconds, and then darting down the alleyway. The fearful expression on his face seemed to indicate he might be looking for help. He had on worn denims, a sweat-stained straw cowboy hat, and cowboy boots.

"Hello." Mattie went on to introduce herself and Stella.

He shook his head, indicating he didn't comprehend, so Mattie switched to Spanish, repeated the introduction, and asked him his name.

"Juan Fiero." He clutched the pitchfork and averted his gaze when she offered a handshake but then took hers in a limp grasp. The proximity brought a whiff of stale cigarette smoke on his breath.

"I'll get the boss," he said in Spanish, turning on his heel and heading down the alleyway.

Mattie exchanged a glance with Stella as he left. "Cowboy boots and a cigarette smoker," she muttered.

"You've just described about half the cowboys in Colorado," Stella responded, keeping her voice low. "But I get what you're saying."

A beautiful, petite woman with black hair and dark eyes hurried toward them in lithe strides while Juan disappeared through another door down the way. She wore riding breeches and a fitted brown jacket that flattered her form. No wonder Cole seemed to be taken with her.

She introduced herself as Carmen Santiago, returning Mattie's handshake with a firm grip. "What a beautiful shepherd," she said, bending toward Robo while looking at Mattie. "May I pet him?"

A glance at Robo showed him alert and receptive, ears pricked as he watched the new person. "Yes, he won't mind," Mattie said. "It's okay, Robo."

"What happened to his shoulder?"

"Got in a fight," Mattie said, not wanting to get into details.

"Oh my, you beautiful young man. You shouldn't do that kind of thing," Carmen murmured while petting Robo and setting his tail in motion. She straightened. "To what do I owe the pleasure?"

Mattie noticed that her smile seemed warm and genuine.

"We're here to talk with you about Adrienne Howard," Stella said.

The smile dropped from Carmen's face, replaced by a frown of concern. "I read in the paper that she died last week. A tragedy."

"Did you know her?" Stella asked.

"Yes. She was doing massage on some of my horses, although she'd only come up here three times. I didn't know her well."

"When did you last speak with her?" Stella asked.

She seemed to search her memory. "I'm not sure. I think it was Monday or Tuesday of last week."

"What did you talk about?"

"We made an appointment for her to come back. I train racehorses, and I decided to make massage a part of my program. I didn't have enough time or visits to evaluate the value of that decision."

Mattie remembered Cole saying that employing a massage therapist to work on a horse tipped the owner into the kind and caring category. She hated to admit it, but so far this woman seemed to fit the mold.

"What day did you schedule Ms. Howard's return appointment?" Stella asked.

"For Friday. It was the same day I read about her death in the paper." Sorrow touched her face. "That was also the day my stallion, Diablo, got sick. Such a bad day."

"I'm sorry to hear that," Mattie said. "How is your horse now?"

"Not well. Dr. Walker is . . . Do you know him?" She looked at Mattie.

"I do."

"Is he good at his business?" she asked, a frown of concern creasing her brow.

"I think so. Everyone says so," Mattie said.

"Dr. Walker is taking care of Diablo, but he's not sure what's wrong. We're treating symptoms as they arise." She shook her head. "My horse doesn't seem to be getting any better."

Mattie could relate to the woman's concern for her animal. "I hope things turn around soon."

Carmen nodded, giving a sad, resigned smile.

"Did Ms. Howard say anything to you about her plans for Wednesday when you spoke with her?" Stella asked.

"No, not at all. She offered a Friday appointment time, and I took it."

"Did she ever speak about plans for her time off on Wednesday afternoon or another client stable that she might visit?"

Carmen shook her head slowly while thinking. "No. I'm sorry, but I don't know anything regarding her schedule or her plans."

"Did your employee, Mr. Fiero, meet Ms. Howard?" Stella asked.

Carmen lifted a hand in a graceful gesture of correction. "I guess you could say they met, although not formally. I worked with Adrienne on the horses while Juan held them or led them to the stocks."

Mattie thought it could be considered odd that the hired man wasn't introduced to Adrienne, but possibly not, considering the language barrier. "Did they share any conversations?" she asked.

"Juan doesn't speak English. As far as I know, Adrienne didn't appear to speak Spanish, so I would guess not," Carmen said.

"Could we talk to him?" Stella asked.

Mattie was glad that the detective hadn't decided to dismiss her concern about boots and cigarettes.

"But he doesn't speak English," Carmen said.

"I can translate," Mattie said.

Carmen looked at her and nodded. "Then of course. I'll go get him."

As she left, Mattie noticed Robo sniffing at the doorway of the stall Juan had been cleaning. Spotting a cigarette butt, she snatched a plastic baggie from her utility belt, turned it inside out, and picked the butt off the ground without touching it with her hand. After zipping the bag shut, she stuffed it into her pocket. She also saw where Juan had left a boot print, clear and clean. Mattie took out her pen and laid it on the ground beside the print.

"I'm going to take a picture of this, just in case," she told Stella, taking her phone out to snap the photo. By the time Carmen returned with Juan, both phone and pen were back inside her pocket.

The hired man trailed behind Carmen. His eyes darted from Mattie to Stella, looking like a mouse caught in a dodgy situation between two cats.

Ears pricked, Robo took a step toward Fiero as he approached, and the man froze, eyeing her dog. Mattie took note of Robo's reaction, wondering if there was something about the man's scent that alerted him.

In Spanish, Mattie told Juan that they would like to ask him a few questions. At that point, she assumed the role of translator, allowing Stella to take over.

"We need to talk to you about Adrienne Howard, Mr. Fiero," Stella said. "I understand you worked with her here on the horses."

Fiero glanced at Carmen, and she nodded encouragement for him to answer.

"*Si,*" he said.

"How long did you work together?"

"Three times," he said, holding up three fingers.

"What was your role when she came here?"

"I held the horses."

"Did she show you how to massage them?"

He looked at Mattie, telling her he didn't understand. She rephrased the question to: "Did she teach you how to rub the horses?" and moved her hands in a circular motion.

"Oh," he said, nodding at Stella. "*Si.*"

"How many horses did you work with?" Stella asked.

"Four."

"How many hours would you work with the horses together when she came?"

He appeared to think prior to responding. "Two hours."

"Did you get to know her?"

"*Si.*"

"What did you think of her?" Stella asked.

He spread his hands. "Smart lady. Very good. Very kind."

"Were you attracted to her?"

He frowned in a quizzical way when Mattie translated. She rephrased using the word love. His expression changed to shock. "No, no. I'm a married man."

Carmen shifted, obviously uncomfortable with the tack the interrogation had taken. "Why are you asking him this? He had nothing to do with this woman's death."

"Is your wife living here with you?"

His eyes darted to Carmen. "No," he said.

"Where does she live?"

"Mexico." He paused and then added. "Juárez."

"Do you have family? Children?" Stella asked.

"Four kids."

"I bet you miss them," Stella said.

He glanced at Carmen again. "Yes, very much."

"When will you go back to Juárez?"

He shrugged, and his eyes traveled to Carmen, evidently passing the question to her.

"He has a one-year work visa," Carmen said. "We've been here three months."

"Are you two related to each other?" Stella asked Carmen.

"No, we are not."

"How did he end up here working for you?"

"He worked for my family in Juárez."

Stella continued to focus on Carmen. "Who has ownership of this operation?"

"I don't see how that applies to this business of Adrienne Howard," Carmen said.

"Humor me. I can find out with a simple computer search."

Carmen shrugged. "My uncle owns the stable. I'm in charge."

"What's your uncle's name?"

Carmen shifted her feet. "Javier Santiago."

"So let me see if I understand this right. Mr. Fiero worked for Mr. Javier Santiago prior to coming here on a work visa to work for you?"

"Yes." Carmen said.

"And are you from Juárez, too, Ms. Santiago?"

"My mother is a United States citizen, as am I."

Stella nodded slowly and then focused her attention back on Juan. "Where were you Wednesday afternoon, Mr. Fiero?"

"He was here, working," Carmen said.

Stella shot a glance at Carmen. "Please let Mr. Fiero answer the questions that I ask him."

Carmen frowned, waving a hand toward Juan.

After Mattie translated the question, his reply echoed Carmen's almost exactly. It made Mattie wonder how much English the man actually understood.

"Mr. Fiero, do you know anything about the death of Adrienne Howard?"

He looked toward Carmen even before Mattie could translate.

"Please forgive me for interrupting again, Detective," Carmen said, her face consumed with apprehension, "but this man has nothing at all do with Ms. Howard other than to hold horses for her to work on. I must express my concern at your line of interrogation."

"It seems to me that he knows Ms. Howard better than you think," Stella said. "Were you with them the entire time she worked on the horses? The full six hours during the three visits?"

Confusion mixed with the concern in Carmen's expression. "Not entirely, I suppose. I was riding the horses to warm them up before the massage. But the two of them don't speak the same language. How well could they know each other?" Looking at Mattie, she held her hands out in a helpless gesture.

"He might know more English than he lets on," Mattie said, observing Juan to see his reaction. His expression became a mask as he stared at the ground.

"Ms. Santiago, do you know anything about Ms. Howard's death?"

"Absolutely not!" Anger chased surprise across her face. Taking a deep breath, she visibly worked to control her emotions, and she spoke with conviction. "We work here with the horses every day. We don't even go into town. I was as shocked as anyone by Adrienne's death, and neither Juan nor I know anything about it. I'm sorry, because I would like to help you with your investigation, but I cannot."

Stella studied the woman while she took her time extracting a business card from her pocket. "All right, Ms. Santiago. I appreciate your cooperation. If you think of anything that might help us, please call me."

Mattie saw nothing but sincerity in Carmen's steady gaze. "I will. But I assure you, we barely even knew her. We can offer no help."

Mattie and Robo followed Stella out of the building. While Mattie loaded him into his compartment, Stella stood beside the SUV, scanning the property and taking in the layout of track, house, barn, and outbuildings. Then they climbed into their seats.

"What do you think?" Stella asked Mattie, as she fastened her seat belt.

"There's a strange dynamic between Carmen and her hired man. It's almost like she's protecting him from something."

"Maybe an immigration issue?"

"I don't think so. She brought up the work visa. I don't think she would have mentioned it to a couple cops if she didn't have her paperwork in order."

"Agreed. Does that boot print look the same as the partial we have?"

"It's hard to tell, but I'm inclined to say yes. But most cowboy boot prints look alike."

"If it matches for size, let's see if we can get a warrant. There's something about this place that makes me want to jump right in and search."

Robo poked his nose through the heavy mesh of his cage when Stella said the magic *S*-word.

Mattie nodded toward him. "Robo agrees with that," she said, starting up the Explorer and shifting it into gear. "Let's go back and send the photo of this print to your lab."

Chapter 26

It seemed like breakfast had set a good tone for the day, better at least than the fiasco from yesterday. Angela had shown up at the table dressed appropriately, though she made a show of saying very little and eating even less. Cole tried to bring her into the conversation but soon gave it up. He could lead a filly to water but could not make her drink. The last thing he'd said to the girls as they left was a promise to meet them after school, like he'd done yesterday.

The morning went by quickly, and as he finished up in the exam room, Tess put a piece of paper on the shelf at the pass through. "Your lab results on Diablo are in."

"Thank you." He scanned the results, searching first for the Clenbuterol screen. He felt a tug at his stomach as he read the number, seeing it was well above therapeutic level. *Shit.* Trace was right—this horse was evidently toxic from dosing with Clenbuterol. And this blood had been drawn several days after Carmen presumably stopped dosing the poor horse. How high would the number have been if he'd tested for it on the first day?

"Did we get that medication order I put in this morning?" he asked Tess, referring to the drug Trace had recommended to counteract the adrenergic effects of the Clenbuterol.

"Yes, the pharmacy courier just dropped it off."

"I need to take it with me. I'll grab some lunch, go up to Dark Horse Stable, and be back by three to meet the kids when they come home from school. Office hours again from four 'til six?"

"You caught a break today. They're only 'til five."

"Great. Feel free to go home when you've finished your work here."

Cole drove down the lane to the house. After parking in front, he dashed in to grab a late lunch. Mrs. Gibbs had already made a sandwich for him, and she was setting it on the table when he entered the kitchen.

"Thank you, Mrs. Gibbs," he said, going to the fridge to grab a soda. "I appreciate you more than I can say. I'm on the run, but I plan to be back in time to meet the kids after school. Office hours are only until five today, so I shouldn't be late for dinner like I was yesterday."

Mrs. Gibbs came to the table and took a seat opposite from him. Cole knew she wanted to say something, but he didn't have the time to sit and wait for it. She'd have to say her piece while he ate.

"I know our young miss is still angry with me. I'm afraid she doesn't want me here," Mrs. Gibbs said.

"I think she's more mad at me right now than she is at you. Today was a little better than yesterday. Maybe she'll have cooled off by this afternoon."

She rested her chin on her hand, evidently pondering that for a moment. "Maybe so. I want to work through this, but I don't want to overstay my welcome if it's not working out for you."

"I hope you're not thinking of leaving us."

"What I'm saying is, I can leave if you think I'm creating more grief for Angela than it's worth."

Cole sat back in his chair, finishing up the last bite of the sandwich that he'd just inhaled. "Let's put it this way: you're worth a lot to me. Our house is running smoothly, for the most part. If this puts too much stress on you, I'd understand if you wanted to leave. But I'd hate to see you go."

"Ach! I raised two daughters, you know. I'm used to their hysterics. But I do worry about Angela and wonder where her head is in all this turmoil she's facing."

"I do, too. In fact, I think I'll talk to her school counselor about it. See if she has any advice for me."

Mrs. Gibbs face lit. "That's a fine idea. She might help us with a way to connect with her."

Cole stood up from the table, picking up his soda can to take with him. "I'm sorry I have to eat and run, but I better get on the road if I'm going to get back by three. I'll call if something comes up and I can't make it. I promised Angela that I would last night, and I intend to keep that promise. I might not be able to spend as much time here at home as I'd like, but I can at least keep you posted if something comes up to change my schedule."

Mrs. Gibbs stood, following him to the sink as he carried his plate to it. "Raising children is not easy, Dr. Walker, and I can see you're working hard at it. You're doing a fine job. You should know that."

Cole paused a moment before going out the door. "Thank you, Mrs. Gibbs. I appreciate you saying that. Sometimes I feel like I can't win for losing."

She chuckled. "Some days are like that, I think. See you at three."

As Cole climbed into the truck, he counted his lucky stars. He'd found a diamond in Mrs. Gibbs. He hoped he could work through this rough patch with Angela and keep them both happy.

★

The hard plastic chair supported Mattie as she slumped down at the table with Stella and the sheriff. Robo circled and lay down at her side. Things weren't going quite as they'd expected.

"Ramon Vasquez passed the lie-detector test with flying colors," Stella said. "That alone doesn't prove he's innocent, but I also heard back from my lab. The boot print we have on file doesn't look like a match for either pair of boots we sent in."

"He might have disposed of the boots he wore at the gravesite," McCoy said.

"True. But my tech said his boots both appear to be wider through the toe than the partial Mattie found. They still haven't compared the print we just sent in for Fiero. They'll get to it as soon as they can."

"So we don't have enough hard evidence to press charges against Vasquez for Adrienne Howard's murder," McCoy said. "We'll have to set him free."

"What about the bow we found at his place?" Mattie asked.

"The medical examiner believes it could be the weapon if it was used at close range, but he can't testify that it was the exact cause of death. We don't have the arrow that killed her, so we can't match it to his supply."

"Jack Kelly from Green Thumb Organics learned about Adrienne's death from Jim Cameron," Mattie said. "And he confirmed that he's the one who broke the news to Vasquez. He says Ramon took it hard."

The door opened in the back of the room, and Mattie turned to see who it was. Brody, frustration wrapped around him like a cloak, entered the room and approached the table.

"I need to talk to you. All of you," Brody said, his eyes an icy blue that sent a chill through Mattie when they touched her.

"What do you want to say, Deputy?" McCoy asked.

"You can't shut me out like this. I need to be a part of this investigation."

"After your behavior yesterday, I think it's best that you be excluded from these briefings," Stella said, locking eyes with Brody. "I'll meet with you afterwards to update you."

"That's bullshit. My duty logs and GPS covered my alibi, so I'm off the suspect list. I can help." His eyes softened slightly as he turned away from Stella to appeal to the sheriff.

"I need to help. I'll control my temper."

Stella waved a hand toward Mattie. "And that's why Deputy Cobb has a black eye? Because you were able to control your temper?"

Mattie needed to speak up. "Chief Deputy Brody didn't mean to hurt me. I think he deserves a second chance. Keeping him out of the loop only leads to misunderstandings."

Brody threw Mattie a grateful glance before turning back to Stella. "All I can do is prove to you I can stay in control. Not knowing the full picture on this is driving me crazy. It won't happen again."

"You're damn right it won't happen again," Stella said, staring him down. "What's your opinion, Sheriff?"

Mattie realized that deferring to the sheriff was a way for the detective to back off while saving face. Maybe it meant something to Stella when Mattie had vouched for Brody.

Sheriff McCoy studied the chief deputy in silence while Brody met McCoy's gaze without animosity.

McCoy finally spoke. "Do I have your word that you'll behave with the conduct expected from an officer of your caliber, Chief Deputy Brody?"

"Yes, sir," Brody said.

McCoy continued to examine Brody for another drawn-out minute. "Detective LoSasso, I believe this man deserves to know," he said, finally coming to a decision. "Take a seat here at the table."

Robo had been watching the entire exchange while lying at Mattie's feet, ears pricked and mouth open in a slight pant. Her dog didn't seem to miss much when emotions were high, and arguing tended to create stress for him. In reality, she might have to admit that arguments caused stress for her, and her feelings went right to Robo. She was glad she'd taken the time after work yesterday to assure him that Brody meant her no harm, and he'd stayed out of the mix during the discussion. Robo was also proving himself capable of conduct becoming of an officer.

Brody leaned against the table behind them. "Thank you, Sheriff. I won't let you down."

"I'm sure you won't," McCoy said.

"You'd better not, that's all I can say," Stella said, crossing her arms and closing the subject. "Brody, we're going to have to release Vasquez. Not enough evidence and we can't tie in the bow as the murder weapon."

Brody set his jaw and nodded.

"The polygraph confirmed the information that he's given us about the Howard family dynamics. Do you know anything more about this?"

"Adrienne didn't talk about her family. I didn't know anything about them prior to her death." Brody crossed his arms over his chest as he leaned against the table, a relaxed posture that Mattie knew was all show. Beneath it lurked a temperament that was wound pretty tight.

"We're working on another suspect," Mattie said. "Juan Fiero at Dark Horse Stable. Did Adrienne mention him or her work there?"

Brody shook his head. "What made you look at him?"

"Phone calls on Adrienne's call list led us to the stable. Robo's nose, and I guess Mattie's too, led us to him," Stella said.

Mattie explained about the cigarette butt and boot print. "Stella questioned both of them, and it seemed like Santiago was protecting Fiero from something."

"Fiero doesn't speak English, so Mattie translated. His story didn't quite match up to Santiago's. He seemed to know Adrienne better than his boss thought he could. She seemed to think the language barrier would get in the way."

Brody's eyebrows rose. "Adrienne spoke Spanish."

Mattie's mind jumped to the next conclusion: Fiero and Adrienne had visited with each other while Carmen exercised the horses.

"Adrienne was fluent in Spanish," Brody continued.

"And I had the impression that Fiero knew more English than he was letting on," Mattie said. "The two of them could have definitely held conversations. Conversations that didn't include his boss."

Brody nodded, apparently taking in the information and thinking it through. Moving out of his relaxed pose, he straightened, and Mattie could feel the tension rolling through him. "What do you suggest we do next?" he asked in a calm voice.

"We sent the boot print photo to our CSI unit to compare with the partial Mattie found at the crime scene," Stella said. "We should hear back on that any minute. If it matches for shape or size, we'll try to get a search warrant and go back to Dark Horse to take a look."

Chapter 27

While Cole drove up into the mountains toward Dark Horse Stable, his thoughts turned to Carmen. What was he going to say to the trainer? He needed to confront her on the issue of dosing and let her know that he planned to report her to the racing commission. No one should be allowed to do this to a horse and get away with it.

He began to wish he'd asked Tess to ride along and make this call with him. He couldn't predict how Carmen would react, especially after she'd made a pass at him. It seemed silly, but a veterinarian became vulnerable when working alone on house calls without a witness.

He also imagined that she might deny the accusation. If so, he'd have to do the best he could to document the conversation. Well, he didn't have time to change the situation now. The log arch that marked Dark Horse was a welcome sight; he could quit thinking about the confrontation and get on with it.

After parking, he gathered his equipment and the new medication, walked past the barking Bruno, and entered the barn. For a change, no one was waiting for him. He paused outside Diablo's stall, remembering the other horse down at the end. He wondered if that red chestnut, like Diablo, had been dosed with the concentrated form of Clenbuterol. He placed his kit beside the stall door and hurried down the alley.

When he reached the last stall on the left, he peeked over the door. What he saw confirmed his suspicion and made him sick to his stomach. The gorgeous red thoroughbred trudged along a worn path that was about six inches lower than the rest of the bedding. He'd obviously been circling like this for days. His sweat-drenched coat appeared dull and lifeless. His sunken eyes spoke volumes, delivering a message of fatigue and anxiety.

Good God, why didn't I come down and check on this horse sooner?

"Doctor!" Carmen called from only about ten feet away, making Cole jump. He hadn't realized she was behind him. "What are you doing?"

Cole faced her. "I ran a test on Diablo's blood for Clenbuterol. It came back positive. You're dosing these horses."

A variety of expressions chased across her face: surprise, anger, deception. "I don't know what you're talking about."

"I think you do. Frog juice."

"Frog juice?"

"I brought the proper medication to counteract Clenbuterol toxicity. We need to get Diablo started on it. And you need to stop dosing this chestnut horse right now," Cole said, and he walked toward Diablo's stall.

She remained silent while he picked up his things, and she followed him inside the box stall. Diablo was lying down, an emaciated version of the horse he'd been a few days ago. The easy boots were in place on his feet; plentiful grass hay wisped over the edge of his feeder.

"Has he stopped eating?" Cole asked.

"Pretty much." Now she seemed shut down and sullen.

"Will he get up?" Cole started drawing the proper dosage of the new med into a syringe. He bent over Diablo and injected it quickly, sending out a request to the powers that be that it wasn't too late to do some good.

"We had him up about an hour ago. He drank some water."

"When did you stop giving him the frog juice?"

"I don't know what you're talking about."

Her refusal to acknowledge the truth and give him the medical information he needed infuriated him. "This horse could die. As it is now, you risk losing your trainer's license. Do you want to face animal abuse charges on top of that?"

She shot him a venomous look. "I have nothing to do with these accusations. I need to question my employees."

"Your employees dosed this horse without your knowledge? I find that hard to believe."

"What is the plan to make Diablo well?"

"I'll leave this medication for you. Otherwise, we need to continue as we have been, supporting him and working through the symptoms. He's probably got damage to his liver, kidneys, and heart. What were you thinking? That it would increase his endurance?"

She stared at him, her face expressionless.

"This drug can break down muscle tissue and compromise vital organs." Cole typically tried to educate clients, but this made him mad enough to lash out. "Dosing horses with it is illegal and cruel."

"I believe Juan is the one you should speak with about this. I'll go find him." She went to the door of the box stall and let herself out.

Right . . . pass the buck. Cole tried to put a damper on his fury and looked around the stall. He went to the hayrack to check the quality of hay and to make sure there was no alfalfa in it. Scooping the hay away from the wall, he examined the dry grass, noticing it was of excellent quality, weed and alfalfa free. He was about to replace it when his eye caught a glint of white from behind the rack.

Peering into the crack, he saw something with a black-and-white pattern. As his eyes adjusted to the poor lighting in the narrow space, he realized he was looking at a laptop computer. With a zebra-striped cover.

His memory clicked on an image of Adrienne Howard typing information into a laptop like that. And he remembered Mattie asking him about Adrienne's missing computer.

He reached into the narrow space. Barely able to grasp the plastic case, he pulled out the laptop and stared at it. *This must belong to Adrienne.*

Did someone put it here? Did she?

The stall door flew open and Juan Fiero dashed inside, frantic. "You must come with me, Doctor. Hurry. She's going to kill you," he said in English.

"What?"

"There's no time to talk. Come with me."

Knowing that the man's panic was real, Cole followed, placing the laptop into the front of his coverall and zipping it in tightly against his chest. Juan ran a few doors down the alley to the opposite side and tugged open a door. He led Cole into a room filled with hay bales.

"There is a door to the outside there," Juan said, pointing. "It's the back side of the barn. Go! She killed the lady. She wants to kill you!"

Stunned, Cole tried to process what he was being told. "Carmen killed Adrienne?"

Juan's eyes darted to the inside door and back. "No time to talk. Get away! Go to the top of the ridge. You can use a cell phone up there."

Cole's thoughts were hazy. Juan began pushing him across the room toward the outside door, his hands shaking with urgency. Cole felt the man's terror, making him believe what he'd said.

"Stop!" Carmen stood inside the doorway, the alley at her back, an evil-looking crossbow in her hands. Cole froze, staring at her as she raised the bow and sighted through the scope. Juan pushed him outside the back door, shouting as he slammed the door shut behind him, "Lock the door! Run!"

Cole stumbled out onto a rocky verge scraped up around the barn's foundation. He had the presence of mind to process Juan's last instruction, even as he heard the man's scream and a thud. He found the latch that secured the door from the outside and slammed the heavy bolt in place.

My God! What the hell's happening? But even with shock making his thoughts disjointed and confused, his instinct for survival kicked in. He scanned his environment: heavy forest upslope about fifty yards. Running for all he was worth, he headed toward the trees.

★

Mattie completed her reports and looked at the clock. Shortly after three. Stella's lab hadn't called back yet on the boot print, and she was tired of waiting. She decided to call Cole to see if he could share any impressions of Juan Fiero. She swiped to her quick-dial list and pressed Cole's cell phone number. She listened to a few dial tones and a click before hearing a female voice answer: "Timber Creek Veterinary Clinic. This is Tess."

Mattie identified herself. "I'm trying to reach Dr. Walker."

"Hi, Mattie. He must be out of cell phone range. Your call transferred to the office."

"Oh. Do you know when he'll be back?"

"He went up to Dark Horse Stable. Actually, he should be home any minute."

A twinge of anxiety worked its way into Mattie's chest.

"He wanted to be home in time to meet the kids after school," Tess continued. "I'm surprised he isn't within cell phone range yet. Do you want me to leave him a message to call you?"

"Tell him to call my cell; he has the number."

"All righty. Talk to you later."

Mattie disconnected the call and took a long breath. The people at Dark Horse had set off her radar. If Cole didn't call back soon, she would try to reach him again.

She went to Stella's office to see if she'd heard from her lab yet. She tapped on the door and entered the room. Stella looked up from her computer.

"I just tried to reach Cole Walker, and his assistant told me he went to Dark Horse this afternoon," Mattie said. "He's late getting back."

Stella nodded, a furrow of concern creasing her brow. "I'll call and build a fire under my CSI unit. I expected them to call back by now." Her cell phone rang, making her pull it out of her pocket and look at the caller ID. "That's them now. Hold on a minute."

Mattie listened to Stella's side of the conversation while a sense of urgency tightened her chest.

"Okay," Stella was saying, summing up the information with the CSI tech for clarification while stating the information for Mattie. "So you're saying that you can't say the boot prints are the same size since one is a partial, but the toe prints match exactly. You're extracting the shape and sole information that you have to see if you can determine the brand of boot that made it. But since the sole is flat and has no tread marks, you consider being able to do that a long shot."

Stella listened, nodding at what she was hearing.

"Okay. See what else you can do," she said, ending the call. She looked up at Mattie. "Toe shape is as close as we can get on that print match, but it's close enough to give us probable cause. I'll get the sheriff started on that search warrant."

Stella headed for McCoy's office while anxiety circled Mattie's chest. She knew her brain had taken a leap from a match on a toe print to labeling Fiero a killer, but she couldn't help herself. The thought of Cole inadvertently walking into a dangerous situation—a situation that she should have uncovered sooner and warned him about—made her shoot into red alert.

She needed to go now and see if she could find him; she couldn't wait the hour it would take to get a warrant. She started after Stella when her cell phone rang.

Relief melted through her when caller ID told her the call came from the Walker residence. But when she answered the phone and heard Angela's voice coming through the receiver, her relief was short-lived.

"Mattie?" Angela asked, her voice sounding high-pitched and tight.

"Yes, Angie. Is something wrong?"

"I don't know. Dad said he'd be here by three and he's thirty minutes late. Tess says she expected him back about an hour ago."

Mattie's throat tightened. "Okay."

"Dad told us this morning that he'd always let us know if he was going to be late. He made a big deal of it, you know. And . . . well, I'm worried that something happened to him."

Mattie knew Cole Walker, and a promise to his children would not be something made lightly. "I talked to Tess about twenty minutes ago. Have you talked to her since then?"

"Just now. Right before I called you."

"And she hasn't heard from your dad yet?" Mattie knew the answer but needed to confirm.

"No. I asked Mrs. Gibbs to drive me up toward Dark Horse Stable to look for him, but she suggested I call you instead."

"She's right. I'm glad you did. You girls need to stay put in case your dad calls. Call me immediately if he does. I'll drive up that way and find him. Maybe he had a flat tire outside of cell phone range or something. I'll let you know as soon as I can."

"Okay." Angela still sounded frightened.

"I'm sure your dad's fine, Angie. Don't worry so much. You'll hear from one of us soon."

Mattie tried to reassure the girl before disconnecting the call, but she couldn't damper her own alarm bells. With Robo following, she went directly into McCoy's office and summarized the situation for him and Stella.

"He's an hour late now," Mattie said. "I think under the circumstances, I'd better drive up that way and see if I can find him." Not intending to wait for permission, Mattie turned to leave.

"I'll go with you," Stella said, falling in behind Robo.

"Get Deputy Brody to go along as back up," McCoy said. "I'll get this warrant request over to the judge and meet you up there."

Chapter 28

Cole sprinted up the hillside. Adrienne's laptop felt bulky against his chest, and he worried that it would slow him down, but he didn't dare leave it where Carmen might find it. This piece of evidence proved that Adrienne had been at Dark Horse Stable on the day she died.

If only I can get out of here and get it to Mattie.

He crossed the fifty yards of open space and reached the tree line in seconds. Pine, spruce, and large boulders gave him enough shelter to slow down and think. He ducked in behind a ponderosa, turning back to look at the barn. No one was following.

He patted his shirt pocket. *I left my cell phone in the truck!* It felt like a nightmare. Juan said that Carmen killed Adrienne. And she seemed willing to kill again. He'd seen her sight down a crossbow at him before Juan shoved him out the door. The disturbing image was burned into his memory.

Had Juan stopped her? He remembered the man's scream. No, he'd taken the bolt meant for Cole. Carmen was still out there.

The open space between him and the barn remained still and lifeless. A hawk wheeled overhead and screeched a haunting call. Could he circle back to his truck?

Suddenly, the Doberman pinscher tore around the edge of the barn, dragging Carmen on the end of his leash. She carried the crossbow and a quiver of bolts on her back. She directed the dog straight to the hay room door. The Doberman swept the area with his nose as he went.

Good Lord! She's using the dog to track me.

Cole gave up all hope of reaching his truck. Maybe he could sneak around Carmen and beat her to his vehicle, but there was no way could he outrun that dog. He snatched the laptop from inside his coverall, scooped aside pine needles, and buried the computer at the base of the tree, making sure it was well hidden by the needles.

Turning away from the barn, he dashed upslope, running as fast as he could, dodging through the trees. The more distance between them the better, but still, he knew he couldn't outrun Bruno. He hoped Carmen would keep him on the leash—anything to slow him down.

Even so, he had to think of something else—something besides running.

Finding a game trail allowed him to increase his speed, and he did a quick mental assessment of his assets. The only thing he had with him that he could use as a weapon was the Leatherman he always carried in his coverall pocket.

He heard the deadly clunk of the crossbow before he felt the searing pain in his arm. The bolt flew past and thudded into a tree. Blood trickled from his left upper arm. He grabbed at the wound where the steel tip had grazed him, trying to stop the blood from leaving a trail on the ground.

Topping a rise and going down the other side for cover, he jerked a bandanna from his back pocket. He wrapped it around his arm, using his teeth to help tie it snug. He kept running and almost stepped on a dead coyote, a wicked crossbow bolt lodged in its side, surrounded by darkened, bloody fur. The stench of decomposition stifled his breath.

She's been using the animals for target practice. And it looks like she's a damn good shot!

Grabbing the bolt, he ripped it from the half-rotten carcass, the razor-sharp broadhead tip coming with it. He'd gained a weapon, for whatever it was worth. He tucked it into a loop on his pants leg.

He searched his surroundings, looking for a good place to get off the game trail. He needed more rocky terrain. There, near a large boulder, he found what he was looking for: shale and flat stones leading into some scrub. He leaped from stone to stone. He grabbed onto prickly rose branches to pull himself up and into the shrubs, the barbs drawing blood that blossomed bright red on his palms.

The Doberman's sharp, staccato bark wafted upslope on a chill breeze. Cole realized he was downwind from the dog. Thank God Mattie had told him about wind interference. How could he use it?

Being downwind was a lucky break. At least the breeze wouldn't carry his scent back to the dog. Cole needed to head across the slope. He paused, thinking of the coyote carcass. Maybe he could use the heavy scent of decomp to distort his trail and slow down the dog.

Leaping back along the stones, he retraced his steps to the dead animal. He picked it up by the shoulders, dragging it along as he backed toward the shale. He rubbed the carcass over his own steps while struggling to keep the decaying flesh intact. When he reached the stones, he arranged the carcass to look as natural as possible, as if it had died in place. After rubbing scent from his hands along the soles of his boots, he crossed over the shale and sprinted through timber.

Spotting a limber pine, he pulled his Leatherman out of his pocket and opened a blade. Taking mere seconds, he sliced a heavily needled bough and stuffed it down the back of his bib overall to block his shirt from sight. Closing the blade on his Leatherman, he continued to run, stuffing the tool into his pocket.

His breath was starting to recover from his mad dash uphill, but he knew he needed to head back upslope gradually to use the wind factor to his advantage. Branches scratched his arms as he sped through the trees. He angled his direction uphill, his feet pounding the rocky surface. Knowing his endurance wouldn't allow him to run uphill forever, he started to think about what kind of terrain would be best to take a stand. He would need the element of surprise to set up an ambush.

The Doberman barked, the sound coming from much more near than Cole expected. His attempt to sully his trail with the coyote's strong scent might have slowed the dog, but it didn't throw him off the trail. He tried to run faster, but his legs were getting tired.

He came upon a shallow stream. *This can mask my scent.* Running full tilt, he leaped into the frigid water. Its icy fingers snatched at his ankles and snaked into his boots, taking away what little breath he had left. Gasping, he jogged upstream, bending to scoop a handful of mud that he smeared on the front of his shirt and as far as he could reach in the back. Another palmful covered the bright blue color he'd been worried about. He smeared it on his face as well.

The Doberman continued to bark, and it sounded like he was closing in. Slogging through the cold water, Cole realized he was almost spent. He needed an area of limited access with protection at his back. Maybe a cave? Too dangerous. He needed a back door for escape.

Scanning the forest in quick snatches, he took his eye off his footing for a split second. His foot slipped off a smooth, wet stone in the streambed, and his boot lodged between two rocks. Pain shot through his ankle. *Shit!*

Cursing himself, he pulled his boot from where it was wedged and hobbled onward. Frigid water swirled up to his calves, numbing the pain. One moment of inattention could be the difference between life and death. Now he'd be forced to find a place to hole up.

Digging deep, Cole trudged uphill. He came upon another dead and decaying animal with a bolt in its ribcage, this time a deer. A crash behind him made him whirl. He prepared for the worst but spotted a buck coming through the trees. The large deer charged past and continued uphill.

He's running from the dog, too.

Breath heaving, Cole stopped, deciding this was a good place to leave the water. As he went up the bank, he yanked the limber pine bough out of the back of his coverall and used it to wipe away his footprints. He rubbed the branch against the deer to load it with the scent of decomposition and repeated his action. After swiping his boots over the carcass a few times, he limped across slope, finding easier footing and hoping to catch his breath.

If he could ditch the dog, he might have a chance. He doubted Carmen could track him herself, but who knew? If only he could stay alive until darkness fell, maybe he could hike out to the road overnight. But first he needed to stabilize his ankle.

Pushing himself, he limped upslope at the fastest pace he could manage.

How fit was Carmen Santiago? Could she follow him up this severe grade at the pace he'd set? Was the Doberman still on a leash, or had she turned him loose to chase Cole through the forest?

The Doberman barked again, this time from a little farther away. Buoyed by hope that the buck had distracted the dog, Cole decided to keep pushing uphill. After a while, he spotted what he'd been searching for—a rocky cliff face that led up to a ridge. It looked like something he could scale, and it would afford a vantage point. The boulders would provide shelter from both front and back, and it would be steep enough to at least slow down the dog. He would climb close enough to the top to provide a back door getaway if he needed it.

Grabbing onto a handhold, he started to climb, gritting his teeth against the pain.

Chapter 29

With blue lights still flashing, Mattie's SUV sped down the lane toward Dark Horse Stable. Her vehicle rocked as she came to a sudden stop beside Cole's truck. It was sitting out front with its hood up.

"I wonder why he didn't call home to let them know he was stuck up here with engine trouble," Stella grumbled under her breath.

Mattie withheld her own frustration as she shut down her engine and stepped out of her vehicle. Brody, who'd followed in his cruiser, pulled up beside her and climbed out.

"This is the vet's truck, right?" he said as he went directly to Cole's truck and peered under its hood.

"Yes," Mattie said.

"Shit! The battery cable's cut."

Mattie joined him at the front of the truck, Stella beside her, to see for herself. "Someone meant to keep him here," she said, urgency growing inside her. She scanned the front of the barn. "The dog is gone."

"What dog?" Brody asked.

"A Doberman they keep chained up out here," Stella said.

As Stella spoke, Mattie headed for the back of her SUV and let Robo out of his cage. He jumped to the ground, waving his tail and looking up at her for direction. "Heel," she told him, striding off toward the barn entrance and releasing her Glock in its holster.

Brody and Stella hurried to fall in beside her, loosening their service weapons as well. "What's the plan?" Stella asked.

"There isn't one," Mattie said. "I have no idea what's going on, but we've got to find out."

"We could be walking into a trap."

"Look for cover as soon as you get inside," Brody said. "Take it if all hell breaks loose. Otherwise, we'll stick together and question whoever we see first."

Getting information from the first person they saw sounded fine to Mattie, but she planned to keep going until she was speaking directly to Cole Walker.

Robo stayed close to Mattie as they entered the building. She scanned the area for places to take shelter. Scarce—a wheelbarrow here, an open stall door there, a few piles of hay and straw. Feeling exposed, she continued down the alleyway, glancing at Robo to read his body language. He was alert and scanning the area, no raised hackles.

When she reached a room that was set up as an office, Mattie could see it was empty. "Let's check the box stalls," she told the others. "Spread out."

Taking the side opposite the office, Mattie headed down the alley, peering into each doorway on her way. Inside one stall, she found a black horse lying stretched out on its side. She paused, staring at its bony frame to make sure it was still breathing. Its chest rose and fell in shallow, rapid breaths. She presumed this was the very sick horse Cole had mentioned.

Going farther down the alley, she came to a closed door. Robo nosed the doorway with interest, nudging it after he sniffed. His actions made her think that someone could be on the other side. Could it be Cole? Or Juan Fiero? She decided to err on the side of caution and drew her service weapon, releasing the safety.

She heard a low moan from the other side. Pushing Robo into a covered position against the wall, she told him, "Sit. Wait."

Taking shelter at the wall beside Robo, she threw open the heavy door and waited a split second. When nothing happened, she peered into the room and spotted a man lying on the floor surrounded by stacks of hay bales. He raised one hand weakly as if beckoning for help.

"Down here," she shouted to the others before entering the room. "Robo, heel."

She could already tell that the man wasn't Cole. It was Juan Fiero. And he was definitely in trouble. He stared at her with desperate eyes. Blood saturated his shirt below where the feathered end of a short, metal arrow was embedded in his right upper chest.

Pushing away the horrible image, she stayed focused. She knelt beside him and spoke quietly in Spanish. "Who did this to you?"

He wheezed as he tried to take a breath but could achieve little more than a shallow pant. "Carmen," he whispered.

Mattie glanced up at Brody and then Stella as they entered the room. Robo crowded in closer and tried to sniff the arrow. "Get back," she told him, nudging him away and leaning over the injured man. "Juan, where is Dr. Walker?"

"He ran." Fiero panted for breath, and he spoke in English. "She wants to kill him."

"That arrow must have collapsed his lung," Stella said, drawing her cell phone from her pocket. "I'll call for an ambulance."

"I saw a landline in the office," Mattie told her. "I doubt if there's cell phone service up here. Call Sheriff McCoy, too."

Stella left. Brody leaned forward. "What do you know about Adrienne Howard?" he asked.

Fiero stared up at Brody, his face haunted. "Carmen killed the young lady," he told him, gasping for breath but clearly wanting to communicate. "She forced me . . . to hide her body . . . but . . . I wanted . . . you to know."

"You called our office to tell us where to find her body?" Mattie asked.

"Yes."

"Why did you act like you couldn't speak English?"

"Carmen." He paused, struggling to breathe.

"You didn't want Carmen to know you spoke English?" Mattie asked.

"Right."

Mattie glanced at Brody. He wore a murderous expression that told her everything she needed to know about his feelings, but when he spoke, his voice gave away nothing. "How could she force you to do something you didn't want to do?"

"*El Capo* . . . her uncle . . . big drug boss . . . in Mexico . . . holds my family. He will kill them." The effort of speaking appeared to steal Juan's breath, and he lay gasping on the floor.

Stella reentered the room. "The ambulance is on its way," she announced as she crossed the room. Squatting beside the injured man, she spoke to him in a soft voice. "We have to leave that arrow in place. We'll try to make you as comfortable as possible while we wait."

"Brody and I have to go after Cole," Mattie said to Stella. "Can you stay here with Fiero?"

Stella swept her gaze around the room, thinking. "Yes, that's best. I'm no good in this terrain. I'll bolt this outside door and build a little shelter with these bales. If Santiago comes back, I'll take her down."

"We're more likely to find her out there," Mattie said, while Brody straightened and started stacking hay bales between Stella and the doorway. Mattie turned back to Fiero. "Do you have any idea which way they went?"

"To the ridge."

"Robo can track them," Mattie said to Brody.

He gestured toward the door with his chin. "Let's go."

She thought about the missing Doberman. "The guard dog isn't out front, Juan. Could Carmen be using him to find Dr. Walker?"

A furrow deepened between his eyes. "He tracks . . . animals."

With a sinking feeling, Mattie stood and gave Stella a hard look. "Take care of yourself. Shoot to kill if she comes through that door."

"You two watch yourselves," Stella said, following them to the door of the hay room and closing it behind them.

Mattie dashed out to her SUV and jerked open the back. From a floor compartment, she grabbed her utility belt, strapping it on while she spoke to Brody. "Do you have Kevlar on under your shirt?"

"Not today."

"Strap it on."

He went to his cruiser and opened his trunk. Mattie put on her own vest and reached for Robo's. "Robo, come," she said, squatting down beside him to place his vest over his back and shoulders and then fasten the straps that held it in place under his chest. She checked to make sure the vest wouldn't rub his wound, and the area that covered it seemed flat and smooth. Hurrying, she splashed water into his collapsible bowl and encouraged him to drink.

"See if there's a scent article in Walker's truck," she called over to Brody as he was completing a thorough check of his AR-15 Colt rifle. "A coat or shirt or something."

Brody slammed down his cruiser's trunk lid and, using the remote, chirped on the locks. He jogged to the front door of Cole's truck, opened it, and searched inside. Mattie finished stashing away Robo's things and grabbed a couple of long-distance walkie-talkies, attaching one to her belt loop.

"How about a hat?" Brody called over to her.

"That's great. Let me pick it up," Mattie shouted back as Brody turned toward her with the item in his hand. She hurried to join him, pulling a plastic bag from her utility belt and noticing his chagrin. She held open the bag. "Not a problem. Pop it inside here."

He dropped it into the bag, and she sealed the zip-lock.

"Ready?" she asked Brody. At his nod, she sprinted toward the back of the barn, calling, "Robo, heel," as she ran. Robo fell into place beside her, waving his tail with excitement.

"Robo and I are lead, and you're backup," she told Brody as they ran. "We'll track Dr. Walker. You watch my back."

"What about going after Santiago?"

Mattie could tell he wanted Adrienne's killer, but Cole's safety was her first priority. "We might run into her on our way to him. If we do, we'll take her into custody. If we find Walker first, we'll secure him and head back to the barn. Then we'll get a scent article for Santiago and track her down."

She glanced at Brody as she ran. "Got that?" It was her way of asking him to follow her command.

"Got it," he said.

They'd reached the only doorway on the backside of the barn, so she assumed this was the door that led into the hay room. "Stella, you hear me?" she called at the door.

"Yes."

"Open the door. I've got a walkie-talkie for you. You're base. We'll be in touch."

The door opened and Stella reached for the instrument. "Good luck out there," she said, standing in the doorway.

Mattie zipped open the bag and held it low for Robo to sniff. He buried his nose in the hat for a split second. "Search," she told him, gesturing toward the ground at the base of the door.

Robo sniffed the ground no longer than the time it took for one heartbeat and then he bolted toward the trees, running down the rocky berm that surrounded the barn and across the cleared grassy space beyond. Mattie raced behind him, and Brody followed. They entered the forest as a unit, as close as soldiers going into a hotspot. Robo kept his nose to the ground, and she knew he was tracking rather than trailing the scent through the air. This told her that Cole was not in the immediate vicinity. She observed the hair on Robo's neck—not raised, no perceived predator nearby either.

She checked wind direction and felt the breeze behind her. Cole had to be downwind from her position. The chances of Robo being able to air scent and go to him directly were slim. They'd need her dog's nose on the ground.

She was able to keep up with Robo, and Brody stayed close behind. Suddenly Robo stopped, forcing her to step to the side to keep from bumping into him. She put out a hand to warn Brody. Robo sniffed off to the right and ahead on the trail. He came back. Bearing right, he kept his nose to the ground.

At the base of a large ponderosa, he used his nose to root among the dead pine needles. In a swift transition, he sat, looking up at Mattie, his grin clearly indicating his joy at finding something.

Mattie stooped and brushed aside more of the needles, unearthing a black-and-white striped cover on a laptop.

"Good boy, Robo," she said, ruffling the fur at his throat and giving him a grin to show him how much he'd pleased her. Then with a more serious expression, she looked up at Brody "Adrienne's?" she asked.

"Yeah." His face was grim.

"We can't carry it with us," Mattie said, covering the laptop again. Drawing out a roll of orange flagging tape, she tossed it to Brody. "Mark this tree with a strip of this. We'll come back later."

While Brody tore off a strip of the tape and tied it to a branch, Mattie sent a transmission to Stella. "K-9 One to base, over."

"This is base, over." Stella's voice came over the walkie-talkie loud and clear.

"Robo just located Adrienne Howard's laptop, buried next to a large pine, beside a game trail that leads up the mountain. We've marked the tree with orange tape." She wanted Stella to know about it, just in case.

"Affirmative."

"Roger that. Over and out."

Turning her attention back to Robo, she stroked his head. He leaned into her hand, gazing up at her with affection. "You're a good boy, you know that," she murmured.

She began some chatter to rev up Robo's prey drive and let him know they weren't finished. Taking out the bag containing Cole's hat, she let Robo sniff it again. This time, he skimmed over the bag with his nose, barely needing a whiff. Mattie knew he had the scent locked into his memory, and she'd bet her next paycheck that her dog knew exactly which man they were tracking: his own doctor.

"Search," she told him.

Robo darted onto the game trail that provided even footing for a short distance, affording a moment for Mattie to scan the forest. Dense pine and spruce, as well as boulders of all sizes, covered the rocky terrain providing plentiful places to hide. This would have given her a small amount of comfort had she not been so worried about the Doberman. The fact that he'd been used to track animals told her he'd received at least some level of training. And the way he strained at his chain to reach visitors told her that the dog was vicious.

Robo kept moving uphill. Slowing to a trot, he led them to a place where shale and rock abutted the trail to the right. On the stones several feet away from the game trail lay a dead coyote, well decomposed. Robo sniffed the area, working his way around the coyote, leaping from one stone to the other and giving each a thorough whiff. Mattie followed, catching her balance on each stone while she waited for Robo to finish his examination. A few feet past a thicket of prickly rose, Robo touched the rock he'd been sniffing with his mouth and then sat. He gazed at her, indicating his find.

Being careful not to jostle her dog, Mattie stretched her legs to cross over to the stone he was sitting on. Brody followed behind, leaping onto the stone she'd left. Mattie squatted beside Robo, placing an arm around him to help her balance. "What did you find?"

She searched, and as her eyes adjusted to the pattern in the gray and black stone, she perceived some spots that didn't belong. Reaching into a pouch on her utility belt, she withdrew a compact evidence kit. "There's something here," she told Brody.

Using a swab, she gently rubbed the spot, and the end of it turned red. She showed it to Brody as she tucked it inside its plastic cover. "Looks like blood," she said flatly, but her heart sank. *Maybe it's Cole's.* He could be injured, and an injury would greatly reduce his chances of escape.

"Good boy," she told Robo, giving him a firm pat on his Kevlar-coated side. "Go on. Search."

Chapter 30

Cole sat on a rocky ledge, peering down into the forest from behind a boulder. Sunlight slanted hard from the west, nearing sunset. He shivered as the cold breeze kicked up, turning the wet legs of his coveralls into instruments of torture. He'd used his Leatherman to cut damp strips of cloth from the bottoms of each pants leg to bind his swollen ankle, but pain still throbbed with every heartbeat. He'd also fashioned a spear of sorts by winding narrow strips of cloth to secure the crossbow bolt onto a solid branch he'd harvested from a pine.

His breath came in full and even cycles, and he felt fully recovered. Had it not been for the ankle, he could run again. As it was, he wasn't sure how much more pounding the injury could take. He stood to test it, bending over to make sure he remained hidden behind the boulder. Pain shot up his leg when he bore weight on it, but he could handle it if necessary. He wished he knew where Carmen and her dog were.

By now, someone should have missed him—Tess, his clients, his kids—someone. The last thing he wanted was for one of them to come looking for him. He wondered if Carmen had given up and returned to the stable. If so, she would be a danger to anyone who came into her vicinity.

He wished he'd called Mattie to tell her about the Clenbuterol dosing before he left home. At least then she would have known he was coming up to confront Carmen about it. It was stupid of him not to. If only he'd known then what he knew now.

Thoughts of his kids sent a chill of a different sort through him. What would happen to his kids if he died? He'd never even made out a will. No appointed guardian. Would Liv come out of her self-imposed exile and take care of them? He didn't want to think about it. Couldn't think about it. He needed to pay attention.

Scanning the steep cliff face above him, he wondered about his plan. With his ankle the way it was, he doubted he could climb any higher. An escape route felt really important, and he didn't have one. He debated going back down and moving on. Staying hidden up here might work if his stalkers were mere humans, but he worried about the dog, Bruno. Just how good a tracker was he?

Searching the forest below, he discovered the answer. What he first saw as movement between the trees soon took form. Bruno trotted across a clearing, nose to the ground, coming closer with each step. Cole's heart rate kicked up a notch.

Who was with him? He studied the forest, trying to find Carmen. Nothing. She'd apparently turned the dog loose.

As Bruno came closer, Cole could see a bulky collar on his neck. *An e-collar.* His mind jumped to the possibilities of what that could mean. Carmen could summon the dog back to her with an electronic signal. Or if the collar contained a GPS, she could allow him to run down prey and then follow him at her own pace. The second option scared the crap out of him.

Without hesitation, the Doberman sprinted up to the base of the cliff, and Cole lost sight of him. He searched the forest—still no sign of Carmen. Cole straightened so he could see around the boulder. *Where is that dog?*

Bruno lunged into view a mere ten feet below. They locked eyes for several scary seconds. The dog snarled and barked, scrambling at the bottom of the ledge in search of a way up.

Now what?

Don't panic.

The Doberman scrabbled at the loose shale, sending rocks sliding to the bottom of the cliff, taking him partway down with them. He continued to bark as he got up and tried again, this time gaining some ground.

Cole scanned the forest. Still nothing.

I've got to do something to stop this barking. He remembered how Bruno had reacted to Sophie's baby talk. He tried to imitate Sophie's sweet talk to the best of his ability. "Hey Bruno. *Guter hund. Guten morgen,* Bruno. *Guten hund,*" he called, most likely butchering the translations of 'good dog' and 'good morning' but doing the best he could. Hopefully the dog wouldn't care about proper syntax or what time of day it happened to be.

Cole kept up the chatter for almost a full minute before Bruno stopped barking. By this time, he'd scrambled back to the base of the ledge. He stopped for a moment, giving Cole his full attention, ears pricked.

Hardly daring to hope, Cole continued to talk to the dog, alternating between a soothing voice and baby talk. Bruno stared at him, his amber eyes unblinking.

Cole's attempt to say "good boy" seemed to make a difference. Doggie confusion came into Bruno's expression, and he whined—a single, confused utterance.

Encouraged, Cole stood and showed Bruno the palms of his hands. "*Das is gut,* Bruno," he repeated, trying to keep the urgency he was starting to feel out of his voice.

He wracked his brain for what to do next. He decided to try a command. "Bruno, *sitz!*"

The Dobie tucked his tail and sat, looking up at Cole expectantly, ears pricked.

Where is a dog treat when I need one!

Taking slow and cautious steps, Cole moved from behind his shelter and began to inch his way down the cliff face, hanging on to shrubs and branches for balance. All the time, he babbled in German, saying any words that came to mind heavily interspersed with "good boy."

Bruno watched him, now looking more curious than confused. Cole tamped down his fear as he drew closer to the dog, because he knew the animal could sense it. Instead, he thought of Sophie's lighthearted trust and tried to duplicate it. When he reached a prominence directly above the dog, he tried a different command. "Bruno, *platz.*"

The Doberman went into a down position.

What is the word for stay? He couldn't remember. Falling back on the tried and true, he repeated the word for 'down' as he continued to ease his way along the rocky cliff. Each step on his swollen ankle sent jolts, but he kept going and soon was on an equal level with the dog, about eight feet away. Bruno watched him without waver, looking eager and expectant. Cole decided he needed to give the dog some form of reward, because it looked like that was what he obviously wanted.

"*Komm,*" Cole said, at the same time using the hand gesture for "come." "*Komm hier!*"

Bruno leaped to his feet and ran straight at him, causing Cole to almost go into cardiac arrest. But the Doberman scurried to sit right in front of his feet and looked up into his eyes with excitement. Cole bent forward and extended a hand for

Bruno to sniff. The dog dismissed it, still eagerly waiting for a treat. Cole stroked the top of his head and then patted his side.

Giving Bruno lots of loving strokes and crooning to the dog in German, Cole gingerly reached for the e-collar and slipped it off. Bruno showed no objection whatsoever. Looking up at the perch on the cliff that he'd abandoned, Cole heaved the collar up toward the ledge. The collar bounced off the rock face, skittered downward, and lodged in the branches of scrub cedar—unseen from below.

Couldn't be better. He patted the dog and hugged him close to his leg, telling him what a good boy he was. He scanned the forest, feeling the urgency of desperation. Befriending Bruno was a major accomplishment, but he still had Carmen and that crossbow to contend with. Deciding to head across slope opposite the direction from which Bruno had come, Cole patted his left leg. "Bruno, *ferse.*"

Bruno fell into heel position as Cole finished the last descent and jogged off as fast as his swollen ankle would allow.

★

When Robo stopped at the edge of the stream and sniffed up and down its bank, Mattie knew that Cole had taken to the water. That's exactly what she would have done if she were in his shoes. Robo leaped over the water and sniffed along the bank on the other side, tentatively heading upstream. It was the first time he'd hesitated since he'd taken to Cole's trail. Robo nosed the foliage along the bank, tracking Cole's scent slowly and carefully upslope. She hoped his effort to mask his route had been enough to throw the Doberman off his trail.

Although she grew impatient to move forward at a faster pace, Mattie let Robo do his work. He continued to give the tall grass a thorough sniff as they moved upward. At times willows and boulders blocked their path, forcing Mattie and Brody to circle around or enter the stream. Robo either edged along the stream or took to the water. When he splashed into the creek, she followed him, the frigid liquid filling her boots and numbing her feet. Brody stayed close at her back.

They toiled upward. Her breath quickened, and she could hear Brody heaving for air behind her. Robo worked the trail, seeming more and more sure of himself. After what felt like a lifetime, they came upon a dead deer with a short, metal arrow lodged in its rib cage behind its front shoulder. The ugly bolt matched the one in Juan Fiero. Gooseflesh tingled along her spine, and it wasn't from the icy water that squelched in her boots.

Robo continued upstream but then turned to go back, sniffing furiously along both sides of the bank.

He's lost the trail. And Cole must have left the water. Trying to think like Cole, she scanned the banks for tracks. Nothing in the rocky shale. Robo must have had the same idea, but he was using his nose, sniffing in widening arcs that brought him over to the decomposing deer. He scurried back and forth with his nose to the ground, moving away from the water. Soon, he headed across slope with greater determination. Mattie and Brody filed into place behind him.

They trooped along, Robo picking up speed. She assumed the scent trail had become stronger here. They jogged through stands of timber and across open spaces. Mattie snatched glances of the surrounding terrain even while she watched her step, placing her feet carefully to avoid ankle-turning stones. They were approaching a cliff face when she noticed the hackles at Robo's neck rise.

"Robo, wait," she said in a quiet voice.

He stopped in place, throwing a glance at her over his shoulder. She could swear he was asking, *What for?*

Brody stopped a mere twelve inches behind her. "What?" he said, matching her quiet tone.

Mattie spoke in a near whisper. "Robo's hackles are raised. He knows Cole Walker. I don't think he'd do that with him. There must be someone else ahead on the trail. Proceed with caution."

Brody was already holding his rifle ready. "Right."

"Robo, search." Mattie followed him as he lowered his nose to the scent trail.

Through the pine, she spotted a small clearing with a cliff face beyond. Robo pushed forward, his neck bristling. She placed a hand on his Kevlar vest, grabbing hold of a strap sewed to its back, and slowed him down. She wanted to avoid breaking out into the open space without seeing what it contained first.

Brody stayed at her back, slightly to the side. "There," he whispered. Evidently his height and position made it possible to spot something. Crouching, he pointed.

Mattie reacted at once, getting low and stepping to the side. She peered through a break in the trees in the direction Brody indicated. Carmen Santiago stood at the base of the cliff face pointing a wicked looking crossbow up at it, a bolt loaded and ready to shoot. Mattie scanned the area above Carmen but could see nothing.

Carmen raised a hand holding an oblong object and pointed it upward toward the ledge.

"What's that?" Brody whispered.

"Looks like a remote for a dog collar," she whispered back.

"What's she doing?"

"I don't know. Where's the dog?"

286 | Margaret Mizushima

"I don't see him."

"She must have lost him," Mattie whispered, watching Carmen continuously press and repress a button on the remote. "She's signaling him. She thinks he's up there."

Brody straightened and scanned the area, stooping low again when he finished. "I don't see a dog."

"Do you know anything about that crossbow?"

"They're powerful. No safety. She can sight down the scope and pull the trigger in a split second."

"Reloads easily?"

"No. It would take some effort. Might take fifteen seconds," Brody said.

"Do you think she has a gun?"

"Can't tell."

Mattie locked eyes with Brody for a few seconds. "I want to take her alive. She's got a lot of questions to answer."

"Agreed." His face was grim. "But I won't let her take another life."

Mattie nodded. Brody could easily hit a target with his rifle at up to one hundred yards. The use of deadly force would be permissible if Carmen was trying to kill one of them, including Robo. Would he jump at the chance to take out the woman who killed his girlfriend?

Removing her handgun from its holster, she whispered instructions. "Let's split up and go in from two directions. You take seven o'clock and I'll take five. Avoid each other's line of fire."

He nodded. "I'll draw her fire. You'll have about a fifteen-second window to take her down."

He started to turn away, but Mattie grasped his forearm to stop him. "Be careful, Brody."

"You too."

She turned off to the right, whispering to Robo to heel and seeking the five o'clock position to home in on the cliff face. Robo stayed close as she crept through the forest, using trees and boulders as cover when she could. She'd recovered her breath during their brief stop, and it came evenly. Her senses sharpened. The wind sighed through boughs overhead, and dead pine needles crackled beneath her feet.

Mattie crept close enough to Carmen so that she could see her clearly. The woman's black hair had been pulled from its braid, messy strands floating around her head. She stood at the bottom of the incline, her back to Mattie and her hand raised to shield her eyes from the setting sun. She studied the cliff face above, holding her crossbow ready.

Mattie searched for Cole in the rocks, but could see no sign of him. She decided to get even closer.

Cover became sparse as she moved to the edge of the clearing, but by now she estimated she was only about thirty feet away from the woman. Robo danced at her heel, ready to lunge forward. Grateful that his training held to remain silent, she gripped the strap on his vest to keep him close. She scanned the seven o'clock position but couldn't see Brody. He would be well hidden, and she didn't waste time looking for him. She assumed he would be in place.

Mattie waited, her breaths coming in short bursts despite her trying to slow them.

"Carmen Santiago!" Brody shouted from off to her left.

Carmen pivoted, training her bow in his direction. But she didn't fire. She crouched and sidestepped behind a boulder at the base of the cliff—still armed.

The boulder sheltered Carmen from Mattie's vision. *Does she have a gun?* A gun would be a huge factor.

"Lay down your weapon!" Brody called. "Come out with both hands raised where I can see them."

Robo tried to surge forward, but Mattie held him back. "Heel," she whispered. "Steady." She felt it critical that Carmen didn't know she and her partner were there. Surprise on their part would make all the difference. Robo settled beside her.

"Why are you threatening me?" Carmen called out.

"I'm here to arrest you for the murder of Adrienne Howard," Brody shouted.

Mattie looked for him, but still couldn't see him. Evidently Carmen couldn't either.

Carmen gave a sharp laugh. "I had nothing to do with that. You should talk to my hired man, Juan Fiero."

"Well . . ." Brody said, drawing out the syllable. "I've done that already. He's alive and talking."

Silence fell over the clearing, and Mattie wished she could see the woman. Then Carmen backed cautiously, crossbow held ready, keeping the boulder between herself and Brody but coming into Mattie's view. She could see the camouflage pattern and black scope on the bow. She couldn't count on Robo's Kevlar to protect him from the deadly bolt. She waited, Robo straining against his vest. She didn't know how much longer she could keep him from barking.

Evidently Brody grew tired of the wait. He stepped out from behind the trees, showing himself at the edge of the clearing. He held his rifle pointed at the sky.

"Come out and let's talk," he said. "We'll both put down our weapons."

Carmen rounded the boulder, sighting through her scope as she came. A heavy clunk vibrated through the clearing as she shot the bolt. Brody fell.

Heart racing, Mattie sent her dog. "Robo, take her."

Robo streaked across the thirty-foot clearing like unleashed fury. Carmen turned, while he leaped at the arm that held the bow and clasped it in his jaws. His momentum sent them both tumbling down into the rocky shale, Robo on top. Without releasing his bite, he leapt off the woman and stretched her out, dragging her away from the crossbow. Carmen's screams and Robo's terrible snarls echoed off the cliff.

Mattie charged toward the two of them. She pounced on Carmen's back, feeling satisfaction when she heard the wind whoosh out of her. Robo continued to tug while she grasped Carmen's free hand and pulled it behind her back.

"Surrender," she told Carmen, "and I'll call off the dog."

With a curse, Carmen quit struggling.

"Robo, out!" She waited for Robo to drop her captive's arm. "Guard!"

Robo loomed over Carmen's head, saliva dripping from his jaws.

"Don't move, or he'll go after you again," Mattie said as she secured Carmen's other arm behind her back.

She started to reach for the cuffs that were secured to her utility belt, but Brody came up from behind with his. Mattie snapped the steel cuffs into place, looking up with relief at Brody but seeing the blood trickling down his forehead. "You're hit," she said.

"Shit," he muttered, gingerly touching a wound on his forehead. "More like I hit the ground."

Mattie shook her head. *You're crazy*, she thought, but kept the words to herself. Letting Robo stay in guard position, she stood and stepped away from her captive. The woman was no longer struggling. "You ready?" she asked Brody.

"Yup."

She released Robo and called him to her side.

Brody bent and grasped Carmen's upper arm, his firm grip apparent even to Mattie. "On your knees," he told her in a gruff voice.

"I have political asylum," she said, struggling to get up on her knees. "You can't arrest me."

"Watch me. Stand up now," Brody growled as he pulled her up. He proceeded to arrest her for Adrienne's murder and read her the Miranda rights.

Mattie wondered why the woman thought she'd have immunity and hoped there'd be no problem prosecuting her. The only proof they had that Carmen Santiago had killed Adrienne was the word of a migrant worker. She hoped Adrienne's laptop contained something even more damning.

Mattie took her first aid kit from her utility belt and handed Brody a sterile gauze pad. "Will you be okay?" she asked. "I need to find Cole Walker."

"I'm fine," he said, pressing the gauze to his wound. "Go ahead and track him. I'll take her down to the barn. Call on the walkie-talkie if you need help."

Mattie gave him a short salute and turned to go, patting Robo and telling him he was a good boy. "But we're not done yet," she said, withdrawing Cole's hat from the utility belt and giving Robo a sniff. She lowered her hand and used a sweeping gesture to indicate the ground.

It took only a few seconds for Robo to pick up the trail, and he followed it across the slope. She heard Brody tell Carmen to walk as she hurried to keep up with her dog. Robo appeared confident, tail waving and happy, while he led Mattie through the forest. Soon, she realized that Cole must be headed for the main road. After about fifteen minutes, she came to the edge of a small clearing and caught a glimpse of him disappearing into the trees on the other side. A large black dog walked beside him. The Doberman.

Such a great sense of relief flowed through her that it was almost overpowering. Breaking into a run, she shouted. "Cole! Cole, it's Mattie."

He reappeared through the pine, and the exuberant grin that she'd grown so fond of lit his face. He dropped the branch he was using for a walking stick and limped toward her, his arms extended. "Mattie! Thank goodness you found me."

She stepped into his arms, and he wrapped her in a hug so tight it took her breath away. Her face came to the level of his chest, and her cheek pressed against the stiff fabric of his coverall. When she inhaled, he smelled of mud and horse and sweat. She held him in a firm embrace and realized that she never wanted to let go. He pressed his lips to the top of her head.

She tried to pull away, but Cole tightened his grip. She let him hold her while she fought the tumult their closeness triggered. When Cole gradually released her, she took a step back and glanced around, looking anywhere but at this man she now knew she loved.

Cole touched her face with a gentle finger, his gaze showing his concern. "What happened to your eye, Mattie?"

She gave him a fleeting glance. "It's nothing. I got in the way of a flying elbow."

He opened his mouth to continue, but the Doberman she'd last seen chained in front of the barn was bouncing at their feet, bowing into a "let's play" position for Robo who was trying his best to ignore him.

Cole laughed. "You wouldn't happen to have a dog treat on you? I owe this guy a few."

Chapter 31

On their way down the mountain, the sun sank behind the westward mountains, and the elk began to bugle—a high, melodious whistle that slid up multiple tones and echoed through the hills. The sound heralded crisp autumn air and usually nourished Mattie's spirit, but this time it resonated with loneliness, taunting her.

While she led Cole back to the stable in the waning light, she stuffed her feelings back into a dark, deep place. His limp slowed their progress, but he insisted he could make it down from the mountain on his own two feet rather than waiting for a four-legged ride to be organized by the sheriff and rescue volunteers. He told her about how Juan Fiero saved his life and accused Carmen of murdering Adrienne, and Mattie told him how she and the others had found the injured man in the hay room.

"So he was still alive. Can we find out how he's doing?" Cole asked, gesturing toward Mattie's walkie-talkie.

Mattie keyed on her remote, connecting with Sheriff McCoy, who had evidently arrived at the property and taken charge. She asked him about Fiero's condition.

"He was alive when he left in the ambulance. Over," McCoy said.

"Copy," Mattie replied before signing off.

"Good," Cole said. "He must have been too afraid of something to report Carmen to the police."

"He said Carmen's uncle has control of his family, and he feared for their lives."

"Good grief. What will happen to him?"

"Essentially, he's an accessory to murder," Mattie said. "But he's also a witness. We'll just have to see if he pulls through."

After that, they were silent as they labored tediously downslope through timber and rocky terrain. Cole appeared to be concentrating on putting one foot in front of the other, while Mattie focused on trying to take the shortest but smoothest route to the barn. Bruno and Robo stayed close despite the slow pace.

When they entered the glow from the yard light, Mattie could see the relief on Cole's face. He hobbled onward, using his walking stick for support. Brody was standing out by the patrol vehicles, and he apparently spotted them. He walked out to meet them, giving Mattie a sweeping once-over before focusing in on her face.

"Are you all right?" he asked, his voice gruff.

His concern surprised her. "Sure. You?"

"I'll live." Brody shifted his attention to Cole and offered a shoulder. "Can I help you, Dr. Walker?"

"I'll be all right. I need to get to my truck, so I can wrap this ankle. Then I need to check on Diablo and that other horse."

"Detective LoSasso will want a statement from you before you leave. Someone cut your battery cable, but I patched it." Glancing at Mattie, Brody added, "LoSasso and McCoy are searching inside the house now. They want you there ASAP."

Mattie nodded. She'd hoped they would wait for her before starting the search, but she could understand their eagerness. "I'll go now."

Cole reached to take her hand, causing Mattie's cheeks to flush. She was thankful for the limited light.

"Do you need my help?" she asked.

"No. It's just, well, I can't tell you how grateful I am that you found me and helped me out of that mess." He touched her cheek, and a wave of tenderness built inside her. "You look exhausted, Mattie. I wish you could go home and take care of yourself."

"It's the eye that makes me look so bad, but I'm okay. Truly. You're the one that's beat up."

"I'll call the kids and then stick around for a while. Go do your work. I'll touch base with you later." He squeezed her hand before releasing it. "And . . . thank you."

She nodded and turned away, not trusting her voice to speak. She struggled to switch off her emotions, something that was becoming harder and harder to do. Walking toward her vehicle, she noticed that Brody seemed to be on guard beside his. She realized that Carmen Santiago sat in the back of it. She diverted her route and approached Brody, signaling that she wanted to speak with him. He met her half way.

"Has Stella questioned Santiago yet?" she asked in a quiet voice.

"She refuses to speak without an attorney. I'll take her to the station after the search."

"Okay."

"But Stella said the hired man talked plenty before the ambulance took him away. Briefing later."

Mattie nodded, went to her SUV, and loaded Robo into his compartment. After taking off his Kevlar vest, she checked his wound, was relieved to see the staples were still intact, and gave him some water. She drove to the fork in the lane and took the one that led to the house. Lights blazed through the large windowpanes, and she could see Stella and McCoy coming down the staircase from the upper level. Taking a deep breath to fortify herself against her fatigue, she slid from the driver's seat and went around back to unload Robo. Time to get back to work.

Before letting him jump down, she put on the collar he wore to search for dope. From the amount of money the property represented, she assumed that would be her purpose. She began talking to Robo in high-pitched patter. Together they entered the house, Robo dancing beside her, tail waving. His unlimited fount of energy never failed to amaze her. For him, his work was a never-ending source of play. She found the sheriff and Stella in the great room.

McCoy greeted her with a question. "How's the doctor doing?"

"He made it down on his own, but his ankle looks pretty bad. He's going to take care of it himself with his vet supplies and then check on the horses."

McCoy nodded.

"Can you and Robo sweep this house for drugs?" Stella asked.

"Sure." Mattie focused her attention on Robo, patting him and holding him against her leg while he shifted his weight between his front feet. "You want to find some dope? Huh, do ya?"

Mattie used the leash and her free hand to guide Robo in a sweep of the house, starting with the downstairs. After receiving no alerts from him there, she led him up the staircase and started in the room that looked like Carmen's home office. Nothing. She'd felt certain that they'd find something in the office, so she was about to give up hope of uncovering a drug stash in the house. *Maybe in the barn or one of the other outbuildings.*

She came to the master bedroom, appointed with heavy walnut furniture—headboard and footboard, dressers and nightstands, a settee near the fireplace—and lush, olive-colored bedding. Directing Robo forward, he made a beeline for the bed. At first he tried to crawl under it, but when he was too big to go all the way, he backed out and scratched at the floor. Then he sat. He looked straight into Mattie's eyes.

Full alert. "He's indicating something under the bed," she told the others.

"We checked there," Stella said. "There's nothing, not even a dust bunny."

"Let's move the bed," McCoy said, crossing over to the far side of the footboard and trying to drag the heavy piece of furniture to one side. Mattie and Stella hurried to help, and soon they'd moved it away from its place.

"Looks like nothing but flooring," Stella said, getting down on her hands and knees and smoothing her hand over the floor. Excited, Robo joined her, giving each board a sniff. He fixated on a small dent in the floorboard, gave it one scratch with his foot, and then sat and stared at Mattie as if to say he'd done all that he could.

"Thanks, Robo," Stella said, probing the dent with her finger. "What are you trying to tell me about this divot right here?"

With a delicate whisper of well-maintained gears, a three-foot square section opened up by sliding down and then under the rest of the floor. Startled, both Stella and Robo jumped away from the widening hole while Mattie and McCoy moved closer.

Stella chortled. "Well, look what we have here!"

Mattie knelt beside Robo and hugged him close, taking her eyes off the glorious sight and burying her nose in the fur at his neck for a brief moment. Looking back at the stacks and stacks of plastic-wrapped bags that could only contain drugs, she watched Stella reach down with a latex-gloved hand to take out one of the wads of banded cash and rifle through it.

"All one hundred dollar bills." Stella took a moment to count them. "Looks like it's sorted into ten thousand dollar bundles. My God, there must be close to a million dollars here."

McCoy stared into the vault, obviously thinking. "This organization reaches far beyond this one property in Timber Creek County. I need to call the CBI on this," he said, referring to the Colorado Bureau of Investigation. "And I'm sure they'll bring in the Feds."

"Mattie," Stella said, looking up at her with a gleam in her eye. "That dog has one helluva nose."

Chapter 32

Wednesday

The Timber Creek officers gathered for debriefing, all staring in glum silence at anything but each other. Disappointment and anger fueled the tension in the room.

Mattie glanced at the clock on the wall of the briefing room. Five thirty: the sun would rise soon. Yesterday had been the longest day of her life, and since she'd still not had any sleep, the endless day was stretching into a two-day marathon. Robo had curled up beside her chair and fallen asleep. He snored lightly.

McCoy spoke first. "So it's out of our hands now. DEA agents are taking our prisoner to their Denver office. I'll be informed of her disposition on a 'need-to-know' basis. There's no guarantee we'll be kept in the loop."

Brody had chosen to sit beside Mattie and Robo, and she could feel him simmering. "Will Carmen Santiago be prosecuted for Adrienne's murder?" he asked.

A pained look touched McCoy's face. "I don't know. I wish I could tell you she will, but . . ." He lifted his hands in a gesture of helplessness. He continued to explain. "They'll use her as bait to get to her uncle, *El Capo*. They've been tracking his activities in the United States for months. This horse stable is believed to be a money-laundering scheme for proceeds from his prostitution and drug operation that extends from Juárez to Los Angeles. The thing is, it's doubtful he'll care enough about Carmen for them to use her for leverage against him in any way."

"So she might get a plea bargain," Brody said, spitting out the words with distaste.

"It's possible," Stella replied, looking grim. "But she won't get away scot-free. She'll serve time for Adrienne's murder. And in her family, getting caught like this will mean a death sentence. I doubt she'll last long in prison."

Brody rolled his shoulders and pushed back from the table, his chair scraping against the tan linoleum. Mattie could tell that Stella's answer held no satisfaction for him. He would want to take part in the woman's prosecution and see justice served with a murder-one conviction. They all would. But they were enmeshed in the downside of federal jurisdiction pulling rank.

"I was able to access Adrienne's computer prior to the Feds taking it for evidence," Stella said. "I found a file that contained her notes regarding the horses. She documented the decline of a horse named Diablo and her concerns about a horse named Red. She suspected drug dosing of some kind."

As she continued, Stella eyed Brody, whose face had turned stony. "Juan Fiero told me what he witnessed. He said the lady, meaning Adrienne, accused Santiago of making the horses sick. Carmen went to her office, came out with her crossbow, and told Adrienne to run. She did. Carmen shot her in the back, and the bolt went clear through her chest. Fiero said she died immediately."

Brody pushed back from the table, bent forward, and placed his elbows on his knees. He stared at the floor, clenching his jaw.

Stella continued. "He said he thought Carmen killed Adrienne because she needed to prove to her uncle that she was committed. He said that compared to her uncle, her evil side is very small. He thinks she's probably as afraid of him as he is."

"How did he call into our tip line?" Mattie asked.

"Adrienne gave him the TracFone," Stella said. "They talked while they worked on the horses. He told her he wasn't allowed to use the phone, and Adrienne gave him an old one that still had some minutes on it. After Carmen forced him to bury her body, he felt so bad about it, he had to call."

"The Feds have taken Fiero into custody and plan to transfer him to a hospital in Denver as soon as they can," McCoy said. "Why did he hide the fact that he speaks English?"

"He said he wanted to hide it from Carmen and her uncle. He believed it gave him an edge in case he could ever make a move to escape," Stella said.

"They're pawns," Brody growled.

Mattie related to his frustration and nodded her agreement. The group shared a moment of silence. Mattie felt like she needed to say something to Brody but didn't know what that could be. Stella beat her to it.

"It pisses me off that we couldn't mete out justice for Adrienne ourselves, Brody. But we have to hope the system will give her the punishment she deserves."

Stella had summed up her own feelings in the best way possible. "I think so, too," Mattie said. "The important thing is that we were able to shut her part of the operation down and bring her to justice, even if what happens next is out of our control. And we solved the homicide case and made an arrest."

Brody shrugged. "Maybe so. But Adrienne's gone no matter what we do about it."

Purely out of reflex, Mattie reached out to comfort him and put her hand on Brody's forearm. His tension was evident in the tight, ropy muscle beneath his khaki shirtsleeve. "I'm sorry, Brody. I wish things were different." She withdrew her hand before it became awkward.

McCoy steepled his fingers at his chin and swept them with an all-inclusive glance. "I couldn't be more proud of the way my officers performed out there last night. I don't want you to lose sight of our accomplishment: it takes a well-trained team of professionals to break up an international crime organization and take down one of its primary players. You can be proud of the way you served our department, our state, and our country." He paused for a moment, letting his words sink in. "I believe the local property owned by this crime organization will be appropriated by the federal government and eventually liquidated, and I can promise you that I'll fight for our share of the asset forfeiture when the time comes."

"What about the animals?" Mattie said. "What's their disposition?"

"Timber Creek County Humane Society has assumed responsibility for the horses, and they'll remain under Dr. Walker's care until he determines if they can be saved or not." He smiled in a slight way, as if recalling a memory. "Dr. Walker made it clear that no one was to even touch the Doberman but him. He put the dog in his truck as soon as he finished with the horses."

It was a relief to know that Cole would be in charge of the animals.

McCoy continued. "I want you all to know that even prior to Ms. Howard's disappearance, I'd been working with the county commissioners to approve a budget increase to add a detective to our staff. There's no question that our increased crime rate justifies the expense." He sent Stella a pointed look.

"I hope you'll consider applying for the position as soon as we post it."

Looking thoughtful, Stella gave him a slow nod.

"Any questions or things you want to add?" When no one spoke, McCoy went on. "I've made arrangements for Deputy Garcia to extend his shift through the morning, and Deputy Johnson will also be on duty. You all can have the morning off, but shifts resume as scheduled at one o'clock this afternoon. For now, you're dismissed."

With fog descending on her brain, it took a moment for Mattie to orient herself to the day. Wednesday . . . right. She and Robo were scheduled to work, so she'd better get home as soon as possible. Right now she'd trade almost anything for a few hours of sleep. When she pushed her chair back and stood, Robo awakened and scrambled to his feet. He stretched and yawned, haunches in the air.

"Mattie, could I have a word in private before you go?" Stella asked.

"Sure," she said, hoping it wouldn't take long. She rested a hip against the table while the men left, closing the door behind them.

Stella searched Mattie's face for a few seconds before she spoke. "I can tell the past forty-eight hours have been hell for you. I can read the pain in your face."

Tears prickled Mattie's eyes, and even though she wanted to argue, she couldn't speak.

"I know you want to deny it, and I know you're pushing yourself to carry on as if nothing has happened," Stella said, the emotion behind her words making her sound angry. "But you're one hell of an officer, Mattie, and I don't want to see you break down. You owe it to your training, your career, and— yeah, you owe it to Robo—to take care of yourself. I'm not going to stand by and watch you self-destruct. You've got to take care of this now that this investigation is over and get yourself some help, or . . ."

Surprised at the detective's vehemence, Mattie looked her in the eye. "Or what?"

Stella put on her too-sweet smile. "Or I'll nag you until you do."

Placing her hands on her temples, Mattie rubbed the tightness that had formed there. "Good to know. Right now I need some sleep." She started to pull away, but the need to tell someone the thought that had truly begun to nag at her made her turn back. "You know what's bothering me the most now, Stella?"

"What's that?"

"The fact that my mother must have known what was going on, and she didn't protect me." Mattie's throat tightened and she couldn't say more.

Stella looked thoughtful. "Yeah, you're probably right. But keep in mind that she was going through her own hell. That's no excuse to fail to protect an innocent kid, but . . . who are we to judge? At least she recognized that she wasn't providing what you needed and did the best thing she knew how to do at the time."

Bitterness flowed from Mattie's chest into her words. "Yeah . . . relinquish her kids to the state."

"Hey, we can piss on our parents as worthless idiots all we want, but ultimately we've got to take responsibility for who we are as adults. You've ended up all right."

It wasn't the time to share that all she'd ever really wanted was to reunite her family, and now she wanted nothing to do with them. Her shattered dream hurt more than anything at the moment, but she was too tired to get into it. She pulled a hand down over her face. "I've got to go home. I'm due back here at one."

"Okay, I'll let you go. But think about what I've said, and we'll talk later. Hey . . . I'm considering that job the sheriff mentioned. I might be your neighbor someday."

Mattie gave her a tired smile. "Worse things could happen."

Stella took Mattie by the arm and started walking her toward the door. "And they probably will."

★

Mattie slept the hard sleep of exhaustion for five solid hours, and so did Robo. When she awakened a few minutes before noon, she lay in bed disoriented. In the split second it took to remember why she was in bed in the middle of the day, it all flooded her mind—the search for Cole, Carmen's takedown, the hideous image of that bolt lodged in Juan Fiero.

And Willie's phone call.

She pushed herself up and sat on the edge of the bed. Robo lay stretched out on his side on his dog bed, and he opened his uppermost eye to stare at her. As if also needing a second to orient himself, he lay still for one eye blink before scrambling to his feet. She realized why the room was warmer than they were used to—she'd forgotten to open the window before collapsing on the bed. And she'd awakened, safe and sound.

"Come here, buddy."

He came and placed his head on her knee for an ear scratch.

"Thanks for always being there when I need you," she murmured. "You're my best friend."

More refreshed than she'd felt for a couple of days, she let Robo into the yard, watched him long enough for him to do his business, and then called him inside. Picking up her cell phone, she took it off vibrate and noticed she had a message.

It was Cole, asking her if she would join him and the kids for dinner.

She took in a breath, thinking about his family. Months ago, she'd believed it to be perfect—loving couple, gorgeous daughters, dedicated parents—and then she'd discovered the flaw in her illusion. No family was perfect. And the pain Cole's kids were feeling over their own mother's abandonment was as real as hers. She wanted to make sure that Cole sought counseling for his daughters without delay.

And what about you? Clearly Stella had weaseled her way inside Mattie's head, because it was her voice that whispered the question.

"Okay," Mattie said aloud, causing Robo to look up at her. "I just might do it, too."

★

The mundane routine of patrol duty and paperwork felt like such a relief, and the last half of Mattie's shift flew by. She clocked out and left the station in time to drive straight to Cole's house for dinner. After parking under the tree in front, she unloaded Robo, who wasn't even trying to hide his delight. Allowing herself to smile, she decided that dogs could teach humans a thing or two about happiness.

Cole opened the front door and stepped out, his friendly grin lighting his face. *Dogs and Cole; they always make me feel welcome.* Bruno and Belle spilled out into the yard to greet Robo, and the chase was on. Mattie climbed the few steps up onto the porch and allowed herself to be swallowed up by Cole's warm hug. She was relieved to feel less complicated emotions than those she'd felt during his last embrace. This time, she recognized joy and affection, pure and simple.

"I'm so glad you're here, but I have to warn you about something," Cole said, releasing the hug but tucking her under one arm. His expression turned serious, his eyes earnest. He spoke in a rush, his voice hushed in the low, confidential tone used for sharing secrets. "Angie is real mad at me for not coming home last night, even though I called her when we got back to the barn to explain that I had to stay to take care of Diablo. I'm at a loss how to tell her and Sophie the real story. How serious the situation was. You know, I can't tell them what really happened, about the danger and all, but they've got to realize I was gone for good reason. What can I say?"

A few months ago, Mattie would have done anything to avoid getting involved in Cole's personal trouble, but tonight she felt better equipped. "Did you tell them Carmen was arrested for Adrienne's murder?"

"Not yet. You know how Angie's been. And I just got home from the clinic."

"Well . . ." She thought for a moment—watching the dogs play, sensing the warmth of his arm on her shoulders and his body at her side, breathing in the spicy scent of his aftershave. "The truth is always best. With kids, withholding the truth is more damaging than exposing them to some of the scary stuff. But after this, you've got to find a professional who can help your daughters deal with their feelings, Cole. They've been through too much lately."

"Agreed. I've already decided that's what we're going to do."

Thank goodness. "Let's tell them about most of what happened and let them talk things over with us. If you want me to, I'll help you sort through how much to say."

"Thank you, Mattie. You're a lifesaver," he said, giving her a slight squeeze. As he released her and stepped back, he raised his brow as if realizing the reality of his statement. "And I guess I mean that literally."

She smiled. "How are the horses?"

"Garrett's been helping by keeping an eye on them up at the stable. Big Red is going to be fine. I'm cautiously optimistic about Diablo. He spent some time standing up today, and he ate a little bit of hay this afternoon. I hope we can transfer both of them to my clinic soon."

"That's great news."

His grin warmed his countenance while he opened the front door with a flourish, inviting her into his home. "And do you want to hear some more great news?"

"Absolutely."

"Mrs. Gibbs baked an apple pie."

Acknowledgments

Many have helped bring *Stalking Ground* to publication, and I extend my heartfelt gratitude to all. From researching to writing to editing to publishing, I couldn't ask for a better support network. I also want to thank readers who have embraced the Timber Creek K-9 mysteries; it's a pleasure to hear from them, and I appreciate their encouragement to keep writing stories about Robo and Mattie.

My sincere appreciation goes to the professionals who helped me research this book; any misinterpretations or fictional enhancements of the information they provided are mine alone. Lieutenant Glenn Jay Wilson of the Rio Blanco County Sheriff's Office answered my questions about officer training and procedures, among many other things. Fellow writer Tracy Brisendine never gave up on answering my continuous questions; Tracy offers information consultation for fiction writers regarding death investigation, police procedure, and crime scenes in workshops and one-on-one. Robert Perce, DVM, and Charles Mizushima, DVM, provided veterinary consultation for this story, and I appreciate their input and guidance in helping me set up challenges for Cole Walker to face. Wildlife Technician Louie Starzel Jr. and District Wildlife Manager Nancy Howard from Colorado Parks and Wildlife shared information regarding hunting, mammal wounds, and related topics. And Christian Cable of Sportsman's Warehouse took time to demonstrate a crossbow, so I could experience the sights and sounds related to loading and shooting this powerful weapon.

Special thanks to my agent, Terrie Wolf, for ongoing support and for tying up all those loose ends; to my editors, Matt Martz and Nike Power, who have taught me such valuable lessons on writing; to my publicist Dana Kaye and her staff, for helping get the word out about the Timber Creek K-9 series; and to Sarah Poppe and Heather Boak of Crooked Lane Books, for everything they do to keep things on track. I'm so fortunate to be able to work with these professionals.

Thank you to my writer friends who make up Rocky Mountain Fiction Writers and who made it possible for me to meet editor Matt Martz at a conference. Special thanks to my writing group, who provide input and support and keep me on task: Catherine Cole, Saytchyn Maddux-Creech, Caroline Marwitz, Liz Stevens, and Brian Winstead. And a note of appreciation goes to Susan Hemphill for helping me proofread.

To my extended family and circle of friends: thank you for celebrating with me each step along the way. I love to party with these folks! Warm hugs go to my daughters, Sarah and Beth, and to my son-in-law, Adam, for believing in me and reading first drafts. And once again to my husband, Charlie, thanks for everything.